Behind Kane, something was stirring

Something large and reeking of amniotic fluid and newness. Something alien.

Kane dragged himself out of the tantalizing promise of unconsciousness. His side hurt, his right arm hurt, his head… He had hit the wall and lay there now, on the floor amid a scattering of fallen drapes and totems and jars, trying to make sense of where he was.

He turned, pain rushing through his neck as he strained his muscles, his breath coming through clenched teeth. An Annunaki stood behind him, large and saurian, larger than any that Kane had ever seen before. He had fought with Enlil and Marduk and others, gone toe-to-toe with Ullikummis, whose surgical enhancements made him a towering pillar among his own kind. But this, an Annunaki of gold and green, was something else. Something huge and muscular, its power barely restrained.

Kane gathered his thoughts, commanding the Sin Eater back into his hand from its hidden sheath. He squeezed the trigger as Anu turned, the light of recognition appearing in the monster's blood-red eyes.

And in that moment, Kane knew just who he was looking at.

Other titles in this series:

James Axler
Outlanders®

APOCALYPSE
UNSEEN

A GOLD EAGLE BOOK FROM
WORLDWIDE®

TORONTO • NEW YORK • LONDON
AMSTERDAM • PARIS • SYDNEY • HAMBURG
STOCKHOLM • ATHENS • TOKYO • MILAN
MADRID • WARSAW • BUDAPEST • AUCKLAND

HUDSON BRANCH

Recycling programs
for this product may
not exist in your area.

First edition November 2015

ISBN-13: 978-0-373-63888-8

Apocalypse Unseen

Copyright © 2015 by Worldwide Library

Special thanks to Rik Hoskin for his contribution to this work.

Printed in U.S.A.

It's not what you look at that matters, it's what you see.
—Henry David Thoreau,
1817–1862

The Road to Outlands—
From Secret Government Files to the Future

Almost two hundred years after the global holocaust, Kane, a former Magistrate of Cobaltville, often thought the world had been lucky to survive at all after a nuclear device detonated in the Russian embassy in Washington, DC. The aftermath—forever known as skydark—reshaped continents and turned civilization into ashes.

Nearly depopulated, America became the Deathlands—poisoned by radiation, home to chaos and mutated life forms. Feudal rule reappeared in the form of baronies, while remote outposts clung to a brutish existence.

What eventually helped shape this wasteland were the redoubts, the secret preholocaust military installations with stores of weapons, and the home of gateways, the locational matter-transfer facilities. Some of the redoubts hid clues that had once fed wild theories of government cover-ups and alien visitations.

Rearmed from redoubt stockpiles, the barons consolidated their power and reclaimed technology for the villes. Their power, supported by some invisible authority, extended beyond their fortified walls to what was now called the Outlands. It was here that the rootstock of humanity survived, living with hellzones and chemical storms, hounded by Magistrates.

In the villes, rigid laws were enforced—to atone for the sins of the past and prepare the way for a better future. That was the barons' public credo and their right-to-rule.

Kane, along with friend and fellow Magistrate Grant, had upheld that claim until a fateful Outlands expedition. A displaced piece of technology…a question to a keeper of the archives…a vague clue about alien masters—and their world shifted radically. Suddenly, Brigid Baptiste, the archivist, faced summary execution, and Grant a quick termination. For Kane there was forgiveness if he pledged his unquestioning allegiance to Baron Cobalt and his unknown masters and abandoned his friends.

But that allegiance would make him support a mysterious and alien power and deny loyalty and friends. Then what else was there?

Kane had been brought up solely to serve the ville. Brigid's only link with her family was her mother's red-gold hair, green eyes and supple form. Grant's clues to his lineage were his ebony skin and powerful physique. But Domi, she of the white hair, was an Outlander pressed into sexual servitude in Cobaltville. She at least knew her roots and was a reminder to the exiles that the outcasts belonged in the human family.

Parents, friends, community—the very rootedness of humanity was denied. With no continuity, there was no forward momentum to the future. And that was the crux—when Kane began to wonder if there was a future.

For Kane, it wouldn't do. So the only way was out—way, way out.

After their escape, they found shelter at the forgotten Cerberus redoubt headed by Lakesh, a scientist, Cobaltville's head archivist, and secret opponent of the barons.

With their past turned into a lie, their future threatened, only one thing was left to give meaning to the outcasts. The hunger for freedom, the will to resist the hostile influences. And perhaps, by opposing, end them.

Prologue

The Earth's first monster was called Anu and he arrived from the heavens in a spaceship. Oh, there had been horrifying things before Anu—dinosaurs and giant things that lived in the ocean's depths and saw in a range beyond the visible spectrum, creatures which one might describe as monstrous. But Anu was a monster inside, where it truly counts.

Anu was a self-styled explorer from an immortal race called the Annunaki, who hailed from the distant planet of Nibiru, many light-years from the planet he dubbed Ki after his sister and consort, the planet which we now call the Earth. Anu was a strange kind of explorer, looking not for new lands or resources but rather for new experiences, ones that might stave off the crushing ennui that threatened to quiet his race forever when time itself had failed. The Annunaki were bored—of life, of experience, of pleasure.

Anu first visited the Earth in a period when the apekin—or humans—were still cowering in the trees from saber-toothed tigers. He landed amid the wild greenery in a starship shaped like a dragon. The starship was called *Tiamat*, and she was a semisentient device as eternal as any of the Annunaki race. The journey across the gulfs of space had exhausted her, which was reason enough for Anu to step from her loving womb and onto the soil of this new planet; a planet that waited untouched and ignored on one of the pale, squid-like tentacles of a barred spiral galaxy that would one day be known as the Milky Way. Such was the impact that *Tiamat*'s arrival would make on the locals that, many years later, she would be erroneously considered responsible for the creation of the Milky Way itself.

Anu strode from *Tiamat*'s bridge and inhaled his first breath of the Earth's atmosphere, taking in the blue-skied vista spread before him. He was a tall creature, nine feet in height, with scales of gold laced with green like brass touched by verdigris, his thick tail circling behind him for balance as he stepped from the widening aperture on *Tiamat*'s shell and out onto the boarding ramp that extended from the ship's nose. He wore an ornate cloak patterned after one of Nibiru's most prominent flowers, its scarlet weave so dark that it was almost black, a perfect match to his red-black eyes. His neck was thick and corded, the ideal plinth for his long head, whose skull seemed to arch back and outward from a curved face with almost flat features, like a visage reflected on the back of a spoon. At the apex of his head, spiny protrusions emerged from his skull, thick, twisted bone struts running in a spiky array that jutted like the spokes of a wheel. In years to come, Anu would be remembered by the Earthlings for his crown, though it was not decorative but a part of his skeleton.

Anu breathed the air as he stepped from the widening, circular aperture. He knew that it could do him no damage; *Tiamat* had already tested and confirmed as much before he had taken his first step from her protective shell. To Anu, the air tasted sweet in that way that water from a different source often tastes different.

He took a moment, the grand explorer, the *alien*, to

survey this world he had discovered like a gem amid the night sky of space. According to *Tiamat*'s sensors, it teemed with life, something that so few worlds did. There were other races, of course—Anu knew as much and had convened with them, as had others of his own race. But, for better or worse, such races were scattered vast distances from each other, as if a law within some grand, hidden design had stated that no two sentient races may coexist within one hundred light-years of one another. Perhaps there was a plan at that, one hidden from all but the most enlightened of the higher beings. Anu had considered this during his long journey to the planet Earth—or Ki, as he was already calling it—but reached no firm conclusions, only more questions.

The Annunaki were eternal beings. And they were something else, too—multidimensional. But it was possible to see the Annunaki through humans' eyes, and as Anu stepped from *Tiamat*'s boarding ramp and out onto the green carpeted plains that would one day become Kenya, he was seen by the first man who would ever have a name. The man cowered behind a deciduous bush, where he had been plucking perfectly round, purple berries that he planned to store for eating later, back at his dwelling—which was admittedly little more than an indentation in the ground, but served to keep the wind from touching him at night. The man had stopped plucking berries, his purple-stained fingers poised in midpluck, as the dragon ship landed and the figure emerged. The whole sequence had taken almost ten minutes, from when the man had first noticed *Tiamat* as she gracefully came to rest, barely making a sound beyond the displacement of the air left in her wake, to now, when the aperture had appeared on the dragon ship's face and the golden figure of Anu had emerged to stride majestically down the tongue that rolled before him to touch the soil. In all that time, the man—we might call him Adam, although that is not the name which Anu gave him—remained in place, unmoving, perhaps unable to move, as he watched an occurrence play out that was so far beyond his comprehension that he could barely fathom it. It was like hearing something in a foreign language, so impossible was it for Adam to interpret.

As Anu stepped onto the planet, Adam coughed, suddenly choking on his own breath, the taste of berries and stomach acid flooding his throat with a hot surge. He doubled over, taking great racking gasps of air as he tried to clear his throat, pressing his arms against his chest and sides, the berries crushed and forgotten. It was shock, seeing this creature from another world, this...*god*...?

When Adam finally managed to draw a breath without coughing—still hunched over like the apes his kind still resembled—he stared at the ground between his feet and saw golden, clawed toes. He looked up, turning his head slowly, still feeling that twitch on his insides where the choking cough threatened to restart.

The creature from the stars was standing beside him, legs widespread, cloak fluttering in the light, warm breeze, watching him with eyes as dark as newly spilled blood.

Anu spoke in a voice the like of which had never been heard on this planet. The words were incomprehensible to the apekin, but the sound fascinated him. It was duotonal, like someone humming against a sheet of paper, split and yet conjoined, a sound that was two sounds at once. The voice, like everything else about the Annunaki, was multidimensional.

Adam heard the sound and did the only thing that seemed natural: he fell to his knees, bowing down before Anu, peering up at those eyes like blood.

Anu peered down at the apekin creature inquisitively, pleased with this new aspect of the thing's nature. "You are not timid, then?" he said. He spoke the words in his own tongue; they left his mouth with a sound like wind through autumn leaves. He reached down then, touching one golden hand to the apekin's head, pressing it gently against the top of the primitive creature's skull. Anu placed just a little pressure there, and the apekin bowed his head, until he was staring at the ground between Anu's feet.

"Better," Anu declared, a thin smile appearing on his wide mouth.

The apekin remained in that aspect as Anu surveyed the lands around him, taking in the new plants, the trees, the texture of the air. Here was a playground that might stave off the crushing boredom of life eternal, at least for a while. He breathed deeply of the air, consuming it through the flat, flared nostrils that resided on his face like the craters of some unknown moon, as he turned back to regard the apekin bowed low before him. This was something he could use and could get used to. These hairy mammals with their smells and their finite life spans could serve to reignite the pleasure centers of the bored Annunaki.

But when to share his discovery? Anu wondered. Perhaps tomorrow or next week or in a thousand years' time. For time meant little to a race that knew infinity and resided outside of its wide borders. First he would experiment a little, see what these apekin were capable of, and what they could endure.

"Come, creature," Anu said, placing a clawed hand

under the apekin's chin until his head tilted to look at
his new master. "Creature. Creature. No, you need an
identifier, a name by which you may be referred." Anu
was already thinking of the Annunaki's slave class, the
Igigi, none of whom had ever earned a name. They were
devoted and simple creatures, superior, Anu suspected,
to the apekin prostrating himself before him, but still
uncomplicated compared to the Annunaki. It pleased
Anu to think that by naming this first man, he might
further subjugate the Igigi, reminding them of their
status as slaves to the eternal race. And so he spoke a
name, one that would survive throughout man's history.
Not Adam, not that—but *Cain*.

THE DOME SAT on the shores of Lake Tiamat. It was four
hundred yards across and perfectly round as if a giant
sphere had been buried in the ground, leaving only its
top third visible. The shell of the Dome was colored the
silver of clouds, making it almost indistinguishable from
the sky into which it towered. Inside, Anu conducted his
trials. He was loath to call them experiments; they were
really just games that put the local apekin through their
paces, testing them to—and beyond—their limits. Anu
might be excused the latter—he had no prior knowledge
of the apekin, and only by testing them could he hope
to determine where their limits were and of what merit
such limits were.

The apekin needed sleep and food, far more so than
the Annunaki, who could go without such things for
months, even years, at a time. The Annunaki lived outside of time, while the apekin were bound to it in such
a way that it afflicted them with a disease called aging.
Aging. The Annunaki had bypassed that millennia
ago, their bodies immune to the ravages of time, their

minds playing host to the memories of all of their race, perfectly held for instantaneous recall. And more, they had invested in the genetic shunt, a download of personality which allowed them to be reborn as they were, over and over, to regenerate their minds into new forms, each genetic template held safe in the wombship, *Tiamat*.

Anu had spent the past six months on Earth, toying with the apekin and the other creatures who existed on this untouched paradise. He had tested diseases, manipulated DNA, made the apekin serve him, service him and entertain him. He had driven them to madness and to death, called upon them to fight with wild creatures for his pleasure and to fight with one another to the death. He had made mazes and traps to test their intelligence, used mirrors and refraction to throw their senses. Simple tricks all, but tricks that were beyond the apekin's understanding.

But the apekin were learning; that was something of which they were eminently capable, Anu had concluded. They took observations from the trials, learned lessons, reached conclusions that made them better at surviving without injury. If they could learn, Anu concluded, then they could be taught.

Cain had survived all of the trials. Anu's first test subject, Cain had proved shrewd and wily, and he had learned quickly how to please his master and never to trust him. Cain was strong, muscular for his species. He could kill a man with his bare hands and utilize simple tools that he fashioned himself—shaped rocks, carved sticks. Cain showed the kind of spirit that Anu associated with the eternal, a spirit that might live beyond his time here on Ki, on Earth. Anu had found one other like him, a female of remarkable intellect for an apekin, and there seemed to be a bond between her and Cain almost from the moment that they met.

Cain was a servant of Anu, which meant he had safety in the Dome, safety from those prowling saber-toothed tigers and their ilk, each one looking for a hot meal that was slow on its feet and wouldn't fight back. Cain was safe inside, and so he served Anu without complaint. Every morning he would run the circumference of Lake Tiamat, an artificial body of water created from the overspill of *Tiamat*'s tanks, genetic ooze, waste product expelled after the long journey across the field of stars. The dragon ship resided beside the lake, disgorging her innards in a display of regeneration comparable to anything Annunaki, her fish-scale skin slowly replenishing where it had become blistered by the heat of atmospheric entry.

Cain seemed to have some ragged notion linking survival to physical prowess, and so, Anu guessed, that was why he ran. He tried to teach the female, the one of remarkable intellect, and she watched him run the circuits around the lake with bright eyes of emerald green.

TIME PASSED AND the trials continued. Until the day that Anu became bored with the Earth and, moreover, bored with the company of grunting apekin with whom he could not hope to do more than play fetch. He wondered about adding a spark to these listless creatures, and consulted with *Tiamat*'s data banks to design a structure within their DNA that might make them more interesting. He implanted that DNA structure into the ova of the female whom he had observed enjoying the company of many males of her tribe. The twist would make her children more rugged, more hardy, more *interesting*. It would spread, in time, though that was time Anu no longer wanted to endure on this blue-green marble. His servants, the Igigi, let the female go, scared and confused, to spread Anu's gift among the apekin. Anu watched her leave, wondering if he might return to Nibiru to tell the others of his discovery here, that they might add texture to the planet and thus make it interesting again.

Anu was not a monster because of his size or his skin or his otherness. He was a monster because of his heartlessness, his callousness. Because of his evil.

Chapter 1

Monsters waited beyond the shadows, monsters of another age.

Located in an underground bunker, the room had no windows and no illumination other than a single flashlight that wove through the darkness in the hands of its lone living occupant. The room was as wide as a football field, and its floor was masked by a deepening pool of stagnant water, the ripples flickering in half-seen crescents as the beam of the flashlight played across them.

Several vehicles protruded from the water like standing stones—a broken-down flatbed truck, a smaller van with its hood open, three jeeps, each in a state of disrepair. And there were other things—crates and boxes stained with mold, human bones that floated in the darkened water, bobbing horrifically into view before sinking down again to be lost in the cloudy swirl. It smelled, too, of damp and rot. It was a place where the things that reach beyond death flourish.

The woman with the flashlight stalked along the edge of the waterlogged room like a jungle cat stalking its prey, one long leg crossing the other as she moved, feet tramping in the shallowest depths of the artificial lake. Each step was accompanied by the splash of water, dark and foul smelling, and each time her black-booted foot touched the floor, the water would swirl over it until it covered her ankles, threatening to rise higher as she hurried on. Moss and pondweed floated across the surface of the water, twirling on the rippling currents caused by each step the woman took.

The woman was called Nathalie. She was in her twenties, six feet tall, slim and dark skinned with dyed feathers hanging from her ears, brushing against the tops of her shoulders. She wore leopard-print shorts and tall black boots that laced corset-like up the back of her calves. She wore a calfskin jacket that wrapped snuggly across her breasts, and there was a knife sheathed at her hip, its blade glinting in the water's reflection of the flashlight she carried to light her way. The knife was as long as a man's forearm, broadening along its length to a wide tip. Her hair was a shadowy halo of tight black ringlets that encircled her head.

She passed a femur washed up on the strange shores of the underground garage, stepped over it with only a moment's pause as she headed for a doorway and into the waiting elevator that was located in the corridor beyond.

Nathalie punched the button for a lower floor and waited as the elevator shuddered and dropped, its lights flickering and dimming as it sucked power from the redoubt's ancient generator. The elevator worked when little else did, a necessity for the redoubt's other occupant, who had lost both legs two years before.

A few seconds later the elevator came to a halt and its door drew back with a squeak on unoiled tracks.

Nathalie stepped out into a new corridor, one like any other in the redoubt, gray walled with a stripe of color to indicate level and area. Already she could hear the sounds of the generator that ran incessantly at the far

end, not for lighting or heat but for that other purpose—
to keep the dead thing from dying.

The corridor was lit by a single candle at the far end,
held in the claws of a four-foot-high holder, its silver
base emerging from the half inch of water that covered
the floor here, just as it did in the motor pool.

Nathalie followed the corridor to its end, and as she
approached the room there, she could smell the incense
on the air, masking the other scents of damp and sweat
and death.

This room was much smaller, barely able to contain the towering metal-walled tank that dominated its
space. The sound of the generator was louder in here,
too, a great thrumming that seemed to thump through
the metal plates of the floor, pounding against the soles
of Nathalie's boots so that it seemed she was shaking,
that her heart was racing.

The room was lit—almost reverently—by a dozen
candles, each one as tall as a child's arm and propped
inside mismatched containers—jars and cups, here the
jaws of a monkey's skull as if it was smoking a lit cigar.
There was no water in this room, though its floor was
stained dark where water had seeped in before. A lone
figure sat in the center of the room, facing the towering
structure that dominated the space. He sat not in a chair
but in a wheelchair, his back to Nathalie. This was Papa
Hurbon, a corpulent figure with wide shoulders and
richly dark skin. His head was shaved and shaped like
a bullet, a bucket-wide jaw tapering upward to a point
at the top of his skull. Earrings dotted his ears, twin
lines of gold studs running up their shell-like curves,
tiny figures suspended from the lobes themselves.

Clutching something small and ragged like an old
woman's knitting, Hurbon's eyes were wide as he looked

at the vast generator that was housed in the room. The unit towered over Nathalie, its curved metal sides buckled in places where something hard had struck them, a single porthole of six-inch armaglass located in the lone door that dominated its front. This was a cold-fusion generator, designed in the late twentieth century to create energy through nuclear fusion and used to power this underground redoubt when it had been in the possession of the US Army two hundred years ago. A spectral light ebbed from that single porthole, its luminescence a pale, irradiated blue.

"Nathalie," Hurbon said without turning.

Nathalie bowed her head in deference to Hurbon, even though he had not turned to see. "My beacon, my guide," she said, her voice shrill in the enclosed space.

She waited then, as Papa Hurbon, leader of the *société*, master of the *djévo*, practitioner of the dark voodun arts of the Bizango Priests, studied the ghostly miasma that swirled and flowed across the glass of the cold-fusion generator. There was a face there, the hint of an eye as hollow as the grave, a smile half formed from mist, strands of hair that swept across cheekbones that never fully formed as they were tossed by the ceaseless winds of the generator. Nathalie had never really understood what the thing in the generator was, only that Papa Hurbon regarded it with unmatched reverence.

"I have been t'inking," Hurbon began without turning his gaze from the ghost in the window, "about what it is to be immortal. Is it a gift? Or is it a curse?"

Nathalie waited as Hurbon seemed to ponder his own philosophical question. She was not given to philosophy; rather, she was young and the blood still ran hot inside her, driving her to action, not to rumination.

"And so I have thought, back and forth, on this topic,"

Hurbon continued after a long pause, "and I have concluded that the key to immortality lies here, in the con-
quering of death." He opened his hands, bringing forth
the little figure that he clutched there. The figure was a
fith-fath, what the ignorant called a voodoo doll, and its
twisted rag body depicted a woman's figure with dark
eyes and long, skeletal limbs. "But to conquer death,
you see—that is a challenge that few can comprehend.
Because to conquer it is to embrace it as my goddess,
Ezili Coeur Noir, embraces it."

He was talking about the figure in the generator,
Nathalie knew, a by-product of the Annunaki wombship that had somehow been granted a second life, one
fractured into separate bodies, broken away from the
wheel of life and death and rebirth. Nathalie did not
know the full story, had only pieced together hints of
it from what her priest, Hurbon, had told her. When he
was a younger man, Ezili Coeur Noir had appeared on
the Earth amid the debris of a spaceship that had been
destroyed outside of the atmosphere. But, driven mad
by the damage that the accident had inflicted upon her
body, she had come to the *société*'s temple in the Louisiana swamps and demanded blood sacrifice. That sacrifice had been wild and desperate and had involved
dancing and fornication and, ultimately, the shedding
of limbs in her name. Papa Hurbon had lost his legs
to his goddess in those crazy days of debauchery, and
in return she had brought him a brief taste of paradise as she set about eradicating all life on Earth. Her
plan had failed when a group of self-designated pro-
tectors of humankind called Cerberus had intervened,
petitioning Hurbon's aid before forcing the broken aspects of Ezili's body to combine in the heart of the
fusion generator. Hurbon had helped, employing his

arcane knowledge to draw the fractured aspects of Ezili's body to one location. And, in so doing, he had gained a hold on Ezili Coeur Noir, weaving her spirit into his fith-fath and so momentarily controlling the uncontrollable. She was unstable even now, locked inside the generator, but at least she was where Hurbon could contain her.

"Death must be bypassed," Hurbon continued, "and to do that we must first embrace it."

"Do you…intend to kill yourself, Papa?" Nathalie asked, her tone wary.

Hurbon turned to her at last, a golden canine tooth in his top jaw glinting in the flickering candlelight, dark gaps in his lower jaw where other teeth were missing entirely. "That would be foolish, Nathalie child," he said with that easy smile of indulgence. "Even if I gained immortality, using the dragon's teeth, what would that be worth if I lost myself in the process? No, we have tested the teeth in Spain, in Italy, in the Congo—"

Nathalie inclined her head, stopping Hurbon in midspeech. "I am still awaiting the results of the Congo test," she said.

"Where the locals see Heaven's Light," Hurbon muttered to himself, shaking his head sorrowfully. Then he looked up at Nathalie once more, piercing her with his dark-eyed stare. "To keep oneself…well, there are risks, as we have seen. Ereshkigal failed, the body never fully holding. Charun and Vanth failed, their portal collapsing."

"And them with it," Nathalie interjected.

"The risks of using the dragon's teeth have been made clear," Hurbon said, "and can be bypassed with a little patience. There is just one risk left. And to counter that I shall need someone from the *société*, someone loyal."

"I know just the person," Nathalie assured him, thinking of a desperate member of his parish whose loyalty was beyond question.

"Bring them," Hurbon instructed, "and together we shall spring the trap that brings Cerberus down forever and grants us immortality and eternal reign over this beautiful mud ball we call Earth."

Chapter 2

Brigid Baptiste awoke with a start.

The sounds of the Cerberus redoubt filtered through the walls and door of her private apartment, faint but offering a reassuring background, reminding her that life goes on. The apartment was located on one of the upper levels, away from the operations rooms, testing labs and other facilities housed within the redoubt, an old military complex that dated back to before the nukecaust and had been retrofitted to accommodate the Cerberus operation.

It was usually quiet here, whatever the time was. The staff at Cerberus worked in shifts, and people respected that someone was always sleeping no matter what hour of the day it was. But the sounds of talking, of laughter, seemed to echo through her door today.

Brigid shifted, turning onto her side and reaching for the lamp. She squinted her eyes as she brushed the lamp's side, switching it on with her touch. Beside the lamp, the notebook she kept at her bedside had been moved. Brigid had an eidetic memory, one that was photographic, and it remembered details like that. The book had been rotated twenty degrees from where she had left it. Her incredible memory could make her a little precise sometimes in the things she did.

She was a beautiful woman in her late twenties with an athletic body and long locks of red hair that curled past her shoulders to a point midway down her spine. Her eyes were emerald green, bright with a fire of curiosity. Her assessing gaze suggested a voracious intellect, while her full lips promised passion; Brigid was indeed intelligent and passionate and much more besides. An ex-archivist from Cobaltville, she had been expelled from the ville when she had helped uncover a millennia-long conspiracy designed to subjugate humankind. The conspiracy dated all the way back to the presence on Earth of the alien race called the Annunaki, who had posed as gods from the heavens and been worshipped and adored by primitive humans. Their intrigues had become legend, their infighting the basis of many of humanity's myths—but the Annunaki were all too real. Brigid could assure you of that fact because she had been there when they had returned to the Earth in the care of their dragon-like wombship, *Tiamat*, and been reborn to subjugate humankind once more. They had failed, not in the least due to the concerted efforts of Brigid and her companions in the Cerberus organization, a military-style group dedicated to the protection of humanity and its freedoms.

Brigid had joined Cerberus after her expulsion from Cobaltville along with two disgraced Magistrates called Kane and Grant, and a feral child called Domi who had been living as a sex slave for a beast called Guana Teague. Their lives had moved on an awfully long way from that early meeting.

Brigid reached for the notepad, saw in that instant that there were words written upon it. She turned the pad slowly, looking at the words. There were two words—"emit part"—written in her hand, albeit shakily. The words were written not on a line but in a circle, like so:

Automatic writing, Brigid realized as she looked at the strange words, presumably written without conscious thought while she was asleep. Well, that was new.

But what did it mean? Obviously, something had disturbed her in the night; something had caused her to write those words on her notebook, an item that often seemed a redundant indulgence when her memory was such a keen tool and yet could sometimes elicit the answer to a nagging problem from the day before. After all, what would a woman with a photographic memory ever need to write down?

She lay in bed, the covers pulled up high to stay warm, holding the pad and gazing at the topmost sheet.

Emit part.

It meant nothing to her. What was the *part*? What did it *emit*? It was dream writing, the kind that adheres to the logic of the subconscious, whose meaning is lost when the waking mind takes over.

Brigid held the pad before her, stared at the letters until her eyes lost focus and stared beyond it into the whiteness of the page, turning the letters into a blur. From outside her suite, Brigid heard familiar voices raised in a friendly discussion peppered with joyful laughter, but the sound barely registered on her consciousness.

Eventually, she set down the pad, pushed back the covers and got out of the bed. The new day awaited, whatever it might bring.

Chapter 3

Kane stepped out of a window in quantum space and into a hail of bullets. He stumbled back under the assault, shouting a command to his three partners before they, too, emerged from the interphase gateway that had materialized in thin air behind him amid the ruins of the Turkish fort.

"Abort the mission!" Kane shouted as his partners stepped out of the quantum ether amid a multicolored swirl laced through with lightning forks. Even as he spoke, he felt the passage of a bullet burn like hellfire across his right bicep, channeling a lance of white-hot pain through his arm.

Behind him, the same bullet—or maybe another from the same source, since it was impossible to be certain amid the hail of gunfire—slammed against the shining surface of the interphaser unit in a shriek of rending metal, sending out a shower of sparks and shattered plating in its wake.

Kane saw the quantum window collapse on itself at that moment, two conjoined cones of multicolored light streaked through with witch-fire lightning, disappearing in the space of a heartbeat, even as his partners stepped from their impossible depths.

The quantum gateway had been generated by the interphaser, a highly advanced device that used a hidden web of pathways across the globe and beyond to move people and objects great distances—even as far as other planets in the solar system—in the blink of an eye. Utilizing principles laid out by an ancient star-born race of aliens, the interphaser was a portable teleportation device which tapped into a network of so-called parallax points to deliver its users to their selected destination. Parallax points were widespread but not infinite, and as such their locations enforced their own strict limitation on where a user might travel—as one could only travel to and from a specific, designated parallax point, not create one at will. These parallax points had often become sites of religious and spiritual interest as primitive man sensed the strange forces contained within them. However, while the interphaser gave Kane and his Cerberus teammates an incredible measure of freedom in their travels across the globe, there was one very obvious problem with any teleportation system, one writ large as life before Kane's eyes as he dived to the ground with the burn of the bullet stinging against his arm: you just never knew what you were materializing into.

"Down!" Kane cried, slamming against the sandy dirt as the roar of gunfire continued all around him, bullets riddling the ground like rain in a monsoon.

Kane and his partners had emerged in the ruins of an ancient fort, roughly sixty miles south of the Mediterranean Sea in the part of the African continent known as Libya. The fort had no doubt been impressive in its heyday, but now it looked like a scattering of sand-colored slabs—some significantly larger than a Deathbird helicopter—sprawled across the sandy scrub of the Bir Hakeim Oasis. The stones reminded Kane of a graveyard, its gravestones created in colossal proportions as if to mark the passing of titans. Appropriate, perhaps, as the place was yet another reminder of how much of history seemed to have been lost with the nukecaust two hundred years before.

There was a wide crack running through the center of the dilapidated compound, twelve feet across at its widest point and deep enough that its sides disappeared into stygian darkness, even under the relentless brilliance of the midafternoon sun. That sun was obscured by dark cloud cover intermingled with the dense smoke of explosions.

There were at least eighty other people here, Kane guessed as he rolled out of the path of another hail of bullets, one hand clapped against the sting of his arm. Two groups—tribes, gangs, armies, call them what you will—using the ruined fort for cover as they traded bullets from automatic weapons, the sound of gunfire like a thunderstorm echoing across the fallen stones and beyond.

The place had been the site of a Turkish fort a long time ago, back when state borders and ethnic groups mattered, before the nuclear holocaust had rewritten everything in the wink of an eye. It was estimated that 90 percent of the world's human population had died in the scant few moments that had constituted the nuclear war, and even though two hundred years had passed since those retina-searing bombs had dropped, it seemed that humankind was still striving to recover.

One of Kane's partners—Brigid Baptiste—was shouting to be heard over the roar of the conflict. "The interphaser's compromised," she said. "It's not respond—"

Another roar of gunfire cut across Brigid's words, a line of dust plumes accompanying each cough as bullets drilled into the ground all around her. Beside her, another woman—older, with a lean frame and short, dark hair that showed a few traces of gray—wove through the barrage, crouched down and closed her eyes, covering her head with her hands. This was Mariah Falk, a geologist for the Cerberus organization who, unlike the others, was inexperienced in combat situations.

"Get your head down!" the fourth member of the team—a gigantic, dark-skinned man called Grant—yelled, scooping Mariah up in one of his mighty arms and part lifting, part throwing her out of the line of fire. As he did so, another swarm of bullets came lunging through the air, drilling into the dirt and rattling against the chrome sides of the interphaser where it waited on the ground. As they struck, Brigid leaped in the opposite direction, diving for cover behind something that looked like a fallen obelisk.

The world seemed to spin around Mariah as Grant released his grip on her. Still moving, she seemed for a moment to dance toward the cover of a fallen stone archway that, even in its ruinous state, still loomed twice the height of Mariah herself. Then she slammed against it, back and shoulders striking it in a solid thump accompanied by a woof of expelled air from her lungs. She wore a camo jacket like the others, pants and hiking boots, and she had a leather satchel hanging behind her, its strap stretching in a diagonal line across her chest and back. Mariah was slight of frame and, though not conventionally pretty, she had an easy smile and a kindly way that put most people at ease. Right now, however, neither her easy smile nor her homespun charm were likely to help save her life. Instead, she took deep breaths and tried to hold down her breakfast as a drumbeat of bullets caromed off the other side of the stone archway she was pressed against. It was cover—

scant but holding—and she knew it was the only thing keeping her alive in those frantic, heart-stopping moments. How did the others cope with this as part and parcel of their everyday lives? she wondered.

Grant scrambled out of the path of the bullets, darting past Mariah and ducking down behind the far side of the collapsed archway. "What the hell did we walk into?" he shouted, raising his voice to be heard over the cymbal crash of bullets.

Grant was a tall man with a muscular body and mahogany skin, his head was shaved and he sported a goatee. An ex-Magistrate in his midthirties, Grant was dressed in a camo jacket similar to his partners', though it did nothing to disguise his hulking proportions, as well as a Kevlar duster. As Grant scrambled out of the line of fire, it was hard to miss the sheer power that was contained within his well-defined muscles—there was not an ounce of fat on his whole body.

"Don't know," Kane answered through clenched teeth, still pressing one hand against his arm where the bullet had glanced off his protective shadow suit, his back against a half-collapsed wall a little way from his partner. "Some kind of local trouble by the look of it."

Kane was a tall man in his early thirties with broad shoulders and rangy limbs. His dark hair was cropped short and his eyes were the gray-blue color of steel. An ex-Magistrate like Grant, Kane wore a light jacket— desert camouflage colors—that reached down past his waist and featured a dozen pockets of various sizes, light-colored pants and calf-high boots whose leather had the satisfying creases of shoes that have been worn in. Beneath this, Kane wore another layer of clothes, the black all-in-one body glove known as a shadow suit, and it was this that had deflected the 9 mm bullet that had grazed his arm like an angry wasp when he'd stepped from the interphase window. Constructed from a super-strong nanoweave, the shadow suit was a skintight environmental suit that could regulate the wearer's body temperature, even in extremes of heat and cold. While it was not bulletproof, the strong weave could repel blunt trauma and deflect small-caliber bullets, minimizing injury. Right now, Kane's arm burned where the bullet had struck a glancing blow, but its full impact had been reduced thanks to the armor-strong weave of the protective suit.

There was something of the wolf about Kane, both in his rangy, loping strides and his personality, for he could be both a loner and pack leader, depending on circumstance. Right now he was here as an operative of Cerberus, the outlawed organization that dealt in the esoteric, with a particular emphasis on protecting humankind from the hidden forces, human and alien, that seemed always arrayed against it. Together with Grant and Brigid, Kane formed one-third of Cerberus Away Team—or CAT—Alpha.

Between Kane and his partners was the interphaser, its square base and pyramidal sides now dotted with the impact of bullets so that it looked as if some carnivorous creature had sunk its teeth into it. Brigid was staring at it from her own hiding place behind a fallen obelisk of stone that lay close to the mighty rent in the ground.

"How do we get out of here now?" Brigid asked, reaching for the weapon holstered at her hip. She was dressed in a similar camouflage outfit to the others. Theirs was a noble pursuit, but sometimes it seemed that walking into a hail of bullets was a too-frequent part of the job. Almost as though to illustrate this, Brigid unholstered the TP-9 semiautomatic that she habitually wore at her hip, unlocked the safety and scanned their surroundings with alert eyes. The TP-9 was a bulky hand pistol finished in molded matte black with a covered targeting scope across the top. "Well?"

"Don't ask me," Kane spit, ducking his head down as another volley of bullets came hurtling past overhead. "I'm fresh out of ideas. Besides, I thought you were the brains of this outfit, Baptiste!"

Brigid glared at him. "Brains, yes. Miracle maker— that's your department, I believe."

"Yeah," Kane agreed. "Belief will get you a miracle, all right." As he spoke, he performed a long-practiced flinch of his wrist tendons. The maneuver activated the catch on a holster located on the underside of Kane's forearm, commanding a retractable blaster to his hand from its hiding place beneath his jacket's sleeve. Kane's weapon was a fourteen-inch-long automatic pistol called a Sin Eater, a compact hand blaster able to fold in on itself for storage in the hidden holster. The weapon was the official sidearm of the Magistrate Division, and his carrying it dated back to when Kane had still been a hard-contact Mag. The blaster was armed with 9 mm rounds and its trigger had no guard—the necessity had never been foreseen that any kind of safety features for the weapon would be required, for a Mag was judge, jury and executioner all in one, and a Mag's judgment was considered to be infallible. Thus, if the user's index finger was crooked at the time the weapon reached his hand, the pistol would begin firing automatically. Kane had retained his weapon from his days in service in Cobaltville, and he felt most comfortable with the weapon in hand—its weight was a comfort to him, the way the weight of a wristwatch feels natural on a habitual wearer.

Back pressed tightly to the wall, Kane poked his head above the edge of the sand-colored bricks and scanned the area. There were people moving in all directions, some in groups, some alone, all of them armed. Some were dressed in semi-military uniforms, cobbled-together outfits that created a ragtag kind of uniformity. Others wore civilian clothing that looked like a cross between a long coat and a woman's nightdress. All of them were scrambling through the ruins and blasting at one another with a wide variety of weapons. Someone must have seen the interphase window open and figured it for a bomb or a rocket launch or something—with the place full of hair-triggered nut balls the way it was, it was little wonder, Kane concluded, that someone had tried to blast the interphaser to smithereens.

Kane continued scanning the area beyond for a few moments, as another rush of bullets came rattling against the far side of his protective wall. Kane spotted a long-barreled machine gun on a tripod mount, hitched above one of the few remaining walls on the second level of the ruined fortress. It was unleashing serious damage on the fighters below in a continuous stream of 24 mm slugs. Four soldiers fell to its assault even as he watched.

Across from him, Grant and Brigid were scanning other sections of the collapsed fort, while Mariah just kept her head down, flinching at each new shout of a gun being blasted, each *pee-ow* of a bullet's flight. They had appeared, it seemed, smack-dab in the middle of the ruined fort—which was smack-dab in the middle of what seemed to be a raging war zone.

"Nowhere to run," Grant concluded, peering left and right, front and back. As he spoke, he pulled a Copperhead assault subgun—almost two feet of thick black pipe with mounted laser scope—from a hidden holster rig under his jacket and was already ducking back behind the cover of a fallen stone archway, scanning for targets.

The Copperhead was a favored field weapon of Grant's. The grip and trigger were in front of the breech in the bullpup design, allowing the long length of barrel to be used single-handed. It also featured an optical image-intensified scope coupled with a laser autotargeter mounted on top of the frame. The Copperhead possessed a 700-round-per-minute rate of fire and was equipped with an extended magazine holding thirty-five 4.85 mm steel-jacketed rounds. Grant favored the Copperhead for its ease of use and the sheer level of destruction it could create.

"We can't fight them all," Brigid reasoned, even though she looked set to try.

"I don't want to fight *anyone*," Mariah added, ducking lower as a bullet clipped the archway six inches from her left shoulder.

Kane nodded in resignation. "Libya," he muttered. "I think I hate the place already and I ain't been here two minutes."

Chapter 4

Several hours earlier and a continent away, Mariah Falk had been running an analysis on some data she had received from her earthquake monitoring equipment when her interest was piqued.

A geologist for the Cerberus organization, Mariah was a twenty-first-century émigré who had found herself in the postnukecaust world after being cryogenically frozen, alongside a number of other top scientists and military personnel, on the Manitius Moon Base. The Moon Base had been rediscovered in the twenty-third century by Cerberus explorers, who had revived its residents and given them a new home on Earth in the Cerberus redoubt.

The redoubt was located in one of the Bitterroot Mountains in Montana, North America, where it was entirely hidden from view. It occupied an ancient military base that had been forgotten and ignored in the two centuries since the nukecaust that initiated the twenty-first century. In the years since that conflict, a peculiar mythology had grown up around the mountains with their mysterious, shadowy forests and seemingly bottomless ravines. Now the wilderness surrounding the redoubt was virtually unpopulated, and the nearest settlement could be found in the flatlands some miles away and consisted of a small band of Indians, Sioux and Cheyenne, led by a shaman named Sky Dog. The shaman had befriended the Cerberus exiles many years ago, and Sky Dog and his tribe helped perpetuate the myths about the mountains and so keep his friends undisturbed.

Despite the wilderness that characterized its exterior, the redoubt featured state-of-the-art technology. The facility was manned by a full complement of staff, over fifty in total, many of whom were experts in their chosen field of scientific study and some of whom, like Mariah, had been cryogenically frozen before the nukecaust only to awaken to the harsh new reality.

Cerberus relied on two dedicated orbiting satellites—the Keyhole commsat and the Vela-class reconnaissance satellite—which provided much of the data for analysis in their ongoing mission to protect humanity. Gaining access to the satellites had taken countless hours of intense trial-and-error work by many of the top scientists on hand at the mountain base. Concealed uplinks were hidden beneath camouflage netting in the terrain around the redoubt, tucked away within the rocky clefts of the mountain range where they chattered incessantly with the orbiting satellites. This arrangement gave the personnel a near limitless stream of feed data surveying the surface of the Earth as well as providing almost instantaneous communication with its agents across the globe, wherever they might be, and it was this stream of data that provided Mariah with cause to investigate further.

Mariah traced the tip of her index finger across her computer screen, which was located in a small, rectangular office with off-white walls and harsh lighting, and set in a large rig that hung from the high ceiling. She was alone, a cup of coffee beside the computer screen.

"A blip," she muttered to herself, frowning, "a definite blip."

She cross-referenced the blip with the location coordinates and satellite feed data from Cerberus's mighty data banks, tapping commands into her computer keyboard. She reached for her cup as the computer whirred, bringing up the data she had requested. It took just a few moments for Mariah to confirm the location of the blip: it was in the North African territory that was still called Libya on her maps.

"Lakesh is going to want to see this," Mariah muttered, tapping the command key to print off the data. As the printer rumbled to life, Mariah swigged from her cup and grimaced, discovering that her coffee had gone cold. Ghastly. Still, if cold coffee had been the worst of her worries today, she could have rested easy.

THE CERBERUS OPERATIONS ROOM was abuzz with activity as Mariah brought her findings to the attention of the founder of the organization. It was an environment where many highly educated personnel operated in harmony, plotting out field missions and surveying data. Mariah had not always been confident here, feeling somewhat intimidated by the array of physics and chemistry degrees possessed by the on-call staff. In the past two and half years, however, she had grown in confidence, beginning with a relationship with an oceanographer called Clem Bryant. Clem had encouraged Mariah to be more involved in the fieldwork that was crucial to her discipline, something she had at first shied away from when she had been faced with this dangerous new world. But Clem had been killed during an enemy infiltration of the redoubt base, and he had died protecting Mariah from attackers. She still thought of him often, a year after his death, and she regretted that their relationship had not developed further, that he was no longer with her to help guide her and assist the Cerberus operation.

The ops room was a huge space with a high roof and two aisles of computer terminals, lit indirectly so as not to distract their operators. Carved from the inside of the mountain itself, the ceiling looked like the roof of a cave. Within that space, twenty-four computer desks ran from left to right, facing a giant screen on which specific findings could be highlighted.

A giant Mercator map dominated one wall—it was dated, still showing the world before the nukecaust had reshaped the coastlines of North America and other locales. The map was sprinkled with numerous glowing locator dots, which were joined to one another with dotted lines of diodes, creating an image reminiscent of the kind of flight maps that airlines had given to passengers in the twentieth century. Those highlighted routes were not flight paths, however, but the locations and connections of the sprawling mat-trans network that the Cerberus redoubt had originally been tasked to monitor over two hundred years ago.

Developed for the US military, the mat-trans network was primarily confined to North America, although a few outposts could be found farther afield at US air bases in Germany, Scotland and other parts of Europe.

A separate chamber leading off from one corner of the operations room, far from the wide entry doors, contained the Cerberus installation's mat-trans unit along with a small anteroom that could be sealed off if necessary. The chamber had reinforced armaglass walls tinted a coffee-brown color.

Lakesh studied Mariah's findings with an inscrutable

gaze. "What am I looking at here, Mariah?" he asked. More formally known as Mohandas Lakesh Singh, he was a man of medium height with dusky skin, vivid blue eyes and black hair threaded with gray who appeared to be in his midfifties. His hair was slicked back from a high forehead, and he had an aquiline nose and refined mouth. A highly skilled cyberneticist and theoretical physicist from the twentieth century, Lakesh had been cryogenically frozen and endured organ transplants to survive well into his two hundred and fiftieth year. He led the Cerberus operation, albeit as more of a manager than an active investigator, guiding its fifty-strong complement of staff in the protection of humankind from threats outside and within. Lakesh wore a white jumpsuit with a blue, diagonal zipper running up its front, as did Mariah and the other people in the room. This outfit was the standard uniform of the base, although some chose to augment the look with their own accoutrements, giving them an air of individuality amid the vast operation.

"I think it's a sinkhole," Mariah said a little timidly. "It's opened up in the Libyan territory, roughly sixty miles south of Tobruk. I found it after we recorded some seismic activity in the area."

Lakesh nodded, comparing the close-up image to a wider map of the area. "And why do you feel this should concern us?"

"Because there's a parallax point at that location," Mariah explained, "or at least very close to it."

Still holding the printed-out sheet of data, Lakesh stroked his chin sagely. "That is certainly a worry." Although Cerberus had originally been dedicated to the use of the man-made mat-trans network, in recent years Lakesh had helped construct the interphaser, which tapped into the ancient parallax-points system to enable instantaneous travel across the globe. Changes at the location points were not unheard of, but changes on a geological level could mean something more significant was occurring there. "Could you explain to me what a sinkhole is?" he asked.

Mariah smiled her sweet smile, comfortable at last to be able to discuss something within her specific realm of expertise. "Sinkholes are depressions in the ground caused by a collapse of the surface layer," she explained. "This can be through human activity—such as mining. Or it may occur through natural changes to the environment, as with suffusion where a buried cave may be revealed due to problems relating to water drainage, for example—the water weakens the rocks over the cave until they collapse, revealing the cave beneath."

"And how large might such a sinkhole be?" Lakesh asked.

"They have occurred at sizes from a couple of feet to over two thousand feet wide," Mariah told him, "and with the same depth variables."

"So this thing in Libya," Lakesh mused, raising his eyebrows in surprise, "might be two thousand feet deep?"

"The data shows it's significant," Mariah said, "which is to say it's deep, but we'd need to put someone on the ground to measure that with any level of accuracy."

Lakesh nodded thoughtfully. "The parallax points frequently occur at sites of specific religious significance," he said, "but they have become so because of their earlier purpose as sites used in alien transportation. If a sinkhole has opened a path into one of *those* sites, then…" He trailed off, but his meaning was clear enough.

"Precisely," Mariah agreed.

Lakesh turned to a man stationed at a nearby desk who was currently poring through screen after screen of computer language, checking each line for a bug in the program. The man had ginger hair that was wild and tangled in front, where he kept unconsciously running his fingers through it, and he wore a permanent expression of worry on his face. This was Donald Bry, computer expert and Lakesh's right-hand man.

"Donald," Lakesh began, "how soon can we scramble CAT Alpha for a recon mission?"

"CAT Alpha," Bry repeated, looking away in recollection. "They're all on-site right now, Dr. Singh. Brigid's fully recovered from her ankle injury, so they should be able to depart inside of ninety minutes."

"Call them," Lakesh said. "I'm going to plot out alternative parallax points in case our preferred destination has—" He stopped, unsure what to say.

"Sunk?" Mariah offered.

"Yes, sunk," Lakesh agreed with a smile. "That's very good, Mariah. A sense of humor; I like that. Sunk."

Mariah followed Lakesh to the mat-trans chamber located in one corner of the room, from which he could activate the interphaser and do a run-through of the parallax points.

KANE HAD BEEN PRACTICING in the Cerberus firing range when the call came through. The range was located in a subbasement, close to the armory, which stocked multiple units of almost every firearm available, from single-shot .22-caliber Derringer pistols to surface-to-air Dragon Launchers capable of taking an aircraft out of the sky. He had a Colt Officer's ACP in his right hand, a compact and lightweight automatic pistol with an aluminum frame, which still handled large-caliber bullets granting it respectable capability for its size. It was a good weapon to use for practice, even though it was not one that Kane would choose for the field.

Before him, three drop-down targets came into view, paper sheets, each showing a life-size, faceless silhouette like a shadow, each silhouette containing a diagram of circles showing particular vulnerable points, head, heart and so on. The targets appeared at random, between sixty and one hundred feet from where Kane was standing at one end of the firing range, and they cycled toward him on an automated track located on a rig above the firing field. Music was playing from large speakers rigged high against the walls, the booming bass and heavy guitars muffling the loud reports of the Colt as it spit bullets from its muzzle.

Kane stroked the trigger as the next set of targets appeared, moving his perfectly straight arm in a swift arc to deliver two bullets to each target as they were winched along their tracks toward him. As the targets trundled closer, wounds now showing in their heads and hearts, Kane worked the ammunition release on the Colt. In an instant he had loaded a fresh clip and switched the Colt into his left hand, before bringing that arm up and sending another rapid arc of bullets into the looming targets, the closest of which was now thirty feet from him.

Kane relaxed as the second clip clicked on empty, watching as the paper targets completed their wobbling path toward the near end of the range. He smiled as he saw the results of his efforts—he had hit all twelve times, scoring the center ring of the target with ten of the twelve shots. His right hand was dominant and so he had little doubt that he could hit the targets with that—

he had been trained as a Magistrate since birth, combination law enforcer and soldier whose sole purpose was to efficiently operate the weapons he was assigned— and to be a weapon himself. But his left was also strong, not quite as fast, nor as accurate, but enough that he could take out a target at forty feet without going wide.

Kane removed the target sheets from their fastenings and tossed them behind him, adding them to the piled-high trash can that was located beneath one of the roaring speakers. Then he flipped a switch located at the side of his booth which sent the command to restart the session, providing clean new targets with which to hone his prowess. When it came to using guns, there was no such thing as too accurate, Kane knew.

As the first of the new targets dropped down, a device called a Commtact came to life inside Kane's skull, sending a radio communication message directly into his inner ear. "Kane, this is Donald," the voice in Kane's head said, drowning out the prerecorded wail of guitars. "Do you think you can prep for a recon mission setting off in the next ninety minutes?"

"Roger that," Kane acknowledged, squeezing the Colt's trigger and sending bullet after bullet into the silhouetted skull of his would-be opponent. The Commtact was a remarkable communications device that Kane and his fellow Cerberus field operatives relied upon for global communications. The Commtact was a small, radio communications device that was hidden beneath the skin. The subdermal devices were top-of-the-line communications units, the designs for which had been discovered among the artifacts in Redoubt Yankee several years before by the Cerberus rebels. Commtacts featured sensor circuitry incorporating an analog-to-digital voice encoder that was subcutaneously embed-

ded in a subject's mastoid bone. As well as offering
radio communications, the Commtacts could function
as translation devices, operating in real time. Once the
pintels made contact, transmissions were funneled directly to the user's auditory canals through the skull
casing, vibrating the ear canal to create sound. This
functionality also meant that the Commtacts could pick
up and enhance any subvocalization made by the user,
which meant that it was unnecessary to speak aloud to
utilize the communication function. Broadcasts from
the unit were relayed through the Keyhole communications satellite to anywhere in the world.

Thanks to the nature of the vibration system used
by the Commtact, if a user went completely deaf they
would still, in theory, be able to hear normally, in a
fashion, courtesy of the Commtact device.

"Where to?" Kane asked as he finished the clip.

"Mat-trans chamber for departure to Libya," Donald
confirmed before signing off.

"Great," Kane said, delivering the last bullet of his
clip into the silhouetted head of one of the targets.

CAT ALPHA ASSEMBLED fifty minutes later in the Cerberus operations room. Kane was joined by his two
partners, Grant and Brigid. All three were being outfitted for the operation while Lakesh and Mariah outlined her discovery and what they would be looking for.

"Big hole in the ground," Kane said, nodding. "I
think we're capable of spotting that. Y'know, if we look
real hard."

Lakesh ignored the man's sarcasm. "If this sinkhole has disrupted the parallax point, then your arrival
may not be possible," he said. "I suggest you travel
prepared."

Grant shrugged, broad shoulders shifting like an avalanche. "We always travel prepared, Lakesh," he said. "Just part o' the job."

"It may be that the floor has dropped out from under the parallax point itself," Mariah outlined, "or that the materialization point is surrounded by damaged terrain such that we are unable to investigate further."

Kane raised an eyebrow. "We, Mariah?"

"Ms. Falk will be joining you, friend Kane," Lakesh confirmed. "I want an expert on-site in case we only get one chance to look at what's happened."

Kane considered bemoaning having to chaperone a civilian, but he said nothing out loud. He liked Mariah; she was trustworthy and dependable, the kind of operative who formed the backbone of the Cerberus team. Instead he said, "We might be better looking on our own for a first visit."

"As I say, Kane, I want Mariah with you in case this is your only visit," Lakesh said. "If there's any sign of danger, I am certain that you will handle it and get her, and your team, out of there."

Kane nodded. "Yeah." It was all part of the mission.

Grant checked his Copperhead assault rifle, securing the ammo clip before slipping it into the holster rig under his jacket. "Are you bringing a gun, Mariah?" he asked, his voice a deep rumble like distant thunder.

Falk shook her head.

"Then stay behind us."

Together, Kane, Grant, Brigid and Mariah entered the mat-trans chamber, outfitted in camo suits to better blend with the terrain they were about to leap into. The interphaser was waiting in the center of the chamber, already powered up and ready to start the jump.

Lakesh spoke from the doorway as the field team made their way into the chamber.

"I've taken the liberty of tapping several nearby parallax points in case your destination proves disagreeable," he explained. "They are highlighted on the screen—you just need to select one of these alternates as required and the interphaser will begin its jump cycle."

"Thanks, Lakesh," Brigid said, running her eyes across the narrow horizontal strip of screen that was located at the base of the pyramidal unit. "Do you know what we're jumping into?" she asked.

"The area's called the Bir Hakeim Oasis," Lakesh said. "It's in a desert and was once the site of a strategic stronghold for the Turkish military, and it was the location of a bloody battle during World War II."

"And what's there now?" Kane asked.

Lakesh smiled. "You can tell me that, friend Kane, in about two minutes."

With that, Lakesh left the chamber and Brigid activated the interphaser. A swirling tempest of color blossomed from the interphaser, forming two cones of light with the mat-trans chamber, one above the deck and the other, somehow, beneath it. A moment later, Kane led the way into those impossible depths, stepping into the quantum window and onward to a ruined fort in the Libyan desert.

Chapter 5

Kane ducked back behind the pillar, pressing himself and Mariah against it as another jarring scatter of bullets rattled against its edge.

"You okay?" he asked, watching the scene playing out all around them.

"Fine," Mariah said, her voice high and breathless. "What about you? That bullet—"

"Shadow suit," Kane said by way of explanation.

Although she didn't consider herself a field agent, Mariah knew what Kane meant. While Kane might be sporting a bruise for the next few days where the bullet had struck against his arm in a hammer blow, it was a preferable alternative to what would have happened had he not been wearing the miraculous armor weave.

Kane remained tense, watching as the two armies—if indeed it was only two, it was hard to tell—exchanged fire, striking down unfortunate soldiers in sudden spills of red blood. It looked a lot like chaos, but then, in Kane's experience, when it came down to it most ground wars did. "They're not moving in unison," he muttered, making a conscious effort to focus on a specific group—platoon or squadron, maybe?—who were all dressed in similar dirty white robes.

"What?" Mariah asked, confused and feeling woefully out of her depth.

Kane ignored her query, instead engaging his Commtact and hailing his partners, who had taken cover less than twenty feet away. "They're not moving in unison, have you noticed?" he asked.

Brigid's voice came back first, the confusion evident. She was crouched on her haunches beside a mangled column of stonework whose top had been sheared through as if bitten away by some gigantic monster, trying to piece the broken interphaser unit back together. "They're not *what*?" she asked.

"Moving," Kane said, "in unison. They're shooting and they're kind of moving forward in one direction, but there's no strategy between the players."

"Inexperienced, maybe?" Grant asked, chipping in on their shared frequency. He was standing close to Brigid's hiding place, his shoulder pressed to another of the mangled stone columns, using a scope to watch the turret gun that had been set up on the upper level of the aged fort.

"Inexperienced could be it," Kane agreed doubtfully, "but usually that brings out two styles of fighting—the gung ho who gets shot the moment he breaks cover and—"

Boom!

A shell struck near the cluster of ruined pillars, kicking up dirt and curtailing Kane's speech for a moment.

"And?" Brigid prompted, glancing up from her work on the busted interphaser to make sure Kane was okay.

"And the coward," Kane averred, "who hangs back and lets the others get shot. But I'm not really seeing those patterns, are you?"

"Uh-uh," Grant confirmed after a few seconds' observation of the running battle. "You might be onto something." He brought the scope away from his eye, glancing across at Kane. "I don't think the tripod cannon's choosing targets. Its operators are firing wild."

Kane nodded, considering what Grant had said. It wasn't unusual for rookies to get behind a big cannon like that and shoot wild, figuring that something with such destructive power would just seek out and obliterate any target. But it was a fool's game operating it like that—you went through ammo much quicker than you went through targets, and could often be caught with your metaphorical pants down when an armed enemy came close. Which wasn't to underestimate the sheer destructive power of the cannon itself—CAT Alpha would do well to take it out of action if they wanted to survive the mess they had walked into.

"Think you can take out the cannon?" Kane asked Grant over the Commtact.

Grant smiled. "It would be my pleasure," he said, edging out from behind the protective pillar.

"I'll cover you," Kane promised, stroking the Sin Eater pistol already clutched in his hand, "and keep an eye on the girls here."

Sharing the Commtact frequency, Brigid glared at Kane with an annoyed "Hey!" before turning her attention back to her work.

GRANT WOVE OUT INTO the melee, ducking his head and scrambling as bullets zipped through the air less than a dozen feet away. His shadow suit and Kevlar coat would give him some protection, but it didn't pay to get slack in a battle zone like this.

Grant ran, muscles moving with the fluidity of a jungle cat, hurrying across the sand-covered ground in short, fast bursts, using every hunk of broken stone and every fallen body as cover while he constantly updated his best route to the tripod cannon. The cannon was located on a second-story balustrade, its two young operators feeding a belt of bullets into its side as they swung the nose back and forth on its counterweights. Grant estimated that the cannon spit its 24 mm slugs at a rate of three or four per second, kicking up dirt and striking down the occasional solider too dumb or rattled to get out of its path in time. The army was moving away from the fort, so targets were becoming more spread out.

Grant crouched behind a truncated pillar resting on its side in pieces, searching the second story for a way up. The level was broken haphazardly, great chunks of the walkway missing. Can't have made it easy to get that beast up there, Grant thought dourly.

A flight of steps caught his attention, winding up behind a masking wall and leading to the upper level of the ancient fort. It was open ground between Grant and the steps, just twenty feet but more than enough to take a bullet and end it all.

Grant glanced around, scouring the combat zone as a group of bloodstained soldiers came rushing past in a flurry of bullets. As Grant watched, one of the soldiers—little more than a kid, skinny and narrow shouldered, wearing camos stained with sweat and dirt—took a bullet to the back from the tripod cannon and went down on his knees, his face slamming into the dirt a moment later. His colleagues shouted something incomprehensible, shooting back at the cannon and all around them in a wild assault before vacating the area.

Suddenly, the cannon stopped firing, and the whole scene was beset with an eerie moment of calm amid the carnage. Grant took that moment to run, ducking low and keeping his head down, closing the twenty-foot gap between his hiding place and the stairwell that led to the second story.

FROM HIS OWN hiding place, Kane watched Grant make a run for it in the momentary quiet between cannon blasts. *Come on, Grant,* he mouthed, his eyes scouring the terrain all around his partner for any signs of a hidden ambush.

For a moment it looked as though Grant's path would remain clear. Then, with no warning, a figure emerged from the shadows of a toppled pillar, holding an AK-47 rifle with a wide bandage wrapped low over his forehead. He had Grant in his sights, Kane could tell. Kane gently let out the breath he was holding, squeezing the trigger of his Sin Eater on the exhale.

GRANT WAS ALMOST at the stairwell entry when the soldier came bungling out from the shadow of a pillar. The man looked unsteady on his feet, and he was dressed in dirty fatigues with the brutal tool of an AK-47 clutched in his hands. There was something else, too, that Grant registered in the first instant he saw the man—he was wearing a white bandage across the top of his head, and the bandage came down to the level of his nostrils, entirely covering his eyes.

"What th—?" Grant asked even as the stranger turned his AK-47 on him.

Before he could fire, however, the bandaged soldier dropped to the ground, the distinctive recoil of a Sin Eater being discharged echoing amid the chaos of battle, a bloom of ghastly red materializing on the man's fatigues where they covered his chest.

Kane!

Grant kept running. He would thank his partner later; right now he needed to get himself behind that wall and up those stairs to knock out the cannon that had already recommenced its incessant song of destruction from above him.

An instant later Grant was past the stone arch of the doorway and scrambling, blaster in hand, up the steep steps that led to the fort's second level.

The archway was made from sand-colored stone, as were the steps. As Grant stepped into the shadows, he felt the heat of the burning sun on his face drop away, a relief of sudden coolness from the shade. In that instant, however, he was momentarily blind, his vision flickering in extremes of green as it tried to adjust after the brilliance of the direct sunlight. He took a moment, just a moment, to blink back his sun blindness, taking a pace forward onto the first stone step. The staircase curved around, winding up on itself as it ascended to the second story.

Two more steps and his vision was still restricted by the aftereffects of the sun…and Grant was in the sights of an attacker. He felt the movement of the breeze as the man stepped forward, lunging downward with the long blade of the knife he held, driving it toward Grant's face.

Grant reared back, sweeping his left arm up to knock the blade aside by instinct alone. He still couldn't see, not fully, his eyes rendering the figure attacking him from the shadows as a kind of dark blur of limbs and torso.

The man—and it was a man—spit something in a tongue Grant didn't recognize. His Commtact tried to translate, came up with a phrase that was doubtless a curse, but sounded somehow ludicrous to his ears.

"Goat of a mother!"

But with the insult came something else—a gunshot, loud in the confines of the stone stairwell, the blast accompanied by the acrid smell of cordite. Something raced past Grant in that instant, and he heard the wall behind him give up a chunk of rock with a sound like walking on gravel.

Grant did not hesitate. Even through the retreating green mire of his eyesight, he brought his Sin Eater to bear, blasting his opponent in the left kneecap, hobbling the guy in an instant.

Grant's attacker cried out in sudden shock and pain, stumbling forward, losing his balance on the steps above Grant. His blaster—a handheld pistol of unknown manufacture—spit again, sending a 9 mm slug at Grant in a roar of explosive propellant. The bullet struck Grant in the same instant, slamming high on his left biceps before reeling away with the impact. Grant grunted, stumbling against the wall to his right. It had been a glancing blow, clipping him below the shoulder with a lot of force but no penetration—his double layer of Kevlar and shadow suit had ensured that. But it still stung like something out of a blacksmith's forge.

Grant raised his pistol and blasted again, sending a second shot into his opponent—now visible as the green wash across his vision retreated to a handful of spots when he blinked. The man was unshaved with an unruly mop of dark, curly hair held in place with a olive-green cap. His uniform—if you could call it that—was too tight across the chest and too large in the pants, and it looked as if it had been sewn together from scraps, albeit in a way that made for effective camouflage.

Grant stepped aside as his attacker sunk down the steps, blood seeping from his open mouth. Dead.

KANE MEANWHILE HAD his own problems. Two ragtag-looking soldiers came hurrying into the partially hidden area where he was hiding out with Mariah and Brigid, their backs to the Cerberus team. The two looked like brothers. Both were young men with dark hair and beards and scuffed uniforms that had seen better days. They each carried an AK-47 automatic rifle smeared with the pale dust of the whipped-up sand.

Kane subvocalized a warning to Brigid where she knelt working on the broken interphaser. Thanks to its remarkable mechanics, the Commtact could pick up such a gesture and amplify it for Brigid's ear canal, turning Kane's subvocalized "company" into a whisper.

By the time Brigid looked up, Kane had stepped silently forward, bringing the nose of his Sin Eater up until it was pressed against the side of the head of the closest soldier.

"One wrong move and I blow your brain all over your companion—*capisce*?"

Whether the foreign soldier did or did not *"capisce"*—and chances were he hadn't comprehended a word Kane had just said—he certainly understood what a blaster pressed against his face meant. Kane smiled as the man lowered his own gun, saying something in his own tongue that the Commtact automatically translated as "No, no, not shoot."

But even as the soldier spoke, his companion spun, alerted by his partner, raising his automatic rifle and squeezing the trigger in a heartbeat.

Kane saw the move coming, that fabled point-man sense of his kicking in like clairvoyance, leaping aside as the trigger clicked and a stream of 9 mm slugs spit in his direction, cutting down the other hapless soldier before the man could even acknowledge what was happening.

Kane dived to one side. This was not the first time his point-man sense had saved his life. He had been renowned for it, all the way back to his days as a Cobaltville Magistrate many years before. It seemed to be an almost uncanny ability to sense danger before it happened, alerting Kane to the threat with just enough time to avoid it. There was nothing uncanny about it, however; it was merely the combination of his standard five senses, honed to an incredible degree, making him utterly aware of his surroundings. A change in wind, the noise of a scuffing boot—a hundred telltale clues gave Kane the advantage in combat, an advantage that could be the difference between life and death.

Kane hit the ground with a whuff of expelled breath, rolling his body even as a stream of 9 mm slugs chased after him across the dirt, always just a handful of inches behind him. As he rolled, Kane brought up the Sin Eater, nudging the trigger and sending his own triple burst of bullets at his attacker.

The first soldier had sunk to his knees as Kane's bullets struck his companion, a choking noise coming from his throat. His trigger-happy companion dropped in a swirl of unguided limbs, the AK-47 swiveling up into the sky and sending off another half dozen shots before it finally quieted. Then the man lay on his back in the dirt, absolutely still, blood blooming on his chest, the automatic pointed upward like a grave marker.

"Poor sap," Kane growled as he picked himself up and brushed dirt from his clothes. "Shouldn't mess with an ex-Mag."

Across from the dead soldiers, Mariah Falk was cow-

ering beside the pillar, her face pale with exhaustion.
"You—you killed them," she said.

"Yeah," Kane acknowledged with a solemn nod. But
experience nagged at the back of his mind, telling him
that something wasn't right here. The excitable soldier
who had shot at him and his partner didn't seem to have
much in the way of aim. Kane had leaped aside and
stayed out of the path of his bullets as much by the man's
inability as his own improbable luck. Furthermore, he
had shot his own colleague, which could be put down
to inexperience or panic, but it still reeked of something closer to stupidity—and Kane didn't have these
two pegged as stupid, just unfortunate enough to find a
fully trained hard-contact Magistrate had materialized
from a wormhole in space in the spot where they hoped
to hide from the battle. No, there was something else
to these soldiers and their recklessness, something he
wasn't seeing yet. And, whatever it was, he didn't like it.

Chapter 6

Grant raced up the last of the stone steps, the sound of his footsteps masked by the cacophony of the tripod cannon as it continued its deadly opera.

He waited a moment at the topmost step, crouching down and peering warily around the edge of the arched wall where it ended. There was a sort of balcony beyond, wide as a Sandcat wag and made of solid stone. There were cracks in the stone, ancient gouges where rocks had been forced together and held in place by tension. There were two operators working the turret, with a third man visible beside them. The third figure had been hidden before by his low-angled view of the balcony, but now Grant could see him and fingered him for a guard or sentry of some kind because of a stub-nosed pistol resting between his hands. The man was sitting on a box of ammunition and surrounded by almost a dozen more.

"Where do these psychos get all their ammo from?" Grant muttered to himself with a disbelieving shake of his head.

Grant brought his Sin Eater around the arch, edging it silently along the wall until the sentry was in his sights.

Pop!

The sentry keeled over as the bullet drilled through his hand, slumping forward where he sat as his right hand was reduced to a bloody smear.

Even as the man slumped forward, Grant stepped out from his hiding place, shooting again. His next bullet ripped through the arm of one of the two gunners, striking the man with such force that he went careening from his position and danced himself straight over the edge of the parapet.

The second gunner said something that Grant's Commtact translated as "Who's there?"

"Hands in the air where I can see them!" Grant snarled in a voice like rumbling thunder, raising the Sin Eater so that the man could see he was in the center of its sights.

Only, the man couldn't see it, Grant realized. He was blind.

"How's that interphaser coming along, Baptiste?" Kane asked, nervously pacing back and forth as he watched the battlefield. Grant had disappeared from view up the stairwell and the general hubbub that they had walked into seemed to have moved on, for it was now playing out fifty yards away from the ruined barracks itself.

"I can't work miracles, Kane," Brigid told him, irritated. "Just let me work."

"I don't like being somewhere without a way out," Kane growled.

"That explains your inability to hold down a relationship, then," Brigid snapped back at him.

"What's that supposed to mean?"

Brigid glared at Kane for a few seconds, an unspoken challenge flickering between them. They were *anam-charas*, these two, soul friends whose relationship reached back through the folds of time, beyond their current bodies. Kane would always be watching

over Brigid and she over him, the two souls entwined
in a dance that stretched beyond the lines of eternity.

Mariah saw the look Brigid shot Kane from her hiding place, wondered what was going on between the
two of them.

"What?" Kane asked Brigid. "You getting broody
all of a sudden?"

"No," Brigid told him. "Just wondering why we keep
fighting these abominable wars for humanity when our
whole lives are geared to nothing but the fight. I've lost
everyone I cared about—Daryl, others. And look at
us—we're meant to be *anam-charas*, soul friends, but
sole friends is about the sum of that. I just wonder how
we can keep fighting for humanity when we're so out
of touch with what humanity really is."

Kane began to respond when Grant's voice came
over the Commtact frequency, interrupting the discussion. "You wanna know why the cannon team are firing
blind?" he asked. "Because they are blind!"

Automatically, Kane looked across to where the cannon was located, realizing that its seemingly incessant
sputter had finally halted. "Say again?"

GRANT WAS STANDING beside the tripod cannon, holding
its operator's arm behind his back with such force that
the man was bent over until he almost kissed the deck.

"I said they're blind," Grant elaborated. "Both operators, I think, plus their guards."

Grant's captive squirmed in his arms, spitting saliva
on the floor as he issued a cruel curse on Grant and his
family. The man's eyes were unfocused, darting wildly
in their sockets.

"The Commtact's not doing a great job with their
language," Grant continued. "Whatever it is they're

speaking seems to be a combination of Bantu, French, slang and some local patois it can't decipher. But from what I can tell, they're either blind or only partially sighted."

"And they're operating big guns," Kane responded, with a clear edge to his voice.

"Maybe by luck," Grant said.

BRIGID SPOKE UP without taking her eyes from the repair work she was doing on the interphaser. "Shoot off enough bullets and you're bound to get a few lucky shots, right?"

Kane shook his head, not disagreeing but just trying to piece everything together. The two soldiers he had dealt with had seemed—well, not real aware of their surroundings, that was for sure. Could they be blind, too?

Kane scanned the area beyond the little enclave, counting the trickle of soldiers still bumbling about amid the fortress ruin. At first glance they seemed normal enough, the usual fretful stalking of people on the edge of stress. But look again, and Kane thought he detected more of an aimlessness to their progress, as though they perhaps couldn't see where it was they were headed, were just drawn to the noise of battle.

Kane scampered forward, reached for one of the two soldiers he had dealt swift justice to mere moments earlier. They looked normal, and even their eyes looked normal. How do you know a man's blind?

"Baptiste, protect the civilian," Kane instructed, referring to Mariah.

Before Brigid could so much as look up, Kane was off, hurrying into the wreck of the fortress, head down and blaster in his hand.

"Dammit, Kane, do you always have to be so blasted impetuous?" Brigid muttered, shaking her head. Then she called over to Mariah, working the catch on her hip holster where she housed her TP-9 semiautomatic.

"Mariah, you know how to use a gun, right?"

Falk looked uncertain, her eyes fixed on the pistol in Brigid's hand. "Um…kind of."

Brigid handed the geologist the gun. "Point and shoot," she summarized. "Anyone gets too close that you don't like the look of, just blast them. Not Kane, though. He can be annoying sometimes, but he'll only get more annoying if you put a hole in him."

Then Brigid turned her attention back to the interphaser, hoping to be able to trigger a pathway out of this mess. Lakesh had programmed in a half dozen escape vectors if she could just get the wretched thing functioning.

KANE SCRAMBLED, GLANCING up at the mounted cannon and seeing Grant's shaved head peeking up over the angle of the deck.

Five ramshackle soldiers were trekking over the ground, finding their way past the wreckage that littered the terrain. Kane dodged past them, spotting a straggler who had opted to stick to the shadows that ran alongside the walls. The young man's rifle rocked in one hand as he felt his way along the wall with the other.

"Kane, that you down there?" Grant's voice came over the Commtact.

"Gonna try something," Kane explained without slowing his pace. "Cover me, okay?"

Kane reached the lone figure in a few loping strides, coming around and behind him to reduce the chances of the guy shooting him. The man was young and dressed in a loose, dirt-smeared top which billowed as the wind caught it. The AK-47 rifle in his hands was scuffed with dirt.

Sending his Sin Eater back to its hidden holster beneath the sleeve of his jacket, Kane sprinted at the man before dropping low so that he connected with him in a long slide across the loose, dry sand. Kane's legs caught the soldier's, tripping him so that he caromed headfirst off the wall that he had been feeling his way along.

The soldier grunted sharply as he struck the wall.

Kane was on top of him in a flash, grabbing the barrel of the AK-47 and angling it away from him even as he pressed his weight onto the man's torso.

"What are you doing? What's going on?" the man spat in a foreign tongue, the real-time translation coming to Kane almost instantly. It sounded like French.

Kane shoved his free hand against the man's jaw, pressing his hand across his opponent's mouth. "Keep quiet and I'll let you live," he snarled, hoping the man knew enough English to follow his gist.

The man struggled beneath Kane, trying to bring the rifle into play. It was a poor weapon for such close combat, its 16-inch barrel too long and too unwieldy for close quarters. Kane fixed his grip on it and yanked hard, whipping it out of his opponent's hand. He slung it to the side behind him, just far enough out of the man's reach that he couldn't grab it.

"Quiet," Kane warned the man, checking around for possible attackers. No one was approaching—the group of soldiers Kane had spotted was close to the edge of the fort now, where the walls had tumbled away.

Kane looked back at the man beneath him, watching his eyes. They were hazel and they seemed normal enough, a little wide in panic maybe but otherwise normal. The man struggled, and Kane pressed his hand harder against his mouth in an effort to hold his head still.

Kane brought his right hand around, clenched it and extended just his index finger. He waved the index finger before the man's eyes, running it swiftly to the left, then to the right across the man's field of vision. The eyes did not follow Kane's finger—not proof positive, but enough to make Kane suspect that Grant's weren't the only soldiers who had lost their sight.

"Can you see?" Kane snapped, using his Commtact's translation mode to convert the words into stuttering French.

The man's eyes remained wide and he refused to answer Kane's question.

"You want me to kill you right here?" Kane snarled at the young soldier. "Answer the damn question. Can you see? Are you blind?"

"I can see," the man replied in French with an edge to his voice that Kane noticed even if the translation program of the Commtact failed to pick up on it. "I see the face of god before everything, lighting every step and every move, showing me the path of salvation."

Chapter 7

"Blind men fighting a war," Kane scoffed. "What part of that even makes sense?"

The battle had moved on. Now Kane, still standing over the soldier he had disarmed some minutes earlier, had been joined by Brigid—still tinkering with the interphaser as she tried to piece its internal mechanism back together—Mariah and Grant. Grant had brought the remaining gunner with him, held in his strong grip in such a way that he was forced to walk pigeon-toed as he was partly shoved and partly dragged across the stone-strewn battlefield.

"It doesn't," Grant confirmed, screwing up his face.

"Maybe it does," Brigid said from where she sat in the shade with the ruined interphaser spread before her. "Perhaps we shouldn't ask about their blindness, but concern ourselves instead with what they do see, or think they're seeing."

The others looked at her, bemused. Brigid had always been "the smart one" of the CAT Alpha field team, and sometimes her leaps of logic took a little bit of explaining before everyone caught up on the same page.

"You said that fish-face here said something about seeing the face of god," Brigid reminded Kane as she worked a screw back in place on the interphaser with her thumbnail. It slipped. The chassis was cracked above and below its resting place where a bullet had struck.

"Yeah," Kane acknowledged, "but I figure that's—y'know—metaphorical. Religious zealot hokum."

Grant nodded. "We've see a lot of religious zealots in our time."

"And a lot of hokum," Brigid accepted. "But what if what he said was meant literally? That he's really seeing the face of god. Or, at least, something he thinks is a god." She looked up at Kane and the others for approval. "You follow?"

Mariah Falk nodded. "But which god?" she asked. Though a geologist rather than a field agent, even she had met her share of beings who considered themselves gods during her time with Cerberus. One such being, the monstrous Ullikummis, had compelled her to commit fiery suicide, and she had only been stopped when one of her colleagues had shot her in the knee, preventing her from throwing herself into a crematorium oven.

Brigid smiled grimly. "That, Mariah, is a very insightful question."

"Insights can wait till we're somewhere secure," Kane reminded everyone, his eyes fixed on the distant battle still under way just past the borders of the ruined fort. "Baptiste, have you got anywhere with getting the interphaser running?"

"I've made progress," Brigid told him, "but it's not responding to my commands yet. I need—"

"Sure," Kane said with a wave of his hand, cutting her off. "Then let's keep moving forward, locate the quake source we came here to check, and try to stay out of trouble."

Grant laughed at that. "Staying out of trouble? You get bumped on the head or something, buddy?"

"I said *try*," Kane clarified as he removed the ammo

clip from his captive's AK-47 and secreted it in a pocket, along with the other ammunition he had found on the man. "No one's expecting the impossible."

"HE SAID THAT he saw the face of god before everything," Kane recalled as the four Cerberus warriors trekked away from the tumbledown fort, away from the ongoing skirmish between the mysterious factions of blind men.

They were following the path laid out by the crack in the earth, tracking along it as it widened and narrowed, widened and narrowed, searching for the source. Right now, the gap was still five feet across, and it was deep enough that you could not see down to its floor.

"He told me it lit every step he took," Kane continued, "showing him the path of salvation. Like I say, normal religious fanaticism."

"But if he meant it literally," Brigid reasoned, "then here is a man who is seeing an entirely different view of reality. The way he described it, as lighting his path, it might be like neon arrows showing him where to move and what to do. I'm speculating, of course, but we've both seen different views on reality, Kane. You know that."

He did. Kane had been drawn into a war with the Annunaki, which had seen him tap into their holistic view of the universe. He had fought in the bordering dimensions of string theory, which his brain had interpreted in the wildest ways, trying to provide input he could comprehend. It had barely worked; only Kane's innate practicality had kept him grounded during—and after—the experience.

Brigid, too, had touched on different ways to view this fragile thing we call reality. She had been mindwiped by the Annunaki prince Ullikummis, and had her thinking rewired into the Annunaki way of seeing the world for a short period of time. She had become a different person then, just to process the new perspective she had been given on the world, and had taken the name of Brigid Haight. That new comprehension had allowed her to shift time itself, stepping outside of its confines long enough to undo the birth of a goddess. It had been traumatic, and Brigid loathed thinking back to those days, had done all she could to mentally distance herself from that dark other her.

"Men fighting wars in a reality that only they can see," Kane mused. "That's…not an easy thing to process."

"I agree," Brigid said. "Reality is a lot more fragile than most of us realize." As she spoke, her mind went back to another occasion, when CAT Alpha had stumbled upon an ancient device designed to bring about a new genesis. Kane had died during that mission, truly died, but Brigid had stepped inside the machine and reworked things, forcing reality to reknit. In doing so, she had brought Kane back from the dead, though she had never told him.

Mariah was walking beside Grant a few paces behind Brigid and Kane, struggling a little to keep up the pace that they were setting. They were soldiers while she was primarily a desk worker—gunfights and traipsing across battlefields were significantly outside Mariah's comfort zone.

"There's a lot of trekking around in what you guys do, huh?" she said, doing her best to ignore the feeling of damp sweat in her hair.

"Seems that way sometimes," Grant agreed. Despite his recent exertion in curtailing the tripod cannon's assault while wearing a long duster made of Kevlar, he seemed to be barely breaking a sweat. The shadow suit he wore beneath his clothes was regulating his body temperature, keeping him cool in spite of the fierce sunshine.

"So, what's the formula you guys use in determining whether to use the interphaser or the Mantas to travel somewhere?" Mariah asked.

Grant looked at her and smiled. "No formula," he said. "If there's a parallax point or an old mat-trans unit, then we use that, unless we figure we might need to switch locations and stay on the move—in which case, we bring the Mantas out of the hangar." The Mantas he referred to were superfast aircraft of alien design, ones which he, Kane and a few other members of Cerberus were adept in piloting.

Ahead of them, the bleak landscape stretched on and on, parched dirt dotted with stones like the debris from a mine, just a few leafless bushes here and there, rooted to the ground like the skeletal nests of birds. The terrain rose gradually, the crack in the ground widening and narrowing uncertainly but never closing to less than a four-foot gap.

The Cerberus team followed the line drawn by the crack in the earth, making their way up the gentle slope. The slope was made up of loose stones of all sizes and shapes, and as they went farther they found it became harder to keep one's balance on the loose ground. Mariah especially needed help to keep moving forward, and Grant put an arm behind her back to prevent her from slipping. Brigid had put away the interphaser by this point, replacing it in its padded carry case, which could be strapped to her back. The unit still wasn't operational; the bullet had evidently sheared through something important.

As they climbed higher, some of the loose rocks were

dropping into the jagged rent that they were following. Once one started to fall, the rocks cascaded like a waterfall. For a frightening moment, Mariah slipped and fell toward the brink where those rocks had disappeared. Grant grabbed her in an instant, held her tightly by the arm as she dropped to one knee and continued to slide toward the rent in the earth.

"Hang on," Grant told her with all the authority of the Magistrate he had once been.

"I'm—" Mariah began, breathlessly. "Can't…" Her kneeling leg slipped out from under her as a landslide of stones began to disappear into the four-foot-wide opening of the chasm.

Grant tensed his muscles, spreading his legs wider to anchor himself in place. Kane and Brigid hurried back to join him, themselves slipping dangerously on the relentless stream of rocks that were now cascading into the pit.

Grant began to slip, his feet sliding along with the loose stones as Mariah's weight threatened to drag them both into the chasm. Mariah herself was thrashing about, trying to keep from sliding into the darkness, her feet so close to the edge.

"Stop struggling," Kane advised as he scrambled across the moving river of stones, struggling to get purchase. "Baptiste, hold on to me!"

"Hold on to you?" Brigid asked, confused.

"Yeah, I'm going to try to grab Mariah," Kane said, reaching forward.

Brigid swiveled behind Kane, placing her arms around his midriff and locking her hands together.

Kane reached his hand out for Mariah, speaking through gritted teeth as he grabbed her flailing left arm. "Grant, you okay back there, bud?"

Grant was on his backside, still holding on to Mariah's right arm as he struggled to stay in place. His grip had slipped down her sweat-slicked forearm, however, and it was now cinched painfully around her wrist. Mariah felt as though her hand was being wrenched off.

"Grant?" Kane pressed.

"Just grab her, Kane," Grant told him. "Don't worry about me."

With Brigid providing counterbalance, Kane leaned in and reached his other arm around Mariah's shoulders, still clinging to her left arm with his right hand. He pulled her to him in what seemed almost a consoling hug, drawing her face toward his left shoulder and chest. Mariah flailed, still fighting the stream of loose shale that threatened to throw her into the pit, and then she had an arm around Kane. Grant let go, anchoring himself in place as the stream of rocks beneath him rushed onward like an avalanche, accompanied by a susurration of noise as they disappeared into the chasm. In a moment he had stopped moving, though the rocks continued to drop.

"No one move," Kane instructed. "Everyone just stay still, let the rocks settle."

Brigid clutched Kane around his waist while Mariah clung on to him like a drowning woman clinging to debris from a shipwreck.

"You're okay," Kane told her, gently. "You're not going to fall."

Around them, the rocks settled finally as the last few fell into the darkness. The ground, such as it was, felt stable again.

Brigid let go of Kane and he let go of Mariah, while Grant pushed himself cautiously back to a standing position beside them.

"Now, let's just proceed with caution, okay?" Kane said. "No sudden moves."

Following his own advice, Kane took wary steps up the slope, testing the ground with his toe before he proceeded, guiding the group in a path that took them a little farther away from the dangerous chasm they were tracking.

The slope continued to rise, taking the group forty or fifty feet above the tallest part of the distant fort where they had materialized. Throughout the climb, they saw no one else, though the sounds of gunfire continued to echo from the distance where two armies—one made up of blind men—fought their lunatic war.

The Cerberus group reached the summit of the gentle slope unexpectedly. Unexpected, that is, because they had not foreseen that there would be an almost sheer drop on the other side. From above, it looked like a sinkhole, a perfectly circular maw in the earth, its sides so steep that they were almost vertical. A few scaffolds were dotted here and there with ladders leading down into the hole itself. There were figures wandering among the scaffolding, and they could see two simple, boxy buildings at different levels where the people here might take shelter. The nearest ladder down was sixty feet away, a quarter turn around the circular hole.

"What the hell?" Grant muttered, gazing over the edge.

Kane looked at his partners, his eyebrows raised. "Watch that first step, huh?" he said.

"It's a mine," Mariah stated, looking at the formations all around them. They now saw that the slope of rock that they had climbed was waste that had been removed from the ground to create the mine shaft. The shaft itself was a perfectly vertical drop into the ground.

"Not natural, then?" Kane checked.

"No, not natural."

Brigid turned to Mariah, quizzical. "Could this be the cause of the quake?"

Mariah shrugged. "Possibly," she admitted. "I guess it depends on what they're using to bore into the earth."

Kane eyed the figures on the scaffold, trying to detect a pattern that might indicate whether they were sentries. "Guess we're going to have to take a look-see at what's inside," Kane told the others, reloading his Sin Eater.

"I think I miss my workstation," Mariah muttered as she followed the Cerberus field team around the lip of the mine.

Chapter 8

The blind soldier's words buzzed around Kane's thoughts as he and Grant led the way toward the mine, creeping down the only ladder that emerged on the lip of the shaft, moving swiftly, hand over hand. Kane had come up with the plan hurriedly and on the fly—standard operating procedure for Cerberus field missions, it seemed. As the most combat savvy, he and Grant would clear the path of any resistance—not that there would necessarily be any; it was just better in Kane's opinion to expect the worst than to be caught with your pants down. Kane's opinion of people in general was low, since he had seen too much both as a Magistrate and as a freedom fighter.

They reached the first level swiftly. The level was made of planks lined up beside one another like floorboards—a scaffold structure held them roughly horizontal, actually at a twelve-degree slope heading down toward the mine. There was no one on this level, and a dozen strides took Kane and Grant to the next ladder, running down the sheer surface of bored rock.

Kane led the way once more, hurrying down the ladder to the level below, those eerie words of the soldier still playing on his mind.

I can see. I see the face of god before everything, lighting every step and every move, showing me the path of salvation. That's what the soldier had told Kane when he cornered him.

Kane reached the next level, another strip of planks running at a rough horizontal. This level supported one of the two basic structures that were presumably used for shelter. Kane waited at the final step of the ladder, ducking his head down and peering at the boxy structure that dominated this level. It was fifteen feet in length with an open, glassless window at the near end. Within, Kane could see someone's head and shoulders, the rest of the person was hidden beneath the sill of the frame. As he watched, the figure in the construct drank from a leather flask.

Suddenly the structure's door swung open, and two more figures came walking out of it while the figure in the window kept drinking. These two were both men, solidly built with pistols tucked through the belts holding up their pants, loose cotton shirts in a kind of grimy off-white. There was something else, too—both men had scarves over their faces, covering their eyes but leaving their mouths and noses visible.

I see the face of god before everything, Kane thought, recalling the haunting words of the soldier.

Kane waited until the two scarfed figures were completely outside and had closed the door. Then, stepping down from the ladder, Kane raised his blaster casually in his hands, enough that the two men could see what it was, and hissed for their attention.

"Hands in the air," he told them. "I'm not here to hurt you if I can help it."

The two men halted, turning to face Kane. He could not see their eyes, which were entirely hidden behind cloth, but he figured they were looking at him in some arcane way he did not understand.

"Who are you?" the one on the left asked, the words automatically translated by Kane's subdermal Commtact.

"What do you want?" asked the other, again translated in real time.

Neither of them had raised their hands, as Kane had requested, but nor were they making any obvious move to reach for their weapons or raise an alert of some kind.

"Hands up, where I can see them," Kane urged, gesturing with the Sin Eater's barrel. "What's going on here? What are you mining?" He repeated the words via the Commtact's translation, waited as it translated the men's response.

"Heaven's Light," the man to the left stated.

Frustration swept over Kane, wondering whether the translation circuit in his Commtact had gone buggy. "You're mining light…from Heaven?" Kane asked, once again trusting the Commtact's translator circuitry.

Both men nodded. "Yes, Heaven's Light."

"Down there," the man on the right clarified, pointing at the mine.

O-kay, so this just got a whole lot weirder, Kane thought. Now he was talking to two strangers wearing blindfolds who assured him that they were mining Heaven's Light. Not exactly just another day at the office!

Kane engaged his Commtact, automatically patching through to Grant—even though the man was just a flight above him. "You hear this?" he asked. "They say they're mining Heaven's Light. Mean anything to you?"

"Could be a nickname for a drug of some kind," Grant proposed, "though not one I've heard before."

"Me, either," Kane agreed.

The two blindfolded men were still—well—*watching*

him was the only description Kane could come up with, their hidden eyes seemed to be locked on him beneath the covering of their headwear. To them he must look as if he was talking to himself, that was, of course, assuming that they could see.

After a moment's consideration, Kane gestured to the man on the right, the one closest to the edge of the walkway. "Lift up the blindfold," he ordered. "I want to see what you're hiding under there."

Both men just stood stock-still, waiting as if they had not heard Kane's demand.

Kane raised his Sin Eater so that it was in clear view of both men, pointing it at the forehead of the man on the left. "Lift up the blindfold or your pal here gets a 9 mm guest in his skull."

Slowly, the man on the right began to raise his hands, reaching for the bottom edge of the blindfold he wore.

"No sudden movements," Kane advised, translating again through the Commtact.

At that moment, Grant dropped down from the lower rungs of the ladder, hands raised and his own pistol tucked away in its hidden wrist sheath. "Better drop it, Kane," he said reluctantly.

Grant was followed down the ladder by a man in his thirties, wearing dirt-smeared fatigues and holding a Vektor SP nine-round pistol in his right hand. Like the men that Kane was facing, he had a scarf pulled low to cover his eyes.

Kane did not turn around, he only asked Grant a question: "This for real?"

"Yeah," Grant said. "Lower your blaster, this ain't the right time for heroes."

Kane lowered his hand, then dropped the Sin Eater so that it fell to the sloping surface at his feet. Before him, the man had got no further in raising his blind-fold, and he pulled it back in place as soon as Kane had dropped his weapon.

"What's going on?" Kane asked, turning his head slowly to glance over his shoulder. He saw Grant stand-ing three steps behind him, a dour expression on his face. As he caught Grant's eye, the bigger man winked at him, his mouth twitching with a hint of a smile. It meant he had a plan.

TWO MEN HAD sneaked up incompetently on Brigid and Mariah as they had waited at the top of the trash heap. Brigid, alerted by their voices, had spotted them as they emerged from behind a clump of piled rocks across to the right of where Kane and Grant had disappeared. They must have been stationed on this pile of discarded rocks, set to patrol it in a basic concentric sweep pattern. Counterclockwise, what used to be called widdershins.

They had been discussing different approaches to goat rearing, of all things, when one of them spotted the Cerberus women and ordered his colleague to hush. Brigid stood out, of course, her long train of vibrant red hair catching in the wind atop the pile of sandy rock.

Brigid leaned across to Mariah, who was a few paces away trying to follow where the crack in the earth led next, and whispered, "Mariah, we're about to have com-pany. Just play along and don't do anything stupid."

Mariah's eyes widened at the instruction. "As if I ever do anything…stupid or otherwise," she muttered with an irritated shake of her head. She had a point, Brigid realized; Mariah was a geologist, not a field agent—quick-thinking and fighting for her life was all a little new to her. She was more used to dealing with rock formations that had taken millions of years to settle into their current patterns.

Brigid pushed the interphaser back into her backpack, masking the movement from view with her body, clipping the protective case closed. It wasn't as though the unit was working, and she doubted that these locals would have the engineering know-how to get it operative again, but it didn't pay to advertise the tech. She listened as the footsteps came closer on shifting rocks.

"You, woman," said a male voice behind her, speaking French with a rough accent, "hands up in the air."

French? Now then, wasn't that interesting? She had expected the man to be speaking Libyan but it seemed he had come from farther afield.

Without turning, Brigid raised her hands. "May I help you?" she asked in fluent French. Brigid did not need the Commtact to translate for her; she was fluent in more than a few languages and, thanks to her amazing eidetic memory, could manage in many more.

As she spoke, Brigid heard the other man call to Mariah, heard the crunch of boots on gravel as he reached for her. Mariah yelped, stifling a scream.

"What are you doing here?" the man who had approached Brigid demanded.

Brigid slowly turned her head until she could see her questioner. He was a man in his thirties, dark skinned, and the stubble on his jowls masked a hint of a double chin. His shirt was a sweat-stained white with an open neck, and he had a yellow kerchief wrapped around his neck. He wore cotton pants and heavy boots that laced halfway up his calves. Most oddly, he had a thin ribbon of red material tied around his head which covered his eyes. A swift glance to his partner confirmed Brigid's suspicion that the other man also had something covering his eyes, his blindfold thicker and colored a brilliant white, wide as a winter scarf. Both men held South African–made Vektor SP pistols in their hands, their dull black finish gave them the appearance of being cloaked in thick shadows despite the brilliant sunlight.

"Well?" the man approaching Brigid pressed.

"Afternoon stroll," Brigid replied. "Such a nice day out here, isn't it?"

The muzzle of the man's gun flicked to indicate the holstered TP-9 semi that Brigid had retrieved from Mariah and now wore at her hip. "You always stroll armed?"

"Hey, who doesn't?" Brigid teased. "You can never be too sure who or what you're going to run into, right? Present company excepted, I'm sure."

"Yes," the man drawled in French. "You will remove the gun—fingertips only, you understand?"

Brigid nodded, reaching slowly for her weapon. She didn't intend to upset this jerk, nor did she plan to get shot—in fact, what she hoped would happen was that this sentry crew would escort her and Mariah into the heart of the operation here and unintentionally reveal just what the heck was going on.

As KANE STOOD there on the scaffold, Brigid's voice came from above them, regretful. "They snuck up on us," she explained, her slender form appearing on the ladder as she made her way down at the end of a gun barrel. Her pistol had been removed from its hip holster, though she still had her backpack in place—presumably with the interphaser still inside. Mariah followed her, looking pale with fear.

A few seconds later the two women had joined Grant

and Kane on the flat level of the scaffold, accompanied
by two more soldier types holding pistols and wearing makeshift blindfolds. Brigid was a capable fighter,
Kane knew—in fact she was far more than that simple
description implied. Had these people gotten the drop
on her because of Falk, or was there something more
to this than he realized?

One of the two men that Kane had ambushed dropped
to his knees and recovered Kane's blaster, shoving it
in his waistband, while the other unholstered his own
Vektor pistol and held it on Kane. "Follow me," the
man said.

Kane inclined his head. "Lead on."

THEY WERE TAKEN down to the lower level of the mine,
where the scaffolding ran out and they instead found
themselves walking down a slope that spiraled all the
way around the outside edge of the mine shaft itself.
This close, Kane could see something metallic waiting
in the darkness, more scaffolding but this time with a
kind of pulley system across its surface. It was an elevator of some sort, Kane guessed, and even as they
dropped into the shadows he saw the elevator car trun-
dling up on its wire, halting below them at its highest
point before a cage door was pulled back and its passengers disgorged.

"Quite a tidy operation you have going here," Kane
said, not bothering to translate it for his captors.

"You be quiet," the man in front of him advised in
French, waving his pistol in a threatening manner.

"So, how do you guys see?" Kane asked, ignoring
the instruction.

"You have many questions, foreign dog," the man said.

Kane eyed the elevator, saying nothing. Its cage was

made from metal piping, with three horizontal bars running approximately at waist height—enough, presumably, to stop anyone from falling out so long as they didn't do anything silly.

The group followed the path down to the elevator, passing another group of men whose fatigues were covered in dirt. Miners, Kane guessed, looking at the smears on their clothes and faces.

Once they were at the elevator, the guard in the front stepped aside and gestured for Kane to go into the elevator cage.

Kane held his hands out, fingers open. "You sure?"

When the man said nothing, he stepped inside and was followed by Grant, Brigid, Mariah and two of the guards. Four against two—good odds, Kane calculated. Okay, so the guards were armed and Mariah could not be relied upon in a fight, but he and Grant were trained as Magistrates and Brigid was wicked in close-combat situations. They could take these mooks if they needed to, just so long as Kane could figure out what the plan was and who had come up with it.

A moment later, the cage door was drawn shut and the car started to descend. Kane watched their captors warily, sizing them up as the elevator car lurched on its cables.

A few moments later they were lost in complete blackness.

Chapter 9

It looked like something Nikola Tesla might have dreamed up centuries ago.

At the base of the elevator shaft was a carved-out cavern, vast and full of dancing twinkles of light. There were people working down here, Kane saw, men in dirty overalls and flowing robes, almost all of them wearing blindfolds, though a few had opted for glasses whose lenses were completely black.

The descent into the mine shaft had taken ninety seconds. During that time, Kane had eyed the two guards, his muscles tensed and ready. With measured subtlety, he had looked to his companions for any hint of what they wanted to do, first Grant, whom he knew could be relied upon to follow his lead, and then Brigid. She had met his gaze with her own and, very markedly, looked to her left and mouthed the word *no*. Her eyes had barely shown in the darkness of the shaft, but Kane had seen the signal, knew he was to do nothing, that she had a plan. That was something they had between them, a kind of catch-all signal for situations like this one. He figured that maybe Brigid had meant to get herself caught, or if she hadn't, then she had at least settled on a way to play her capture to their advantage. They were, after all, in the shaft, which was where they wanted to be.

"Out," one of his captors said. The metal of the blaster

in his hand just barely caught a flicker of light because there was no light down here, no artificial light anyway. The people here were working in darkness, where the glint of the things they mined was enough to find their way.

"Where are you taking us?" Brigid asked in French. She spoke a lot of languages fluently, one side effect of her eidetic memory.

"Keep moving," the guard said as they filed out of the elevator cage. "You'll see soon enough."

That's not very reassuring, Brigid thought, judging by the sneering tone of the man's voice. She wondered if she had done the right thing, surrendering so easily to these local thugs.

Once down in the mine, the Cerberus crew were guided toward a side shaft, past towering hunks of whirring machinery. Constructed from scaffold and tubing, the machinery had a skeletal appearance, as if its shell had been removed to reveal its insides.

"What are they mining here?" Mariah asked.

"Diamonds, looks like," Kane replied, as one of their guards instructed them to remain silent.

"That doesn't make sense," Mariah said, ignoring the guard's instruction, though she knew enough French to understand it. "There aren't any diamonds in Libya."

"None?" Kane queried, turning to face her, brow furrowed.

The guard beside him jabbed Kane in the ribs with the nose of his pistol, sending a sharp stab of pain through his side. "Eyes forward, no chitchat," the guard growled at him in heavily accented French.

Kane saw Mariah shake her head in a definite no.

No diamonds in Libya according to our resident geologist, Kane thought, and yet here we are in the center of a huge diamond mine. Something's not right.

Kane and his companions had traveled far and wide, even beyond the reaches of the globe itself; they had seen a lot of strange and near-inexplicable things. But there were some fundamentals that you simply could not change, Kane knew, and creating diamond mines out of thin air was one of them. Unless maybe this was an effect of the fallout from the nukecaust—Mariah was a freezie, she had spent two hundred years in cryogenic stasis before being rewoken on the Manitius Moon Base. Could be that her knowledge of the area's geological resources was out-of-date, maybe. But then, Kane didn't hold a lot of hope in that theory—Mariah may be old-school but she wasn't dense. And whatever else he knew about diamonds, he was pretty darn sure they didn't just materialize in new locations without warning.

The group was ushered down a side passage that had been carved directly from the rock. Tools and machinery had been left to the side of the broad passageway, whose walls and roof were roughly circular. Sparkling facets glinted here and there in those walls, like stars in the night sky. A bright light emanated from the far end of the cavern, catching the flecks of brilliance in swirling patterns.

The artificial passageway opened out into a larger cavern. Ever-changing eddies of light streamed from a towering, insubstantial pillar located in the center of the space. The pillar seemed to contain a rapid yet graceful turnover of all the colors of the spectrum, with impossible depths that gave the impression that those colors emanated from beyond infinity. Laced through that swirl of color were forks of lightning like witch fire, playing across its impossible depths. Kane and the others had seen its like before. It was an interphase window, a wormhole in space exactly like the one that they had used to reach the fort aboveground less than two hours before.

But, in Kane's experience at least, interphase windows did not remain open, or they shouldn't. They were locked in place by parallax points, sites of significant arcane power dating back into prehistory, but they were not like physical doors that remained open indefinitely. Instead, these quantum wormholes had to be tapped— by a device like the interphaser that Brigid was still carrying on her back.

"What is this...thing?" Kane asked, feigning ignorance.

"This is your pathway to new knowledge and an understanding of the world that you cannot begin to imagine," the French-speaking guard closest to him explained proudly.

Kane winced as his Commtact translated the guard's grand words. In Kane's experience of men holding guns, grand words like that generally preceded something nasty that, more often that not, involved the word *sacrifice*.

The group halted before the shimmering pillar of light. Up close like this, there was no question in Kane's mind—it was an interphase window, all right, and he felt certain his partners recognized it, too, though they were smart enough not to reveal that knowledge to their captors out loud. After all, the interphaser was unique to the Cerberus operation—no one outside of the redoubt's walls should even be aware of the existence of the interphase windows known as parallax points, with the very rare exception of their most trusted allies.

The guards continued to hold the Cerberus team at gunpoint as they stood before the towering column of light.

"Wh-what is it we're looking at?" Brigid asked, as if she didn't know.

"It's a door," one of the guards explained dismissively.

"Most funky, crazy-ass door I've ever seen," Grant muttered, loud enough to be heard. Like Brigid, he was keeping up the pretense of not having seen an interphase window before.

"Now, if you would be so kind, ladies, gentlemen," the guard to their right said, "I require you to step into the door."

"Into that?" Brigid asked, faking incredulity.

As she spoke, Kane made a swift, subtle gesture of his hands where Grant and Brigid could see them, briefly flicking three fingers to indicate that they were to all move together on his command and turn the tables on their oppressors. They had come this far, as far as Brigid had wanted to explore, and learned nothing yet about the crack in the earth except that a diamond mine was located at its center; a diamond mine that *should not* exist.

"Do not be afraid—it's like stepping into a rain shower," the guard explained in response to Brigid's concern. "It looks quite spectacular to your eyes, but it is just light that illuminates another place."

In your eyes? Kane picked up on that and so did Brigid, he noticed, raising one ginger eyebrow with interest. Yup, there it was again—that suggestion that these people, like the soldier in the fort, were seeing things in an entirely different way.

"Now, step through," the guard to their left commanded, "and gaze upon the face of god."

Grant glanced across at Kane, waiting for his signal. But no, Kane wanted to see what was waiting on the other side of that window in quantum space first. Curiosity may have killed the cat but it also served to uncover a lot of mysteries at the heart of the Annunaki conspiracy to subjugate humanity.

Kane took a deep breath and stepped through.

FOR A MOMENT, the world seemed to whirl, as that restless miasma of wonderful colors obliterated all sense of self.

A moment.

Eternity.

THEN KANE WAS THROUGH. The first thing to strike him was the change in air temperature. It was cooler here, with a stillness and silence that the mine had not afforded them.

Kane took in his surroundings in a glance. He was standing in a great chamber with four walls slanting upward to an apex, like the inside of a grand pyramid. Set into the apex, Kane saw a huge iris-shaped hatch, over twenty-five feet in diameter and encircled by a metal collar. The whole chamber was lit by the swirling tapestry of the interphase window, picking up the glyphs that had been carved into the walls many millennia ago, along with something else—tiny flecks like rhinestones dotted the walls.

"Wait a minute," Kane muttered as he took in his surroundings. He'd been here before.

Kane spun back to face the interphase window as his companions stepped through. Mariah came first, gritting her teeth as she passed through the wormhole in space—she was less used to interphase travel than the others and doubled over as if she might vomit. She was followed by Brigid, then Grant, the latter hanging back close to the interphase gateway as their two captors stepped out from its impossible depths. Even as they stepped out, Grant brought his raised arm down in a chop, knocking the pistol from the hand of the closest guard. The pistol skittered across the hard surface of the floor, and Kane leaped for it.

The second guard stepped through, his own pistol raised and ready. His companion was still reeling from Grant's surprise attack—naturally, he had expected all of the Cerberus team to be momentarily laid low by the journey through the interphaser, little suspecting that they had significantly more experience with the devices than he did. The guard turned to Grant, bleating in surprise as Grant drew back his left fist and drove it hard into his jaw. The guard staggered back into his emerging companion, and the two of them existed for a moment both in the mine in Libya and here, inside the pyramidal structure that Kane had visited years before…if only he could slow down long enough to remember when.

Kane had the gun now, was working the safety and turning it on the two guards as they hurried back through the interphaser gateway and into the chamber.

Kane shot immediately, sending a 9 mm parabellum bullet between the two guards as they came charging into the room from the rainbow swirl. "The next one goes through your skull, *mes amis*," Kane told them, training the Vektor SP on the one guard who remained armed.

"You would be well advised to drop your weapon, monsieur," Brigid told the man in flawless French.

The guard stood stock-still, a cruel smile twisting his lips. "Are you really so shortsighted?" he asked, speaking to himself.

"What do you—?" Brigid began, but Mariah's voice interrupted her.

"Guys, I think you need to look at this—like, now!"

Kane took a step back, still holding the blaster trained on the two guards. "Kinda busy here. What is it, Mariah?"

"I… I don't think I can describe it," Mariah replied, a definite tremor in her voice.

The guard who remained armed held his gun out, rested on his palm, not pointing at either Kane or his companions. "Here. I am doing as you asked," he said. "It doesn't matter now—you have the gun if you want it."

Grant stepped forward, plucking the gun from the man's outstretched hand, wary of any tricks. "I've got it," he confirmed, working the pistol's manual safety catch.

Kane began to turn, and as he did so something illuminated behind him, at the opposite end of the chamber from the interphase gateway. Kane saw the figure sitting there as the shadows were bleached away, something that looked half alive, half dead—and all lizard. It was clearly an Annunaki, one of the cruel race of aliens who had tried to subjugate the people of the Earth and turn them into slaves. It wore a few strips of material like bandages but most of its russet-colored scales were on show. Its skin had dark patches on it, like fungus on a tree's bark, and the typically defined muscles of the Annunaki were nowhere to be seen. Instead this Annunaki appeared to be wasting away.

But its face, its head…that was another matter. As Kane turned he realized just where that increasing bright light was emanating from—and it was the creature's head, like a great ball of white lightning propped atop its neck. As Kane looked, the intensity of that brilliance became a hundredfold brighter, not just dazzling but absolutely blinding. His eyes seemed to scream inside his head as his vision winked out like a television switching to standby, and for a few, agonizing seconds, the brightness was so overpowering it seemed to make a sound as he tried to process it.

Beside Kane, Brigid Baptiste was holding her hand up against the growing luminance of the Annunaki's skull, but already her eyes were hurting, her vision wiped out in a cluster of sudden, painful seconds.

Mariah saw what was happening but all too late to respond. Even as she tried to turn away, her eyesight winked out, images around her switching from bleached out to blurred to a kind of wash of orange and yellow as thought she were looking at the sun through closed eyelids. She dropped to the floor, her hands reaching up for her face.

Even Grant, who had not turned, was caught in the sudden display of brilliance, unable to avoid its spread as the rays bathed the room and its diamond-encrusted walls with sheer radiance. He heard his colleagues drop to the floor, the triple thump of Mariah, then Kane and Brigid almost in unison. "What's happening?" Grant asked, screwing his eyelids closed against the magnificent glare.

But that could not protect him; eyelids could not protect him against a light so pure it burned itself into the very surface of the retina.

Within the interior of the hidden pyramid, four Cerberus rebels were rendered unto unconsciousness as their sight was utterly overwhelmed by the uncanny radiance.

Chapter 10

"Will my sweet prince be joining us later?" the woman asked in her musical voice as she met with the figures boarding the gangplank of her private yacht.

The yacht was located on the still waters of the Bayou Lafourche, a broad river that wound through Louisiana all the way to the Gulf of Mexico and had, historically, provided much of the shipping traffic to the region. The yacht was an impressive beast, part old-time riverboat, part modern-age tech, its blue-tinted chrome-plated sides were like something from a 1950s vision of the future. It was a popinjay's vessel, the kind that screamed "Look at me, look at me!" and would have stood out among ships larger and more practical than it, had there been any such about. This stretch of the Bayou Lafourche, however, was empty save for two other boats, smaller vessels that featured three-man crews and ran up and down the quarter mile or so surrounding the blue riverboat in a steady sentry circuit.

The woman, like the boat, cut a striking figure that drew attention. Her name was Ohio Blue, and she was a tall, slender woman in her late thirties, with thick, long blond hair that ran down her back in a perfectly straight line and was styled to fall over her left eye in peekaboo style. Her clothes, like her name, were blue—a long ball gown of sapphire, strapless with a cinched bodice that clung to her body like paint, hiding her long legs down to the ankles where two booted feet were revealed. Blue opera gloves covered her arms to above the elbows, and she wore a bracelet of pearls around her right wrist as her only ornamentation.

Three figures were stepping from the gangway to join Ohio Blue, a man and two women. The man was called Edwards, and he sported a closely shaved head that drew attention to his bullet-bitten left ear, a shirt and jacket that could do nothing to disguise his broad, muscular shoulders and a pair of combat pants with bulging pockets running down their length.

Edwards was accompanied by Domi, an albino woman who had grown up in the Outlands and sometimes struggled to portray an aura of civilization when in company, and Sela Sinclair, a dark-skinned African-American woman with short hair wound into ringlets and a stocky, muscular frame. Both women were dressed in similar attire to Edwards, although Domi had chosen to skip the jacket in favor of a tight T-shirt that clung to her upper body as if it had been sprayed on. The women could not have looked more different—Domi was petite, elfin, with a pixie haircut, and had the striking chalk-white skin and bone-white hair of an albino, her eyes two vivid scarlet orbs burning beneath her brows; while Sela Sinclair had skin the color of coffee, an easy smile and a weight to her movements that made it clear you didn't want to mess with her.

The three mismatched colleagues were long-serving members of the Cerberus organization and had arrived here via mat-trans at the behest of the woman trader who owned this luxury yacht.

"Kane?" Edwards asked in response to Ohio's query. When she nodded, he shook his head. "Kane's otherwise engaged, he can't make it right now."

Ohio Blue dipped her head sorrowfully as she led the way across the deck of the yacht. "How regrettable," she said. "Far too much time has passed since I last saw my sweet prince."

Quite why Ohio Blue habitually referred to Kane as her sweet prince no one really knew. He had saved her life once, over two years ago, when he, Brigid and Grant had met with the elusive trader to obtain much-needed medical supplies for the Cerberus redoubt. The deal had threatened to go sour until enemy agents representing Blue's estranged brother had appeared on the scene, cutting down her men and targeting her. Kane had stepped in and rescued the trader, and she had considered him her sweet prince ever since.

By her own admission, Ohio Blue was an independent trader, what some people called a bandit. She traded in various commodities—"never slaves, too gauche"—and had a vast network of connections and hideaways in the black market of the Louisiana Basin. Blue had stuck her neck out for Cerberus once before, helping them hide personnel in safe houses across the region when they had been exiled from their own headquarters and been forced to go on the run. Whether she was truly trustworthy remained open to debate, but her connections and eye for a profit made her a useful ally.

This time, she had contacted Cerberus through one of her many networks with news of an informer who may have information that the team might be interested in. Ohio never gave anything away in remote communications, distrusting the fragile security of such systems—most likely because a part of her own vast operation was geared to tapping and decoding those very same "secure channels."

Thus it was that Cerberus had sent CAT Beta, the

three-man field team made up of Edwards, Domi and Sinclair, to liaise with the mysterious black marketer.

"Can't help you, ma'am," Edwards said, keeping pace with the beautiful blonde trader. "So, what have you got for us?"

"A woman came into my circle last night," Ohio explained as she led the way to a set of double doors made of glass engraved with bluebirds. Two men waited at the doors, opening them as Ohio and her guests approached. "Distraught, in need of medical assistance, she prevailed upon a gentleman of my acquaintance—a sawbones— to provide her with said assistance, and when he heard her story, he felt it prudent to inform me."

"What's her story?" Edwards asked. He was an ex-Magistrate like Kane, but he wondered how Kane had the patience to deal with this woman, who seemed to always speak in slow reveals and dramatic pauses.

"Why don't you ask her yourself, Mr.—?"

"Edwards," Edwards told her as they passed through the doors and entered a sunroom within which was located a small swimming pool full of clear, blue water. He had told her his name once already, as he and his team had requested permission to board. He had also been patted down and checked for hidden weapons, though he had been reticent to relinquish the Sin Eater pistol he had locked against his wrist in its spring-loaded holster. He had given his weapon up, as his colleagues had theirs, recalling Lakesh's words when they departed for this mission: "Ohio Blue is wary of strangers and very security conscious, but she has been a valuable ally to us. Don't upset her, just remember that she's harmless so long as you play along."

Edwards was playing along as best as his fiery temperament would allow. "What? She in here, taking a dip?"

"No, through here," Ohio said, pacing along beside the pool in long-legged strides. "My, but you are an impatient one, aren't you, Mr.—?"

"Edwards," Edwards reminded her—again.

"Yes, that's right," the woman acknowledged, a patronizing smile crossing her lips.

A few paces behind them, Sinclair turned to Domi and raised her eyebrows. A transplant from the twentieth century who had been trained by the US Air Force, Sinclair had seen a lot of impressive ships in her time, but nothing like this. This was a floating example of astonishing craftsmanship.

In response, Domi rolled her eyes. She had visited great places and crappy ones. What did it matter to her unless they planned to stay?

Ohio halted close to the door on the far side of the pool, kneeling down to run her hands through the crystal clear water. "Do you swim, Mr....Edwards?" she asked.

"I *can* swim," Edwards assured her, "but right now we're on a tight schedule. I'm sure if Kane was here he'd want you to hurry things up."

Ohio nodded. "Of course," she said, rising once more and leading Edwards and his team through a door, located at the end of the pool room, with a gleaming brass handle within which Edwards could see his own distorted reflection.

This woman's a game player, Edwards told himself. He had experience of the type, both from his days as a Mag and in his capacity as an operative for Cerberus. The deeper you became involved with the thriving black market here in the Outlands, the more levels of gamesmanship you needed to master. Edwards wasn't good at that, not the way Kane and especially Brigid Baptiste were. He didn't have the same patience they did, was more inclined to bluster his way into a situation than negotiate.

Edwards followed Ohio Blue into the tastefully decorated corridor beyond the pool room—simple but expensive in design—with Domi and Sela Sinclair stealthily bringing up the rear. Both women remained alert, eyeing every corner, every door, every shadow for an ambush. Kane might trust this woman—and the emphasis was very much on *might*—but no one else did.

Ohio led the group to an unremarkable door located midway down the corridor. There were six doors at intervals along this corridor, two of which were open as the group passed. A man called Baxter sat guard on a bar stool at the end of the corridor, working a curious wooden box with his hands. The Cerberus personnel glanced into the open doorways as a matter of course while Ohio answered Edwards's queries about where they had picked up the woman, how she been brought here and what her medical condition was now—through a friend, by road and physically satisfactory but mentally unbalanced. The rooms beyond the two open doors had revealed a galley where a chef and two cooks were working at a grand gas-lit stove, and a large bedroom with unmade bed, its black sheets ruffled back in a jumble.

Ohio stopped before the closed door, its top portion a series of wooden slats designed to promote air flow while retaining privacy and rested her hand on the brass handle. "The woman *du jour* is in here," Ohio said, fixing Edwards with her sapphire-blue eye.

"You said she was mentally altered," Edwards said. "She conscious?"

"I believe so," Ohio said, and she worked her free hand on the wooden slats that dominated the top half of the door, opening them a fraction before placing her eye close to the gap. "Do you wish to take a look before you enter?"

Edwards dismissed the offer. "She can hear us out here, right?"

Ohio showed her straight, even teeth in a momentary smile. "No doubt."

Edwards nodded toward the door. "Let's go see what this mystery woman has to tell us."

Ohio worked a lock within the door handle and swung the door open. Within was a medium-sized cabin which featured a porthole beneath which was a writing desk and chair, a second wicker chair that had been placed in the shade beside a whirring fan and a wheeled trolley upon which were the remains of a meal—several plates, bowls and a glass jug of water. A woman sat in the wicker chair flicking through a handmade book that was bound in leather, its pages yellowed, its threads frayed. She was of mixed race, with pale skin and full features, and she was probably somewhere in her midfifties. She wore a badly fitted wig of longish ginger-colored hair. The glinting lines of cheap necklaces circled her neck, their trinkets hidden beneath the neckline of a dress that was made up of layers of autumnal colors, like leaves fallen from the trees. The dress fell past her ankles. She looked up from her book as Ohio led the Cerberus warriors into the cabin.

"You are the people of the three dogs, yes?" the woman asked without preamble.

Edwards frowned, but before he could speak, Sinclair butted in. "She means Cerberus. Yes, yes we are."

The woman in the chair nodded, wincing with the

effort, patently in some discomfort. "You have people here, have visited here before?" she asked in an accent strong with Creole French.

Edwards nodded. "Go on."

"My name is Dagmar Gellis," the woman explained. "I followed the path."

"The path?" Edwards queried.

"She means voodoo," Ohio Blue stated quietly from where she stood with her back to the room, peering through the porthole.

"Voodoo," Edwards repeated. "Right."

"The *société* broke up when Papa Hurbon left us," Dagmar said. "Dwindled, like ice left out in the noon-day sun. I want things to be like they were. Simple, uncomplicated."

As she spoke she moved in her seat, and Edwards realized for the first time that the woman called Dagmar Gellis had only one leg beneath the flowing trails of her skirts; her left leg was missing below the knee. He recalled something that had been mentioned in CAT Alpha's report on an investigation in the Louisiana Bayou two years before—a group of voodoo worshippers had been mesmerized into cutting off their limbs to provide blood sacrifice for their living goddess, a monster called Ezili Coeur Noir. Noir, it transpired, was actually an Annunaki called Lilitu who had been killed and subjected to a failed rebirth program on the Annunaki wombship, *Tiamat*. Kane, Grant and Brigid had managed to trap her in a cold-fusion reactor located inside an abandoned military redoubt that dated back to the twentieth century.

"What does this have to do with us? With Cerberus?" Sinclair asked, picking up on the line of questioning.

Dagmar sucked her teeth, browned with age and jagged like a wild animal's. "Something lives," she said. "Papa Hurbon, he lives still—with the other thing."

"We know Hurbon's alive," Edwards said. "What's this 'other thing'?"

"The goddess," the woman said fearfully, barely breathing the word.

"Ezili?" Edwards asked, turning to his colleagues. "Can't be. Kane's team dispatched her sorry ass. That's what Brigid's report said."

"Where is this 'other thing' that you speak of?" Sela Sinclair asked, leaning down so that her face was closer to the woman's. Close up, the woman's breath was bad, like something that had died.

Gellis spoke some more, about her life and how things had become messed up. She was clearly in an addled and anxious state. It seemed to Sinclair that the woman blamed everyone else for her own failure to face reality, and that most of her talk was in paranoid riddles where she was the only good person caught in a conspiracy of evil.

"Hurbon holds surgery, sometimes, with Mike," Dagmar concluded, "down under the earth, where the dead things still live."

They could get no further sense from Gellis. She spoke of things she had mislaid or places she thought she had been, but most of it seemed like the ramblings of one who was deluded, unable to tell fantasy from reality. As far as Edwards could tell, the woman was a dupe who would never amount to anything but a bit player stuck on the sidelines of her own life. He almost felt sorry for her.

Eventually, the Cerberus group left the cabin escorted by Ohio, holding their opinions until they were away from the closed door.

"You make any sense of that?" Sela Sinclair asked her partners as they paced down the corridor to another set of doors.

"I figure Mike is Redoubt Mike," Edwards proposed.

"Sounds likely," Sinclair agreed.

Redoubt Mike was located in Louisiana and had been the final resting place of Lilitu in her guise as Ezili Coeur Noir. The cold-fusion generator that powered the redoubt had been utilized to bring her fractured aspects back together before crushing them into nothingness, or so Brigid's report had explained. But what if that was not the case, the Cerberus team had wondered as they had listened to the anxious ramblings of the one-legged woman. What if Hurbon was involved in something designed to bring Ezili Coeur Noir, the voodun loa of death, back to walk the Earth again?

Domi shook her head as Ohio led them into a room with a large wooden table at its center surrounded by eight chairs. A further set of double doors was open on the far side of the room and led out onto the portside deck. Two men waited in the room, both visibly armed with pistols and both smartly dressed. The Cerberus warriors ignored them.

"You're trying to make sense of the ramblings of a mad lady," Domi spit.

"Redoubt Mike was where—" Sinclair began to explain.

"I know what happened at Redoubt Mike," Domi assured her.

Ohio took a seat at the head of the table and gestured to one of the armed men to get her a drink. The man opened up the twin doors of a drinks cabinet and began preparing a martini.

"What happened at Redoubt Mike?" Ohio asked as she waited for her drink.

"A lot of voodoo hoodoo," Sinclair told her, explaining nothing.

As Sela spoke, Edwards stepped out onto the deck and engaged his hidden Commtact to hail the Cerberus operations base. "Cerberus, this is Edwards," he said, staring up at the cloudless blue sky.

A moment later, the familiar voice of Cerberus operative Brewster Philboyd was channeled through Edwards's ear canal by the Commtact. "Go ahead."

"Can you triangulate on this position, Brewster, and tell me how far we are from Redoubt Mike?" Edwards requested.

"Already triangulated," Philboyd confirmed, working at his computer desk over twelve hundred miles away. Every Cerberus operative had a biolink transponder surgically inserted into their bloodstream. This transponder could be accessed remotely to monitor heart rate and other metabolic functions, and it could also be used to triangulate an individual's position to within a few feet. It was just one of the miraculous tools at Cerberus's disposal in its quest to protect humanity. "I have you at forty-two miles out, almost directly to the north of the redoubt."

"What's our easiest way of getting there?" Edwards queried, but even as he asked he realized that the answer was obvious.

"Mike has a mat-trans unit, the same as the one you used to meet with Ohio's people a mile away from your current location," Philboyd answered, as if he had read Edwards's mind. "If you return to that unit, I could run a remote jump sequence and send you straight there."

Edwards smiled. "See, I knew I stayed friends with you desk jockeys for a reason."

Sela Sinclair looked up as Edwards reentered the yacht's conference room. She had taken a seat at the table, but declined the offer of a drink. "You have anything?"

Edwards smiled. "Sure do. Let's go investigate this one from the inside."

Domi was perched on a seat, not sitting but rather resting on her haunches atop it. She smiled a feral smile at Edwards's words and turned to Ohio Blue. "I'm going to need my gun back," she said. "And my knife."

Chapter 11

Using flashlights, Edwards, Sinclair and Domi entered an abandoned military complex located in an underground facility close to the Bayou Lafourche. The facility was well hidden from prying eyes, located in a bunker between city streets that could only be accessed via a service alleyway. That alleyway, like the streets around it, was covered with a dense carpet of vegetation.

The city itself was unpopulated and partly demolished, an overgrown ruin dating back to a civilization that had been toppled by the nukecaust of 2001, as much a ghost monument as Machu Picchu or the underworld city of Agartha.

"No civilization ever expects it will come to this," Sela Sinclair said regretfully as the Cerberus trio ducked past the overgrowth and into the stairwell that led down to the hidden redoubt. Thanks to cryogenic hibernation, she was a twentieth-century émigré; she remembered places just like this when they had been vibrant with human life.

Edwards turned to her, offering a grim smile. "Everything ends sooner or later," he said. "Even Cerberus."

Domi flinched at that as Edwards led the way down the steps and into the belly of the redoubt itself. "Do you really believe that, Edwards?"

"It's inevitable," the shaved-headed ex-Mag said. "Either our organization's mission will be completed or someone will get the jump on us—either way Cerberus will disappear."

"It's not like you to indulge in gallows humor," Sinclair observed, shaking her head.

Edwards fixed her with a piercing stare of his blue eyes. "Who said I was joking?" he challenged.

Maybe he's right, Sinclair thought. Maybe there was something in the air; or maybe it was just seeing places like this and the depression that they seemed to engender.

Within a couple of minutes, the group had reached the mat-trans chamber hidden in the bowels of the underground bunker. The chamber was a small, hexagonal room with a tiled floor and armaglass walls tinted the rich pink of cherry blossoms.

The chamber was adjacent to a larger room which featured a line of consoles at which its operators had once sat, a little like the monitoring room at NASA.

The mat-trans room featured a locked door with a numerical keypad beside it. Edwards punched in the code, waiting at the door as Domi and Sinclair trotted inside. As they did so, Edwards engaged his Commtact, hailing Brewster Philboyd at the Cerberus ops center.

"Okay, Brewster," Edwards said as he pulled the heavy door to. "We're all in and ready to jump."

BREWSTER PHILBOYD WAS sitting at the comms desk within the Cerberus redoubt, tucked away amid the Bitterroot Mountains. He was a scarecrow-thin figure whose lanky body seemed to be a little bit too large for the seat and desk he sat at. He had blond hair, thinning a little and receding from his high forehead, and he wore round-framed spectacles perched above his acne-scarred cheeks. Like all the personnel in the room,

Philboyd wore the regulation Cerberus uniform—a white jumpsuit with a blue zipper. "Accessing now," he told Edwards via the headset mic he wore hooked over his left ear.

The comms desk was found within the large operations room, where twin rows of a dozen desks each ran from one wall to the other. Most of the desks were occupied by operators at this time of day, and Lakesh was sitting at his own desk to the rear of the room, drinking tea as he supervised operations.

Philboyd worked the keyboard of his computer, his fingers running over it with speed and precision as he brought up the remote overrides for the mat-trans network. He had already run through the procedure and coded in the details of the remarkable trip beforehand. As he worked on the final commands, Lakesh joined him at his desk, watching as new data flashed across the screen.

Suddenly aware of Lakesh's presence, Philboyd turned for a moment and glanced at his colleague, mouthing the word *okay?*

Lakesh had that haunted expression on his face, one that Philboyd had seen too many times before. But after a moment, he nodded, offering a wide, if not entirely genuine, smile.

Philboyd tapped the key command and, in an underground room hundreds of miles to the south, the three Cerberus warriors were suddenly bathed with a wash of light and sound as the mat-trans fired up and launched them across quantum space to their destination at Redoubt Mike.

THE PHYSICAL SENSATION of having one's atoms thrown across the quantum ether to a receiver station many miles away was not for the fainthearted. Traveling via mat-trans had once been described by Lakesh as being similar to the feeling of waking up to discover you'd just been punched repeatedly in the gut. He had been one of the very first technicians to work on the project, and when he said things like that, it amazed his colleagues that the network had ever gotten off the ground.

The way the system worked was via fixed points, artificially constructed as sender-receiver stations and located across the old United States of America and beyond. The sender-receiver stations, known as matter transmitters or mat-trans, would reduce travelers to their component atoms before sending them in a targeted beam to a designated receiver station, teleporting them instantaneously from point to point. The system had been developed by the US military toward the end of the twentieth century, and its existence had never been revealed to the general public.

The mat-trans stations were located deep within military compounds where they could be kept secure. That, of course, had been over two hundred years before, but the redoubts had by and large remained undiscovered, which meant that even today they remained the province of the Cerberus organization. That said, the mat-trans had been compromised before, such as when a group of technological shamans from Australia had cut into the signal and split it from its original destination, causing Cerberus some degree of turmoil.

There came a rush of white mist and the sense of physical assault and internal bodily pressure. And then Edwards, Sela Sinclair and Domi were standing in a new mat-trans chamber inside the confines of Redoubt Mike, a chamber of the exact same proportions as the one they had entered in Bayou Lafourche, only with armaglass walls a golden yellow.

"Everyone okay?" Sinclair asked between slow, deliberate breaths.

Edwards nodded, pale where the blood had drained from his face, his lips pressed together. "Yeah."

Beside him, Domi had adopted a crouching position and pulled her Detonics Combat Master pistol from where she had holstered it at the small of her back. Her eyes were narrowed, watching the sealed door to the mat-trans chamber, and her shoulders trembled slightly as she brought her own breathing under control. The small, silver barrel of the blaster in her hands, however, remained steady, despite her heavy breathing—Domi was a professional. "Let's go," she said, motioning toward the door.

The door was off center and, like the one in the underground chamber forty miles distant, was locked via numerical keypad. Sinclair took point, working the code and smiling at the satisfying click of the magnetic locks being released. The door swung outward, releasing the last of the white transportation mists, even as overhead fans within the chamber itself drew away the rest.

Outside, the redoubt was in six inches of water and smelling of mildew. It was silent, too, eerily so, and the automated lights that were designed to come on whenever the mat-trans received a package or traveler flickered and dimmed, several bulbs burned out completely.

"Looks like a friendly place," Sinclair muttered as she stepped from the mat-trans chamber, her own pistol now in hand, a Colt Mark IV. The Mark IV was a compact pistol, which featured an eight-and-half-inch matte black barrel and set-back grip. It was the kind of weapon she had grown up with, trained with, two hundred years before when she had been a part of the US Air Force.

Edwards tried his Commtact as they exited the mat-trans chamber. "Brewster, you read me?"

Nothing.

He tried again, but again there came no response.

Sometimes the Commtacts did not work in certain circumstances; deep underground was one such circumstance.

"We're on our own for now, people," Edwards said grimly, reaching for his flashlight. "Keep your eyes open."

Beneath flickering overheads, the trio trod quietly through the waterlogged ops room and beyond into a corridor that was almost entirely lost to darkness. Edwards flicked on his flashlight, bringing the bland, gray-walled corridor to bland, gray-walled life. There was moss growing on the walls, showing where the stagnant water had idled for months. The water was dark, almost black, and it smelled of rotten eggs.

"What happened here?" Domi asked, keeping her voice low.

"Kane's team flooded the place," Edwards explained, "to stop the release of a biological weapon that had been developed here."

"Flooded," Domi repeated as her feet swished through the water. "Huh."

"Water diluted the biological weapon while it was still in the nurturing aspect of its growth cycle," Edwards said. "Saved a lot of people a lot of trouble."

"Sounds like Kane," Sinclair said as they trekked away from the mat-trans ops room and into the belly of the redoubt.

THE CORRIDOR RAN for two dozen yards, rooms running off it, each one waterlogged like the ops room. They reached a T junction at the end, where a cross corridor ran perpendicular to the one that the Cerberus teammates of CAT Beta had started in, and a bank of elevators, including a wide-doored goods elevator, was before them. A map located beside the elevators showed the different levels and areas highlighted with different colors.

"Which way?" Sinclair asked. "Left or right?"

Edwards ran his flashlight over the map, reading from the key.

BO51...

BO52...

BO53...

Beside Edwards, Domi listened. Domi's senses were keener than the average person's, and she sometimes seemed more animal than human. But even she could detect little in the flickering light or over the smell of mold and stagnant water, only the near-subliminal sound the ripples of water made where the group had disturbed it.

After a moment's thought, Edwards pointed to the right where a heavy fire door was situated. "Stairs," he said. "We'll head up and see where the action is."

Sinclair agreed, though she felt uncomfortable with Edwards's turn of phrase. Something about these Magistrates left them hungry for action sometimes, and she worried that made them reckless.

The group moved to the indicated door, stepping through and into a stairwell that was pitch-black apart from those things the beam of Edwards's flashlight illuminated.

The stairs were hard concrete, as were the walls. The

whole place felt cold and it echoed every movement into an orchestra of thumps and swishes. There was water on the steps, pooling on the lowest one, with just a sheen of it on the first few, and more pooling where they reached the next level.

Edwards waited at the door, peering warily through the small grilled-glass window located at eye level in its center. He had a Sin Eater pistol hidden in a wrist holster under his sleeve, and his fingers twitched a little in nervous anticipation at the thought of drawing it. Gently, silently, he pushed the door open.

THE CERBERUS WARRIORS checked two more levels and found nothing, just water, mold and fritzing lights. There were bodies here and there, dead bodies, long rotted, just skeletons really, though the grimy water made them bob and move, giving them the illusion of life in the flickering light.

On the third level up from the lowest subbasement they found the woman. She was young, dark skinned and wearing leopard-print shorts, black boots and a calfskin jacket. She sat on the edge of a stage-like platform in a large motor pool, and when Edwards pushed open the door from the stairs, her head twitched and she looked up at him through her wild halo of ringlets.

"Oh, bless you, sir," she said in a voice heavily accented with French Creole, "you have found me. I thought maybe you never would."

Glancing left and right, Edwards led the way into the motor pool with Domi and Sinclair holding back just a little as they followed him. There were broken-down vehicles here, all of them military—jeeps and flatbed trucks with rotted tires that bloated flatly in the thin carpet of water.

"You're expecting me?" Edwards asked gruffly.

The woman smiled. "Oh, yes," she said, her white teeth bright in the infinite darkness of the room. "You're here to take me back to the surface, aren't you?"

"You're lost, then?" Edwards asked, feeling increasingly uncomfortable with the disconnect between the girl's story and her joyful expression.

"Perhaps," the woman replied, pushing herself to her feet. She had long legs, Edwards noted, the legs of an athlete.

"I'm Edwards," Edwards told her. "And you?"

"Nathalie," the woman replied, taking a step forward as Edwards and his allies came to meet her. There was something on her hip, strapped there, glinting in the beam of Edwards's flashlight as it played across her taut, muscular body.

"How did you get down here?" Edwards asked, walking to meet with the woman.

"How did you?" she shot back, smiling to take the edge off her words.

Edwards shook his head with obvious irritation. Beside him, Domi and Sinclair had spread out, keeping their distance, surveying the darkened room. Anything could be hiding there—*anything.*

"If you want my help, you're going to have to talk to me," Edwards said, trying to keep the irritation out of his tone.

The woman was standing ten feet from Edwards now, her hands held loosely at her sides. "Who said I needed your help, *Cerberus?*" she asked.

"Wha—?" Edwards spat in shock.

The woman called Nathalie had pulled the knife from its sheath at her hip even as he reacted, drawing and throwing it in one swift, well-practiced action. The knife was long and broadened along its length to a wide tip. It flew from Nathalie's hand in an arc, cutting the air and darkness before embedding in Edwards's chest with a sickening thump.

Edwards half scrambled, half dropped backward, his shocked utterance turning to a scream in his throat even as he sank to the floor in a splash of water. For a moment the room was thrown into disarray as Edwards's flashlight left his grip, painting long shadows across the ceiling, the jeeps, the water, in a deranged dance of confusion.

Nathalie moved instantly, even as Sinclair shouted a command and both she and Domi tried to track the woman with their blasters. Nathalie had crossed the distance to Edwards's fallen form in a second, reached down as she ran, snatched her knife's bone handle and pulled it from the ex-Mag's chest. As she did so, Sinclair fired her Colt Mark IV, launching a .45 mm hollow-point bullet out into the semidarkness at the woman as she scrambled across the deck. The bullet missed, going wide of its target in a burst of angry sound.

As she plucked the knife from Edwards's body, Nathalie had launched her legs into the air, flipping over Edwards as Sinclair's bullet went hurtling past. She twisted her lithe body in the air so that she was facing the direction she'd come from…and facing Sela Sinclair, who had trained the Colt Mark IV on her.

"Drop the knife, lady!" Sinclair shouted as the woman landed on her booted heels with a splash.

Nathalie paid her no attention; instead she was running like a whirling dervish, spinning and launching her long knife again in a whip-fast toss even as Sinclair's gun spit once more. The bullet went rocketing past Nathalie, missing her by inches rather than feet, closely followed by a second shot.

Domi was tracking the woman in the darkness, too, her keen eyes better suited to the insubstantial light that was cast by Edwards's dropped flashlight. She took a steadying breath, Detonics pistol held in both hands, and watched as the woman called Nathalie leaped high into the air to deliver a cruel kick to Sinclair's face even as her monstrous knife struck the dark-skinned Cerberus warrior between the second and third ribs. Sinclair toppled back in an uncoordinated flop, her blaster firing again in a random shot that roared off into the darkness before embedding itself into the high ceiling.

Domi fired, sending a 9 mm slug charging toward the gymnastic woman as she bounded away from Sinclair's falling body. The bullet went over Nathalie's head as she landed on the slick decking and dropped down into a panther crouch.

An instant later, having never stopped moving, Nathalie scampered back to where Sinclair was lying and reached for the handle of her blade. Sinclair was moaning, clutching at her side where the knife had pierced. There was enough quick-acting poison on the blade that it slowed down Nathalie's opponents when it got into their bloodstream. Sinclair was alive right now, as was Edwards, but they were barely able to move.

Domi tracked the woman with the sight of her Combat Master, waiting for the moment. Domi's night vision was superior to the average person's. But here, with the rolling flashlight beam and the occasional flicker of the overheads, it was hard to keep track of Nathalie, let alone keep up with her.

Nathalie was on her feet again, spinning up from the

ground, kicking up splashes of water as she bounded and leaped and sprang across the decking, cartwheeling to create a constantly changing target profile.

Domi fired, the noise from the Combat Master echoing loudly in the motor pool.

There was a spark in the air, a sound of metal striking metal, and Domi realized that the other woman had deflected the bullet with her knife, cutting it out of the air.

Nathalie kept charging toward Domi, an ugly, cruel smile of determination on her face. Domi squeezed the trigger, fired again and again.

Now the woman was fifteen feet away.

Bang!

Now she was twelve.

Bang!

Now eight, seven, six.

Bang! Bang! Bang!

And then the Combat Master clicked on empty and Domi simply let it drop, no time to reload. Domi knew instinctively that the empty Detonics would have been a hindrance for what came next.

Nathalie drove the knife at Domi, point first. It gleamed as it caught the beam of the dropped flashlight, a momentary flash of white in the air.

Domi sidestepped, left arm up, meeting the knife hand at the wrist, deflecting it. Hits and misses would be measured in fractions of an inch now, strikes and blows and flesh on flesh as the petite Domi and the statuesque voodoo warrior clashed.

Nathalie jabbed with her knife, driving it toward Domi's face. Domi ducked her head to miss the cut, then charged forward, butting the taller woman high in the chest with her crown. Nathalie stumbled back, but regained her balance in an instant.

In that brief respite as her foe was wrong-footed, Domi drew her own knife from its sheath at her ankle. It was a combat knife with a six-inch, serrated blade. She had had this knife when she had lived in Cobaltville as a sex slave to Guana Teague, had used it on her master in a frantic escape attempt that, tangentially, had led to her joining the Cerberus team. She had lost any reckoning of the amount of blood spilled by its edge, the bodies it had defiled. Now, Domi ran at Nathalie, taking three long strides before driving the knife at her gut.

Nathalie leaped back, launching her left fist around in a vicious swing which almost caught Domi in the face. It didn't—instead, Domi reacted in the flickering darkness by dropping her head forward until her chin met her chest, the blow sailing over her, ruffling her hair.

As her punch missed, Nathalie continued the swing, keeping up her momentum and kicking out and back with her right heel. The heel connected with Domi's chest, knocking the albino girl backward into the water.

Nathalie did not stop moving; she just kept coming for Domi like an out-of-control freight train. The heel strike was followed by a spin into a vicious double kick. Domi rolled out of the way of the first, but did not move fast enough to avoid the second, getting clipped across her right ear by Nathalie's booted foot.

Domi sank back onto the deck, splashing into the shallow water, a femur bobbing beside her head, as Nathalie stood over her. But as Domi crashed down, she jabbed upward with her knife, stabbing it into Nathalie's inner thigh and driving it there with all her might. Nathalie toppled backward with a shriek of agony, keeling over, Domi's blade protruding from the inner thigh of her left leg.

Domi forced herself to get up. Her clothes and hair were damp, her back sodden—everything was slowing her down.

The woman called Nathalie could be seen in the tight beam of Edwards's discarded flashlight, rolling on the deck in agony, her hands clutched around the protruding handle of Domi's knife. As Domi strode toward her, she saw Nathalie sit up and yank the knife from her thigh, hissing painfully through her gritted teeth. Blood spurted out in a fierce jet, the result of a severed artery, its redness clouding the water as it slapped the pooling water and mingled beneath the surface.

Domi stamped down on the woman's left leg—the same one where the blade had been buried—sending a new wave of pain through her attacker. As Nathalie shrieked, Domi kicked out with her other leg, cuffing the woman across the side of her head with such force that Nathalie crashed back down into the deck with a resounding splash and thud.

Still standing over Nathalie, Domi scanned the deck, searching for her knife. The blade shimmered like a silver-scaled fish where it waited just below the surface of the water. She reached for it and—

Jab!

Something pierced Domi's side, striking her in the fleshy part just below her waist and above her hipbone. She shrieked; fell; hit the deck with a splash, blood pouring from the wound.

Nathalie was ten feet away, still on the floor, but sitting up and with one arm outstretched where she had thrown her knife. Domi saw her as water washed into her right eye where she had struck the floor. Pain seared down the whole of Domi's left flank where the poisoned knife had embedded in her flesh.

"No…" Domi said weakly. "No…"

Chapter 12

Grant awoke in a small, poorly lit room with stone walls covered in carved hieroglyphs…and there was something else in the room with him. The room was cool and windowless. Grant was lying on a plain wood cot, just a plank suspended from two chains that held it against the wall.

Remaining motionless, he looked around through narrowed eyes, searching the room for clues as to what had happened and where he was. The reason he did not move was because of the other figure in the room, that something else that he had caught the moment his eyes began to scan across the hieroglyphics.

"You're awake," the man said in French.

Inwardly, Grant cursed before turning to him and opening his eyes more widely. The man was sensitive— *real* sensitive. He must have detected the change in Grant's breathing.

The man was leaning back against a wall beside an open doorway, one whose lintel was low. He was of average height and build, in his fifties or sixties with mahogany skin and a buzz cut. On his left hip he had a gun—either a revolver or a pistol, judging by its length—held in a pancake holster whose top was sealed. He wore white clothes—shirt, pants, shoes—loose fitting to better alleviate the heat, which was doubtless warmer than this room. He wore something else, too, a narrow strip of ribbon that was strapped over his eyes and colored white as snow. The ribbon didn't seem to affect his ability to locate Grant, for his face was angled toward him as though he were looking directly at him.

"I'm awake," Grant said.

"Anglais?" his companion said, making it a question.

"American," Grant replied tersely.

Speaking French, the man instructed Grant to get up. Grant remained lying down, looking at the man with an expression of confusion drawn on his face. His Commtact could, of course, translate the foreign tongue in real time, but Grant figured that was a secret he best keep to himself for now; in his experience, captors were often free with their words if they thought their captive could not hear or understand them.

The man at the door tried again. "Okay," he said, "you get up now. We have places to go." He was speaking English with a thick accent now, in deference to Grant's seeming ignorance. "Don't try anything rash," he added. "We disarmed you—your knife is gone."

Maybe my knife is gone, Grant thought, feeling the familiar weight of the Sin Eater resting in its hidden holster pressed against his wrist, but I still have an ace up my sleeve. Grant pushed himself up from the cot, taking in as much as he could of the hieroglyphs that marked the walls. It was as though someone had had a lot of time to graffiti the place, a prisoner perhaps, held here for a long duration.

Beside the doorway, Grant's captor stood up straighter, watching the Cerberus man. "You have a name, monsieur?"

Grant turned and nodded. "Yeah. Grant." His head felt heavy where he had been knocked unconscious,

though damned if he could remember how. All he recalled was the bright flare in the dark pyramid room.

"Come, Grant," the man at the door said. "Things
you are to see."

Grant nodded again, moving slowly, still taking in all
the hieroglyphs. Though he was not an expert the way
that Brigid was, he saw something he thought he recognized here: a symbol showing a sitting figure wearing a crown like an upturned sieve and dressed in a
robe that came down to his ankles. The figure in the
engraving had what appeared to be one enlarged hand
that was shaped like a woman's fan. Grant recognized
it as an Annunaki, though he could not pull a specific
name from his memory. Brigid would know; he just
had to get the information to her without being noticed.

Grant was ushered through the doorway and into a
corridor beyond, windowless like the room of hieroglyphs and lit only by what little light trickled in from
its far end. Grant had to duck to get beneath the low
lintel of the door, and he took that moment to look at
its edge, spying a chiseled hole in the side of the stone
frame where a lock had sat but was now missing.

His dark-skinned captor followed Grant from the
room, not threatening, just accompanying him. He stood
to Grant's right, keeping his gun and holster on the far
side of his body from his captive. Grant considered
overpowering him…but then what?

"Where are we going?" Grant asked as they trudged
down the ill-lit tunnel-like corridor.

"You shall see," the man said, then laughed just a
little as if he had made a joke.

The corridor ended in a small flight of steps. The
steps were carved from stone, ancient and well-worn.

Daylight poured down from the opening above as Grant reached them.

"Ascend," the man beside him ordered.

Grant did so, squinting at the harsh daylight after spending so long in the semidarkness. He emerged into an open space surrounded by leafy trees. People were waiting at the edge of the tree line—fifty or more—with still more sitting in the trees. Many of the figures wore ribbons or thicker blindfolds over their eyes. They were mostly men with just a few women, all of them with dark skin that suggested African descent. It was hard to tell more than that, as everyone had the feeling of being a silhouette to Grant, the colors around him were still drained and muted as his eyes continued struggling to adjust to the sheer brilliance of the sunlight.

The open area formed a roughly marked circle of about twenty feet in diameter, the area behind Grant cast in shadow where a structure towered behind him. He began to turn, his eyes still squinting against the brilliant sunlight. But it wasn't just the dazzle of sunlight that was affecting Grant—oh, no, this was something entirely *other*.

Slowly, realization dawned. Grant's eyes were not adjusting properly. There was a problem, a limitation to his vision. The color was drained from the scene he was looking at, leaving only a kind of off-gray wash to the vista. The grass underfoot was the dark gray of charcoal, while the sky was brighter, a kind of platinum gray with the faintest trace of blueness, so infinitesimal it was like something seen only from the corner of one's eye.

Grant turned, trying to process what he was looking at, and as he did so something drew his eye. There, sitting almost directly above the entrance he had just emerged from, was a figure whose body glowed with brilliance. It was like a magic trick—the muscular figure was luminous with color when everything else here was grayed out. It shone with rainbow brilliance, sitting on a throne that had been placed on a step of a towering stone pyramid, head an impossible ball of ever-swirling color. It was hard to look at the figure, but harder still to look away—such was the magnetic draw of that beautiful crown.

The luminous figure was surrounded by others, ordinary men and women—*ordinary*, the term was so utterly perfect yet failed to encompass just now average, how mundane, these people were by comparison in Grant's eyes. They were all shades, shadows, silhouettes with features. Men and women, all of them wearing the blindfold over their eyes like his jailer, like some kind of cult or weird, unsettling magic trick.

"Where am I?" Grant asked, facing the brilliance of the seated figure on the pyramid steps. The figure was achingly beautiful to look at, beautiful and awe inspiring.

"You bring the tribute, apekin—" the figure said in an otherworldly voice that sounded like a monk's chant heard in a cathedral's echo.

"Tribute?" Grant muttered, failing to understand.

"—to my brother, Ninurta," the luminous figure replied in a voice that seemed to cross dimensions.

Grant's mind raced. Ninurta, Ninurta—the name was obviously Annunaki, though he could not place it.

As the brilliant rainbow figure spoke, Grant heard the scuff of feet on dirt behind him. Grant peered over his shoulder—much as it pained him to draw his attention away from this beautiful creature poised before him—and saw figures emerging from the surrounding crowd. Four of them stepped forward, indistinct amid the other silhouettes of the crowd, and began to stride closer, spreading out to approach Grant from all sides. Grant knew an ambush when he saw one, and if he had had any doubts about the strangers' intentions they were dashed when he heard the clank of metal on metal and saw a thick chain droop from one of the figures' hands.

Grant tensed, ready for anything, wondering just what the hell he and his teammates had stumbled into this time. What the hell—and *where*?

THE CONGO, KANE remembered now, the thought so vivid it woke him up without his even realizing it.

· He had been dreaming of that mission—was it three years ago? Four maybe?—when he and Brigid and another Cerberus operative, a physician called Reba DeFore, had become caught up in a mystery concerning a mystical object called the Mirror of Prester John. The mirror was a kind of remote view screen designed by an Annunaki overlord called Utu, through which great Anu himself had gazed upon clandestine meetings and secret trysts. The Cerberus warriors had found it inside a hidden chamber, one which could only be accessed via some kind of teleport door, or at least that's how Kane had understood it.

In his dream, people had mistaken his colleague Reba DeFore for one of the indigenous locals because her skin was tanned. It was a dream and it abided only by the laws of dream—that desperate need to change the facts to make something belong. Idiocy. In reality, DeFore was ash blonde, with tanned bronze skin. Only the stupid or the blind could have mistaken her for a local woman.

Kane pushed the dream away, letting his senses settle as he tried to figure out where he was and what the heck he was lying on. Because he was lying down, and he sure as shooting didn't remember going to sleep.

Something had hit him. Something bright, a light, a dazzling light. So bright it had struck like a physical blow, the way sound can be felt when it's loud enough and deep enough, the way music can shake a room.

He listened for a moment, playing possum, stretching out with every iota of his fabled point-man sense to try to get a feeling for where he was, who was with him and whether he was in danger. Well, the last was a given, but there was danger and there was *danger*; Kane knew the difference.

He heard the sound of a room, hard walls, not a breeze, not the sounds he would associate with being outside. Nothing played across his skin, either, no wind on his face or on the hairs of his forearms. So he was inside—somewhere. Maybe still inside the pyramid chamber? No, it felt too small for that. He was in a smaller room than that; he could feel the way the air came back to him when he breathed, the tiny trace sound it made as it echoed about the room. These subtle tells were the kind he had used to his advantage all his life.

Was anyone else here? He couldn't say. He held his breath, listened for the telltale breathing that someone else would perform. Nothing.

Behind the lids, his eyes seemed to be staring at the sun, a bright—almost organic—orange painted across their backs.

He opened his eyes, listening as much as looking, still reaching out with his senses like a blind man with a stick. When he opened his eyes he saw the same thing as when they were closed: an orange swirl whose vibrancy changed subliminally with each breath.

He wanted it to be something in front of him, a trick, a screen, a light shone directly into his eyes, but instinctively he knew it was not.

What was it he was thinking about Reba DeFore just a few moments before, the way she had been mistaken for a local in his dream, how only the stupid or the blind could have made such an error. Be careful what you wish for, Kane, he chastised himself bitterly.

Without moving, he tapped on his Commtact and hailed his partners, subvocalizing his words. "Baptiste? Grant? Can you hear me?"

BRIGID BAPTISTE HEARD Kane's voice through her ear canal where the subdermal Commtact channeled it through her jaw bone. "Kane?" she asked, her voice barely a whisper.

"Baptiste, you okay?" Kane asked. "My eyesight's been compromised, I'm blind. I'm gonna need you to—"

"I'm blind, too," Brigid replied, cutting Kane off in midinstruction.

"What?"

"Well, not blind maybe," Brigid said. "I can see colors…a color anyway."

"Orange?" Kane guessed.

"Green," Brigid corrected. "Luminous green. Like when you stare into a lightbulb filament."

"Yeah, mine's more a kind of noonday sun," Kane told her, "but the same basic effect, I guess.

"You alone?"

"Hard to say for sure," Brigid replied. "I think so." Like Kane, she had listened to the space she was in, trying to sense where she was and whether she was being watched.

"Grant with you?" Kane asked.

"No." She thought for a moment, listening intently to her surroundings. "I'm inside a room. Small room. I can't hear anyone else, no breathing."

"No snoring?" Kane asked. "Grant snores."

Brigid's mouth twitched with a smile. "You two spend way too much time together. You know that?"

Kane grunted an acknowledgment, then went on. "Any idea what happened?" he asked. "I remember seeing that figure appear from the darkness. Looked like a snake face to me—"

Snake face was one of Kane's nicknames for the Annunaki, as accurate as it was disrespectful.

"I barely saw it," Brigid admitted. "But it was definitely Annunaki."

"Was it Utu?" Kane asked, recalling the would-be god the pair had met here the last time that they had visited.

"What makes you say—?"

"Didn't you recognize where we are?" Kane asked, sounding somewhat smug through the Commtact link.

"Should I have?"

"We're back in the Congo," Kane said. "You remember…the Mirror of Prester John, Utu, Princess Pakari? All of that?"

"Yes, I remember," Brigid said, taking a condescending tone.

"Then you're slipping," Kane told her. "We were in Utu's little storeroom, just like before. Sure, someone had put a new coat of paint on the place, twinkling diamond wallpaper and so on, but it was definitely the same spot. I'd know it a mile away."

Brigid thought about this for only a second, recalling Kane's point-man instinct and the way he could sometimes intuit things that even her eidetic memory could miss.

"Then it was an interphaser, all right," Brigid stated. "But why would we be brought back here? When we left the place, the mirror had been destroyed and Utu had been—" she stopped, gripped by sudden realization.

"Blinded," Kane finished after a moment's pause. "Utu was blinded by the flash of energy that came from the mirror when it blew. It literally burned out his eye sockets."

A sinking feeling struck Brigid as she started to put things together. "Kane, do you think that…maybe… Utu came back somehow?"

Over the Commtact, Brigid fancied she could hear Kane's sharp intake of breath.

MEANWHILE, GRANT STOOD in the dirt arena—because he realized now that that's what it was—as the four figures approached, weapons in their hands. He was still seeing everything in gray tones, a washed-out shadow world to the one he was used to. Inside it hadn't been so bad, but out here he was struck by the absence of color.

Grant could hear the conversation playing out over the Commtact frequency he shared with Kane and Brigid as the figures paced around him, edging closer. They were talking about being blinded, and now he recalled the figure at the far end of the room they had stepped into via the interphase pillar, the way that its head had been a brilliant corona. He had turned, seen the figure only for an instant, caught only at the edge of his sight. Could that be what had changed his eyesight? Likely. And was that stolen glance the reason he was not blind when his companions were?

There was no more time to think, however. Even as

Kane and Brigid's conversation played out across the Commtact, the first two figures made their moves. They were tall men—in fact all four were tall, the shortest of them as tall as Grant. They approached from opposite sides, holding their bodies bent to keep their center of balance low as they drew their weapons. The one to Grant's left had a broad knife with a hooked design, the kind of blade one might use to cut through long grass. The one to Grant's right was wielding the chain he had first detected, looped around his clenched fist, letting its links hang down almost to the ground, the gray, gray ground.

"Now, fellas," Grant said, holding his hands loosely out at his sides in a gesture of surrender, "I hope this isn't what it looks like. I don't want any trouble."

Even as the last word escaped Grant's lips the two men charged at him, weapons ready. Grant took a half step to his left, taking him deliberately closer to the knife man. He was the primary threat, Grant calculated, because a knife like that could do a whole lot of damage in next to no time, even in the hands of an amateur.

LIKE BRIGID, KANE had been surreptitiously exploring his cell as he spoke to her—or at least as surreptitiously as a blind man could. His eyesight had not returned in any measurable sense. He still saw that dazzle of orange in place of anything more definite, and there was no change whether he waved a hand in front of his face or blinked repeatedly.

He checked the cell—he figured it was a cell judging by the locked door and the lack of windows—by a process of bumping into things and playing his hands ahead of him, running his fingers across whatever he met.

He estimated the room to be about eight feet square, with rough walls whose crevices and indentations suggested to him that a design had been carved into them. There was a door with no handle on the inside, detectable only by the seam at its edges where it sat almost flush to the wall.

There were two items of furniture in the room. One was the bed on which Kane had been lying when he had awoken, which was a simple wooden slab chained to the wall, and the other was a backless chair or stool carved from wood.

The floor, like the walls, was made of stone. A gutter ran around the room, two inches wide and parallel to the walls, jutting out just a little at the door. The gutter was roughly an inch deep, sloped so that it ran into a small gap at the bottom of the wall with the door in it. The gap was roughly the size of a brick. Kane guessed that this gutter was used for the sanitary purposes of prisoners, but realized it could also be for more sinister reasons, reminding him as it did of the gullies sometimes found within slaughterhouses designed to let the blood wash away.

Once he had a better idea of where he was, Kane raised his voice and called for attention. "Hey," he shouted. "Anybody out there? Who are you? Where am I? What do you want with me?"

The only response came from Brigid. "Kane, you're close," she said over the Commtact. "I can hear you."

IN THE DIRT CIRCLE outside the pyramid, the knife man took the bait, driving the knife, tip first, at Grant's chest. Grant twisted, bringing his left arm around to meet the knife hand just behind the wrist, flipping the man's arm out and up even as Grant's other arm came around in a powerful swing, fist balled. Grant's punch connected brutally with the man's nose, breaking it and knocking the man back with a shriek of surprise and pain. Grant was still tangled with the man's knife arm, and he brought his left arm down, forcing the man's arm with him, knife and all. As he did so, his second attacker launched his own attack, playing out the length of chain like a whip, cutting it through the air until it struck Grant across the back.

Grant grunted, still hanging on to his first opponent's arm as the chain struck him. Whoever his captors were, they had stripped away his duster but left him wearing his shadow suit and shirt. The shadow suit absorbed the impact of the chain, dissipating the blunt trauma so that it felt more like a hard tap. In that moment, Grant relieved his first foe of the knife, drilling a second punch into the man's face as he struggled to fight back.

Then Grant turned as his second opponent drew back his whip for a second try. The chain whip came hurtling toward Grant's face, and the Cerberus warrior sidestepped—more by instinct than anything else, for his sight remained faulty and indistinct out here.

As he dodged, Grant spoke, piping his words over the Commtact frequency. "I'm alive," he said, keeping his words intentionally vague.

IN HIS CELL, Kane tensed as he heard his partner's words. "Grant? Where are you?" he asked.

"It's cool out here," Grant replied with a grunt of expelled breath, "wish I was wearing something warmer!"

Outside. Kane got the code straightaway; it hardly needed a genius to work out that Grant wasn't able to talk and so was disguising their conversation as something else.

"Me and Baptiste have been blinded," Kane said emotionlessly, keeping professional about the situation. "How about you?"

"Not great," Grant responded as he ducked below the swinging chain and snatched it from the air before its user could draw it back.

As Grant moved, he became aware of a shadow—black on gray grass—crossing behind him. He switched direction at the last instant as something came hurtling toward him from behind. It was a long-handled hammer, swept through the air by his third opponent. It missed Grant and struck the chain wielder instead as he tried to get out of its path.

The chain wielder crashed backward with a painful expulsion of breath accompanied by the sound of breaking ribs. He slumped to the ground in anguish, arms around his legs in a fetal ball.

Grant, meanwhile, had dived and rolled, yanking the chain free of its user as he fell, still scanning for attackers. There were two of them on their feet, still armed. The third, who had used the chain, was lying on his back with his hands on his chest where the hammer had knocked the wind out of him and maybe cracked a rib in the process, while the fourth—the disarmed knife wielder—was just pushing himself up from the dirt, wiping blood from his nose—gray blood, like everything else Grant saw.

Hammer man pulled his weapon back by a short leather thong attached to its handle, before whipping it around his head in an arc. The sound of the hammer whirling was like the blades of a helicopter, a deep vibration that carried through the air.

"You ever hear of someone called Ninurta?" Grant muttered, subvocalizing into his Commtact pick up.

Kane and Brigid replied in unison, repeating the name. "Ninurta?"

"The Annunaki god of war," Brigid summarized. "Where did you hear that name?"

There was no time for Grant to reply. Right now, all of his concentration was fixed on timing that hammer as it cut through the air in a lethal rotation.

The hammer bearer launched it as it reached the apex of its spin, and the hammer came hurtling toward Grant with a howl of parting air. Grant's left arm snaked out, sending the chain whip he had just acquired out to meet the hammer, wrapping around it in an instant with a clash of metal links. A fraction of a second was all Grant had to pull the chain taut, altering the direction of the hammer by a few degrees as he ducked out of its path.

The hammer raced over Grant's shoulder, missing him by the smallest of margins and almost pulling his arm from its socket in the process—before he let go of the chain.

Hammer man was on him in an instant, chasing after his weapon with arms stretched out to his sides, throwing a haymaker at Grant's face.

Grant blocked with his right arm, the knife he held flashing momentarily as sunlight caught it like a streak of silver on the miasma of gray.

"I think Ninurta is behind this," Grant huffed as he crossed his forearms to block a second blow. "Something about my being a tribute to him…?"

Grant's opponent drove down with both arms, using his superior height to try to overwhelm his foe. Grant wove backward, pulling himself just fractionally out of the line of fire.

At the same moment, the remaining combatant joined the fray, two thick metal gloves on his hands with a long length of chain between them.

"I told you I saw one of the snake faces before everything went white," Kane growled over the shared Commtact frequency.

There was no time for Grant to respond. Death came hurtling toward him at an astonishing rate.

Chapter 13

Brigid began recounting the story of Ninurta as she checked the room she was in, running her hands blindly over the walls to try to discover where she was.

"Ninurta was the Annunaki god of war," she recited over the shared Commtact link, "whose city was Lagash in ancient Babylon. His parents were Enlil and Ninlil, so he came from pretty tough stock."

Kane sighed as he heard this. The Cerberus warriors had suffered seemingly endless trouble from Enlil. Enlil was the cruelest of the Annunaki and had been reborn from the genetic material of Baron Cobalt, once Kane and Grant's ultimate superior in the city of Cobaltville back when they had been Magistrates. The Cerberus rebels had rallied to turn back Enlil after he and his brethren, the royal family of the Annunaki, had re-emerged on Earth with a plan to subjugate humanity. But Enlil had proved particularly tough—and had reappeared in the Middle East where he had attempted to re-grow the organic spaceship, *Tiamat*, from a single seed. Eight months ago, in their most recent clash, Enlil had almost died after losing a leg during the fight. Where he was now, if he was indeed still alive, nobody knew.

"Ninurta," Brigid continued, "was an incredible warrior who used a mace called Sharur in battle. Some descriptions of Sharur suggest that it could talk with its master and take the form of a winged lion. From what we know of the Annunaki, that implies there was some kind of technology involved—perhaps it was a computer-aided weapon or vehicle of some sort."

"You said this guy was a superwarrior," Grant said, his words staggered, his voice breathless. "Can you tell me more? 'Cause—"

"—I'M WORRIED I'M about to face him." As he spoke, Grant kicked out at the warrior in the arena with the chain-mail mittens, driving him back toward the watching crowds.

There was no time to catch his breath, however. Even as the gloved warrior stumbled backward, the now-disarmed hammer wielder lunged for him, grabbing his arm and pulling him off balance. Grant danced uncomfortably to his right before bringing his left arm around in a swift punch to the man's face. His opponent went backward with the blow, but still managed to cling on as he stumbled, drawing Grant with him to the ground.

"Ninurta defeated a cycle of beasts named the Slain Heroes—presumably after he had killed them—to reach a monster called Anzu," Brigid elaborated over the Commtact. "These Slain Heroes included the Warrior Dragon, the Mermaid, the Six-Headed Ram and the Seven-Headed Snake, among others. Anzu himself was some kind of massive bird who could breathe fire and water and had stolen the tablets of destiny from Ninurta's father, Enlil."

A shadow loomed over Grant, heavy footsteps getting rapidly closer. Kane's voice piped over the linked Commtacts with a query then, while Grant tried to extricate himself from the other warrior's grip. "You have an interpretation for all that?" Kane asked.

"Most probably Anzu was an aircraft of some sort,"

Brigid reasoned, "and the description of its breathing fire and water could be a primitive understanding of its weaponry."

"Great," Grant deadpanned as he pulled free of the other warrior's grip. At the same moment, the warrior's colleague with the metal gloves reached around Grant's throat from behind and cinched the chain tight. Suddenly Grant was pulled backward, the chain locked around his throat.

Grant still held the dagger he had taken from his first opponent, and he twisted it in his hand as he was pulled back by his enemy. The length of chain pressed painfully against his neck, choking him as he fought against it. Grant stabbed backward, driving the knife into his opponent's leg with as much strength as he could muster.

The man behind him yelped as the knife buried itself in the tendons of his upper leg. His grip faltered momentarily, and Grant used that instant to thread his fingers between the chain and his throat, grabbing it and tugging it away.

The moment's slack in the chain gave Grant enough leeway to drive his head backward, striking his opponent in the nose with the back of his head.

Grant's opponent yelped again as his nose cracked, blood pouring almost instantly from his right nostril. The strength seemed to drain out of him in that moment, and Grant dropped down out of the clutch of the chain, pulling the knife free from his opponent's leg.

Grant's opponent keeled backward, blood spurting from his leg wound and lines of blood emerging from both nostrils now. Grant kicked out, sending his booted foot into the man as he fell backward, driving him hard into the gray-colored grass. The man lay there, eyes shut tight in agony, blood oozing over the grass and dirt.

Up above, sitting on his throne on the pyramid steps, the glowing Annunaki clapped his hands together thrice in brief applause—or at least it seemed like applause, but it was accompanied by no sound.

There was no time to celebrate the victory. Already the two remaining warriors were circling Grant, looking for an opening. Grant stepped back, watching sharply as both men circled toward him. They were scared now, scared of him—for they had seen Grant in action, seen all those years of Magistrate training put to swift, violent use.

The man to Grant's right—whose knife Grant had taken at the start of the bout—saw his opening and hurried forward in a jog. He incorporated his momentum into a swinging punch, one which Grant blocked and pushed aside. The man's other fist came up with a follow through, rabbit fast and aimed to strike Grant hard in the gut. Grant twisted, taking the blow in a glancing strike against his flank before pounding his own fist forward at his attacker's face.

Behind Grant, his second attacker was approaching now, having picked up the hammer that his colleague had lost. One part of Grant's agile brain tracked the man's movements, even as he tackled the first attacker.

Grant's opponent tried to block, taking his punch on his forearm. But Grant struck with such force that the blocking arm was knocked backward, causing his opponent to strike himself across the face.

Grant followed up, bringing one bent knee up into the man's groin, striking there with bone-breaking force. His opponent gasped in pain as he was lifted three inches off the ground before staggering back toward the waiting crowd. Grant let him go, turning to face his other attacker.

As Grant turned, the head of the long-handled hammer came sweeping through the air toward him, its wielder clutching it by the end of its handle for the mightiest swing. Grant ducked instinctively, missing the hammer by an infinitesimal margin, stepping in again during the follow-through as the hammer arced away.

Grant shoved forward, striking his mallet-wielding opponent with a powerful blow that wrong-footed him and forced him backward. The weight of the whirling hammer contributed to the man's stumble, and suddenly he found himself dragged to the left and anti-clockwise in a kind of half step, half jump dance, clinging to the hammer's shaft. Out of control, the hammer slammed against the ground, drawing its user with it so that he rolled across the dirt, tucking his body for protection.

Grant chased after the warrior's retreating form. Three long strides and Grant was delivering a hard kick to his opponent's torso, flipping him over onto his back. The man lay sprawled before him, dark gray blood washing across the teeth in his open mouth, eyes still hidden by the now dirt-smeared ribbon. The man's hand eased on the shaft of the hammer, dropping it as he struggled to remain conscious. Grant pressed his foot against the man's neck as he stood over him, watching his colorless face. Then Grant turned, facing the figure on the pyramid for whom this bout had clearly been organized.

The figure on the pyramid shone with brilliance against the grayness around, pressing his bandaged hands together. "You are war master," he said in a voice that seemed to emanate from the distant end of a long, echoing tunnel. "The blood you shed shall appease my brother. Be proud, apekin warrior, for you are the chosen of Nergal."

Nergal? Grant thought, bowing automatically to this mysterious, dazzling figure. "Lord Nergal?" he pressed, his head still bowed in supplication. "I am your loyal servant. What do you wish of me?"

The figure in the throne took a moment to consider— everything it did seemed slow and very conscious, in fact, as though it struggled with some great burden. Then it answered, tangentially confirming who it was to Grant. "Blood sacrifice is needed to spill the materials required for my brother," Nergal said. "Bring forward the blood sacrifice," he commanded.

Grant swallowed hard. Sacrifices? Unless they were chickens—and he suspected they wouldn't be—then things had just taken a very unpleasant turn.

WAITING IN HIS CELL, Kane had adopted a position beside the door. He could not be certain which way the door opened, nor whether or not he was being watched, but he at least could try to stay ahead of his enemy.

When the door pulled back, outward from the cell, without a moment's warning, Kane moved immediately, lunging toward the entrant with a ram's-head punch, aiming it by the sound of the man's breath, the smell of his sweat.

Framed in the doorway, the guard was momentarily surprised, and then Kane's fist struck him in the center of his chest. The man sagged backward, dropping onto his butt with a loud thump.

"Where am I?" Kane muttered, maneuvering through the doorway by touch alone. "What have you done with my friends?"

Though Kane could not see it, the guard on the floor smiled, a broad slash of white teeth appearing in his face. "You still have some life in you," the man said with a chuckle, speaking in French. As he spoke, he reached for the pistol that he had shoved into his waistband, pulling it free.

Kane pressed his advantage, if he could call it that, kicking out hard at the location of the noise. Incredibly, his toe struck the man's hand as he pulled his pistol from its holster, and, with an "ouch," he almost let the weapon go. He clung on, again more surprised than hurt by Kane's blow—it had been poorly aimed and had struck in a glancing manner, nothing that the guard could not endure.

"I have a gun trained on you, monsieur," the man explained in heavily accented English. "You try anything else and I will shoot you."

Still standing in the doorway, Kane considered his options rapidly, running through his scant choices as a blind man. There were none worth trying, the odds were too heavily stacked against him—unless he could bluff his way...

"I warn you," the fallen guard added, "I have no compunctions about shooting a blind man. None at all."

So he knows, Kane realized. Knows I'm blind.

Reluctantly, Kane raised his hands above his head, looking straight ahead with eyes that could not see. "You got me," he admitted. "But I have to warn you—if we're going anywhere, you're going to have to guide me."

"Don't worry about that," the guard said in accented English. "Your eyesight will improve soon enough." Kane did not like the way he emphasized the word *improve*, as if he meant something more than it implied.

Sightless, Kane was led through a long, cool corridor with stone walls that were cold to the touch. He knew that it was long by the echo his footsteps made, felt the coolness of the stones when he brushed against them with his outstretched hands. "Where are we going?" Kane asked.

His companion said nothing, merely tsked between gritted teeth.

They soon reached a flight of steps. Kane knocked his foot against the first and tripped, reaching for the wall before he fell. "A little help, man," he said to his guard in a harsh tone.

The guard only laughed sadistically.

"Kane?" Brigid Baptiste's voice came from somewhere behind him.

Kane turned automatically, but his vision was no better. He still only saw that haze of brilliant orange, changing a little as if it were something organic. "It's me," he said. "You okay?"

There was no point disguising that they had entered here together—they had been brought through the interphase pane together and been incarcerated at the same time. However, Kane chose not to give his ally's name freely—if they needed it, they could ask, and maybe beg, for it.

"I'm all right," Brigid said uncertainly. "Do you know where we're being taken?"

"Shut up!" a rough male voice demanded harshly from the same location Brigid's voice was emanating from. So, Kane thought, she's got a guard, too. Just one?

"You brought company, I hear," Kane encouraged.

Suddenly something cold pressed against his temple, accompanied by the sound of a safety being cocked. He figured it for a gun.

"Enough chitchat," his guard warned, his breath hot on the side of Kane's face. "Get up those steps."

Feeling the gun pull away from his head, Kane stepped warily forward, toeing for each step as he ascended. As he did, Kane heard more movements behind him, two sets of footsteps emerging from a side passage—he guessed it was Mariah Falk and her guard.

Five steps later and Kane was out of the corridor and could feel the sun's rays on his face. Feel, but not see.

"Keep walking," Kane's captor instructed from behind him, pushing him between his shoulder blades.

GRANT WATCHED THE six figures emerge from the steps that ran down below the pyramid, recognizing his companions, Kane, Brigid and finally Mariah, as they stumbled up into the light along with three guards. Like everyone and everything else here, they looked gray and washed out, as if in a photograph that had spent too long in the sun.

"It's okay, guys," Grant said. "I'm here."

"Yeah?" Kane replied. "And where is here? I'm having a little trouble with my eyesight just now on account of being blind."

At the same time as this exchange was occurring, Brigid subvocalized a query to both men via their linked Commtacts. "Grant, is Ninurta here now?"

"Annunaki sitting behind you," Grant subvocalized, covering the subtle movement of his lips by pretending to study the blood on his hand. "Calls himself Nergal, not Ninurta. Maybe an alias?"

"No, Nergal is another child of Enlil and Ninlil," Brigid confirmed. "Ninurta's brother."

Kane, Brigid and Mariah were now in the center of the roughly marked circle, and as Brigid spoke, they were forced to turn around until they faced the pyramid. As they turned, they became aware of something that could only be described as miraculous. Despite their ruined eyesight—for Mariah had been blinded, too—they could all see the figure sitting before them, glowing with a brilliant, ever-changing rainbow of churning colors, his head exuding a brilliant whiteness. That burning whiteness seemed to purify their vision, eating away at the damage that had obscured their sight, pushing it back from its center in an expanding, circular wave. As it did so, Kane, Brigid and Mariah discovered, to their surprise, that they could see again—after a fashion.

Now they saw Nergal, the glowing figure they had first spied, where he sat atop his throne on the steps of the pyramid. A wash of bland figures, as insignificant as shadows, stood about him, their blindfolded eyes fixed on the three strangers who had entered the circle of combat and execution. And there was another figure, not standing but hovering, legs together, arms outstretched, floating behind and to the right of Nergal, over his left shoulder.

We are in the presence of gods, Kane thought as he stared at the impossibly majestic figures poised before him, so brilliant that everything around them seemed like an unfinished sketch by comparison.

"If Nergal's sitting down, who's the dude hovering beside him?" Kane subvocalized as he tried to process what he was looking at.

"What are you talking about?" Grant asked, his surprise evident even in the secret communiqué.

Kane studied the figure hovering behind the Annunaki Nergal, a sinking feeling clutching at his chest. The figure had a spiny crest jutting from his long, Annunaki skull and his hand was shaped like a fan.

"Ain't no one there, Kane," Grant stated with utter conviction. "Not that I can see."

Chapter 14

"You sure?" Kane asked incredulously over the Commtact link as he stared the floating figure up and down. "Big guy, Annunaki, hanging in the air and glowing colors every which way to Sunday. You don't see him?"

"I see him, too," Brigid confirmed even as Grant denied it. "Ninurta."

It was a disconcerting thing, to learn that your view of reality was genuinely different to that of the people around you. Grant struggled to comprehend what his teammates were saying, that they could see a figure that he could not, like some kind of ghost hanging in the air.

For Brigid and Kane, they had the uncomfortable reassurance that at least both of them seemed to be seeing the same thing—the figure of Ninurta, Annunaki god of war, floating above the steps of the pyramid at the shoulder of his brother, Nergal. Brigid's mind went back to a discussion she had had over a year before, when she had first fallen under the thrall of the Annunaki god-prince Ullikummis.

"YOU FOUGHT WITH my father," Ullikummis had intoned, his voice like rocks grinding together. The voice matched the face, for it, too, was constructed from rock, carved as much as grown, as if the god-prince had been brought to life by erosion. "I saw this when I imbibed time in the Ontic Library. You fought with my father, and others of our race, of the Annunaki."

Brigid had been strapped to a seat made of rock. She squirmed against a pain that seemed to stretch down her back like claws. Ullikummis was doing something to her; only later did she learn that he had removed the biolink transponder that she carried within her at that moment, nullifying its nanospores, which were hidden in her body.

"I saw there," Ullikummis continued, "that you have exceptional knowledge for an apekin, a—" he stopped, as if trying to recall the word "—human. And yet you never questioned what it was you fought."

He was talking about the Annunaki, speaking to Brigid in a way she had never spoken with the enemy before, in a manner that was both patronizing and oddly respectful.

"Tried," Brigid replied, the single word coming out as a gasp rushing between her gnashing teeth.

"They acted like you," Ullikummis said. "My father, Lords Marduk, Shamash, Negra, Utu, Zu. Aliens to your world, yet they behaved like you, like actors on a stage, dressed in masks and rubber suits. Humans in everything but appearance," he mused, adding as if in afterthought, "and perhaps stamina. Yet you never questioned this."

"They had technology," Brigid began, her words strained, "they differed from…"

"No, they did not," Ullikummis interrupted her. "The Annunaki are beautiful beings, multifaceted, crossing dimensions you cannot begin to comprehend. Their wars are fought on many planes at once, the rules of their games intersect only tangentially with Earth and its holding pen of stars. What you have seen is only a sliver of what the battle was, and the Annunaki have shamed themselves in portraying it thus."

Brigid had listened, wondering what Ullikummis was telling her. In that moment, she had recalled traveling to the distant past via a memory trap and seeing the Annunaki as their slaves, the Igigi, perceived them. They had been beautiful, just as Ullikummis was telling her, shining things that seemed so much more real than the world around them, color things amid a landscape of gray. But when she had faced Enlil, Lilitu and the others in her role as a Cerberus rebel, they had been curiously ordinary. Yes, they were stronger, faster, supremely devious, but they were—what?—the thing that Ullikummis called them? Actors on a stage? Players dressed in masks and rubber suits like some hokey performance designed for children? Had Brigid and her companions been taken in by a performance, a show designed to entertain the feebleminded?

The thing that is alien, she had realized as the interrogation went on, is a thing that cannot ever be comprehended, only seen in fragments, its entirety hidden in impenetrable darkness.

The interrogation had ended in brainwashing. Brigid had been changed in those moments, her human mind retreating as something new and hateful took its place, something alien. She had taken the name Brigid Haight in those dark days, and had seen the world in the way the Annunaki saw it—nonlinear, less restrictive, bigger than the spaces her human eyes could endure. She had shifted into solid rock to take a hidden pathway into the underground city of Agartha, not through mechanical means or supernatural ones, but through a unique understanding of the world, one that ensured she was no longer fully constrained by its three dimensions. This was the way the Annunaki functioned, their presence on Earth like an iceberg's tip, only a tenth of their actuality ever emerging.

Or at least, that was how Brigid had understood it when her mind had been possessed of Annunaki thinking. A new comprehension of reality, one entirely removed from the comprehension her companions, her fellow humans, had.

AND PERHAPS HERE it was again. Something in Nergal's brilliance, something in the so-called Heaven's Light, had changed her perception and Kane's. Shifting realities. But what would do such a thing?

And just what were the people in Libya mining? It was obviously tied to all of this, the same flecks of diamond that lined the walls of Nergal's base, which had been Lord Utu's just a few years before, were being mined in Libya; glistering things of silver, like shards of broken glass.

MARIAH, MEANWHILE, WAS not privy to the conversation that her companions were having via Commtact. She could only tremble in fear at the thought of what was happening, and what would happen next.

As they tried to process what was going on, Nergal spoke in a voice that sounded like distant thunder booming from the darkest clouds. "War master," he said, addressing Grant, "your sacrifices are here. Spill their blood, open the pathway for my brother to attain dominion."

Grant may have been disconcerted but he sure as hell understood what sacrifice and spilling blood were all about. This bozo wanted him to ritually kill his partners—something he could not do.

Grant stood there, dumbstruck, as Kane, Brigid and Mariah were forced to kneel. For them, whose eyesight remained in a state of flux, neither wholly comprehensive nor entirely restricted, there seemed nothing they could do but drop to the ground and bow their heads. There were eighty people here, many of them armed and all of them devoted to Nergal—that much was clear from the blindfolds they wore as some strange mark of what had been done to them. Did they see through the blindfolds? Was what Nergal did here, with his so-called Light of Heaven, changing their perceptions so far that they no longer needed to open their eyes to see? Like the soldiers that they had discovered in Libya, where all of this madness had started, were these Congo locals blind, but seeing things in an entirely new way?

"Bow your heads in appreciation of your gods," one of the guards instructed Kane.

Kane could see him, kind of. He was a wraith, a dark shadow in place of a man, but he had a presence in the brilliance of orange that dominated Kane's vision.

At that moment, Mariah spoke, her voice a timid squeak. "Please don't—"

"Silence," one of the guards spit in French.

"Mariah, that you there?" Kane asked.

"Kane," Mariah said with a wash of relief. "Do you know what's happening?"

"No," Kane admitted as he bowed his head. "Baptiste? Is your eyesight improving?"

"Somewhat," Brigid said tentatively.

"Silence," the guard beside Kane ordered, shoving him from behind, pushing his head down so that he sagged forward.

A FEW FEET AWAY, Grant was handed a broad-bladed sword by one of the members of the crowd, a hunched-over man of older years who seemed emaciated in comparison to the local warriors whom Grant had been forced to fight earlier. "Sword of Heaven," the old man said in French.

Grant accepted the sword, looked at it with interest. Unlike almost everything else he saw, the sword was not a dull, washed-out gray. Instead it had a luminescence to it, a network of what appeared to be diamonds entirely covered the surface of the four-foot-long blade.

Grant realized then, instinctually, that his eyesight had been tricked, mangled and adapted by some outside force. He had not been blinded like his other companions, presumably because he had only glanced sideward at the rotting Annunaki overlord who called himself Nergal, rather than staring at his impossible face of light. Nergal was rotting, though; Grant could see that much now that he could look at the brilliant figure without flinching. Something had ruined his body, was eating away at it in dark sores that Nergal had tried to bandage. It reminded Grant of something else he had seen recently, in the Spanish city of Zaragoza. There, another Annunaki had been reborn, a female goddess of the underworld called Ereshkigal; but her body was unstable, as were those of her creations. Ereshkigal could command the living to die and the dead to walk, but she could not command the rot to leave her fragile body. In the end, she had proved too weak and, freed from the nutrient bath that sustained her, she had disintegrated to dust.

"Blood shall be shed," Nergal instructed as Grant was ushered forward, his voice two voices, two tones, the voice of the unseen from the darkened end of a Neanderthal cave.

On the one hand, Grant felt almost compelled to obey this beautiful, rotten, wicked creature that presided on his throne. On the other, his friendship with Kane and Brigid was so strong it vied for his attention, warring inside him.

At the same moment, Kane, Brigid and Mariah saw something glowing before them, long feet pointed toward the ground just a foot away from them. Kane peered up from under his bowed head and realized it was the figure that Brigid had identified as Ninurta, the war god. Up close he wavered, insubstantial, like a pattern seen in a kaleidoscope.

"Something ain't right here," Kane muttered, broadcasting the observation through the medium of the linked Commtacts. "Ninurta isn't complete."

"Just like Ereshkigal," Grant replied, subvocalizing the words.

"I don't think we're going to be much help," Brigid pleaded. "Do you have a way to get us out of this, Grant?"

Grant took up a position behind the three kneeling Cerberus rebels and the insubstantial shade of Ninurta, raising the sword over Kane's neck. "Oh, yeah," Grant subvocalized. "I've got an ace up my sleeve."

The emaciated old man stood before Grant on the far side of the bowed Cerberus exiles, dipping his head curtly to Nergal before addressing Grant. "Like this," he said in French, entwining his hands and drawing them up over his shoulder. Then, as if he was holding a sword, he swept his clenched hands down in a swift arc, ending at Kane's shoulder. "One strike, crosswise, swift and clean. You understand?"

Grant nodded, his stomach muscles clenched in anticipation. He drew the Sword of Heaven up in a two-handed grip so that it was poised above his right shoulder, staring down at Kane's neck. Around him, the members of the crowd seemed to all draw breath, eighty people all inhaling at once, holding their collective breath in expectation.

Grant swept the blade down toward Kane's neck.

Chapter 15

Kane fell forward as the blade of the sword struck him, dropping and then moving again, leaping forward like a runner from the starting blocks. Grant had hit him with the sword, but had turned it at the critical moment, twisting the blade as it cut toward his partner, so that only the flat of the blade had struck Kane across his shoulders. It still hurt, but that pain was momentary and, crucially, it allowed Kane to literally keep his head.

Kane scrambled forward, moving from crouch to full run in just three steps, rushing toward the steps of the black pyramid. Around him, he heard the sounds of surprise and shock as the crowd reacted to what was happening, realized that the sacrifice had somehow got free.

THE OLD MAN who had offered instruction to Grant on the fine art of beheading, gasped in surprise, his gaze sweeping from the sword to Grant in a fraction of a second. *"Ça va?"*

Grant stepped the two paces that divided himself from his instructor, jabbing out with his left fist to deliver a brutal blow to the man's jaw. The old man went down like a sack of potatoes.

KANE WAS UP the steps of the pyramid in an instant, shoving grayed-out crowd members aside as he reached for Nergal and Ninurta where they waited in glowing brilliance at the tall throne. Kane reached for the hovering figure of Ninurta, grasping for the Annunaki's ankle with the intention of pulling him back down to earth. But his grasping right hand went straight through the fantastic figure, sweeping through it with no more consequence than passing through mist.

The unexpected effect of the move unbalanced Kane and suddenly he was tipping sideways, stumbling to regain his equilibrium as he lunged against nothingness. In that moment, the mob around him surged, reaching for Kane with gray-washed limbs.

THE OLD MAN went down, and Grant spun around, tracking the circle of figures who had been watching, dumbfounded, as he had failed to behead his prostrate ally.

The tone of the audience had changed, Grant sensed. A moment ago they had held their breath in sweet anticipation of Kane's beheading and the glorious sacrifice it would make to their sick god. Now, that breath was released in a mixture of surprise and fury, as the watchers realized that Grant had somehow shrugged off the mental hold that Nergal should have over him. Their god could not be fallible, of course, which meant instead that the man who had been granted the rank of war master was some kind of demon sent to test their faith.

They began to shift then, moving forward fearfully as Grant watched. Beside him, Brigid Baptiste was just getting to her feet, encouraging Mariah to do the same.

"You have a plan?" Mariah asked.

Grant handed Brigid the sword as the mob began to close more confidently toward the three of them. "Not really," Grant admitted. "More a kind of hope. But we'll wing it." As he said this, he stepped forward to meet the first of the crowd.

"Wing it?" Mariah repeated, unable to hide the shock from her voice.

Brigid flashed Mariah a smile, one that neither of them could see with their compromised eyesight. "We do this a lot," Brigid said in as reassuring a tone as she could muster. "Just keep behind us and try not to get hit by anything."

"But I can't see properly!" Mariah protested.

As Mariah spoke, the crowd surged toward Grant like a river that had finally broken its banks. Grant raised his right arm, crooked his index finger as he performed that well-practiced flinch of his wrist tendons, the one that would command his Sin Eater pistol into his hand from its hidden holster.

The foremost member of the charging mob went down an instant later, his left kneecap exploding in a burst of blood as a 9 mm bullet carved a path through it from the starting point of Grant's hand. It seemed almost magic, that instant, as the man went down in a flurry of spurting blood, tumbling over himself as his forward momentum met with the opposing trajectory of the bullet that had been fired from a gun that hadn't been there an eye's blink before.

To the lead runner's right, a second man went tumbling over himself as his right knee was shattered by another bullet from the Sin Eater, arms flailing wildly as he suddenly lost all balance and went crashing into a man to his right.

To the left, another member of the mob stopped and turned in place as Grant's third bullet found its target like a nail being pounded through his lower leg.

It had been the work of two seconds, three shots felling the lead members of an enraged, sixty-strong crowd. The crowd halted as one, stopped fearfully in their tracks as three of their own tumbled to the ground with painful wails, blood in the air where it had not been an instant before.

"Everyone had better calm the hell down," Grant ordered, his voice as hard as it had been when he had been a Magistrate. "Next time I'll be aiming for your heads. And I never miss."

From behind him, Brigid translated Grant's words into French and then the lesser-spoken Bantu of the region, ensuring that everyone in the crowd understood her partner's meaning.

As Brigid finished the second translation, Kane's voice shouted from the pyramid steps.

"Little help!" he yelled.

Brigid, Mariah and Grant turned, the latter slowly, making it clear to the crowd before him that his threat had not been an idle one. On the black steps of the pyramid, Kane was struggling as Nergal's closest assistants held him by his arms and legs. They held him upright, pulling his limbs in disparate directions so that he struggled one way and then the other like a man caught on the tide. He hung there in the air, unable to get purchase to free himself.

Grant squeezed the trigger of the Sin Eater, sending a shot over the heads of the crowd on the pyramid steps.

"First one's a warning," Grant said. "After that, I start picking targets."

For a moment, everything seemed to fall silent. Then the group holding Kane resumed yanking him this way and that, straining as if to pull his body apart. Kane howled with the strain, struggling in their grip.

Grant fired again, delivering a 9 mm bullet to the shoulder of the man holding Kane's right arm. The man dropped back with a cry of pain, his shoulder erupting in what seemed to be a gray wash of blood.

Kane lurched as the man let go of his arm, reached across to one of the figures to his left and dragged the man off his feet so that he fell to his knees.

Grant had his next target lined up, blasted again, taking down the man pulling at Kane's left arm.

Boom!

The man fell back with an agonized gasp, and suddenly both of Kane's arms were free. Kane swung there a moment, arms flailing as more of the mob descended upon him. There were about twenty people on the steps of the pyramid surrounding Nergal, twenty people all poised to attack him.

As Grant's hand gun blasted a third shot, Mariah called out another warning: "Guys, the locals are getting a mite restless!"

Brigid turned, glancing to the place Mariah was indicating. The crowd that had been waiting at the edge of the rough arena were beginning to move again, the braver of their number stepping forward, their altered eyes fixed on the Cerberus group.

Grant turned once more, firing a triple burst of bullets at the approaching locals as Brigid charged their ranks with the sword. Gray silhouettes of men fell before the assault.

MEANWHILE, KANE FOUGHT with the last of his captors on the pyramid steps. He drove a kick at the man who held his left leg, clipping his jaw with his other foot so that the man's head tipped back like something from a fairground game. The man's grip faltered, and suddenly Kane found himself dropping to the steps, arms outstretched to halt his fall.

Nergal spoke again in a voice that seemed pulled from the grave. "War master!" he intoned. "My brother. Blood."

Kane shrugged off another attacker, moving forward once more and this time grasping for Nergal's arm. As with Ninurta, Kane's hand went straight through the Annunaki figure. "What the hell is going on here?" he muttered as he reached again for Nergal.

At that moment, one of Nergal's human servants grabbed Kane from behind, pulling him away from the throne.

Kane threw the man, shifting his balance and tossing him over his shoulder. The man sailed over Kane's shoulder and went crashing into Nergal's throne, landing precisely where Nergal himself appeared to be seated.

For one eerie moment, both figures—one human and one reptilian—occupied that same spot in a way that defied Kane's vision to comprehend.

Then, the strange image resolved itself, and it was the human and not the alien who sat in the throne, solid and real where the other had been a ghost or—

"A hologram!" Kane realized, spitting the words as if they were a curse.

TWENTY FEET BEHIND KANE, Grant and Brigid were doing their utmost to hold back the surging mob while Mariah cowered behind them. The mob were trying to coordinate themselves now, realizing that they were facing just two—or maybe three—people and that Grant's blaster could not hold an infinite number of bullets. Added to this, Brigid's severely restricted vision—from her point of view she was swinging a sword at shadows with substance, fighting in the dark—and Grant's slightly better but still hampered sight, was making it seem that the Cerberus warriors could not hope to hold out for long.

Grant was still choosing targets as charitably as he could, shooting at legs and shoulders, knocking people back without killing them. He didn't know the full story behind the mob, couldn't know if they were devoted to Nergal or simply captured in his thrall, and he did not want to kill unarmed innocents on principle.

As Grant drew a bead on his next target and Brigid delivered the flat of her blade to another man who was rushing at them, the whole mob seemed suddenly to freeze. Murmurs were running through them, hurried proclamations in French and Bantu.

"Overlord Nergal has died?"

"Lord Nergal is gone!"

"The overlord has left us all!"

Shoving away the man with whom she had been dueling, Brigid turned and peered up the pyramid steps. In Nergal's throne she saw the man whom Kane had thrown there, saw Kane standing before that throne with a look of disbelief on his face. Nergal still glowed there, but the glow faltered, like a weak television signal failing to tune in. Beside Nergal, still hanging in the air, Ninurta seemed to watch all from his hovering perch of brilliance—to watch, but not to react, not to respond or act. Even as Brigid watched, Ninurta shimmered and glitched, his smooth form turning jagged as if seen in some strange, fun-house mirror.

At the same time, something else happened, something even more remarkable. Brigid's eyesight, along with that of her companions and everyone else clustered around the pyramid, reverted to normal.

Chapter 16

The effect was humbling.

Around the pyramid, voices were speaking hurriedly in bewilderment.

To the people outside the black pyramid, the sky was suddenly blue where it had been silver-gray before. The shadows were shadows still, but they were edged by things of color, browns and greens and sandy yellows. The black pyramid was not black at all, more a slate-gray with highlights and abrasions, patches where the light caught, adding depth to its surface.

But even as the Cerberus team watched, the figure of Nergal became complete once more as the man Kane had thrust into his throne pulled himself up. Hanging in the air above, Ninurta shimmered back, too, a final glitch running through his body, bottom to top.

Something else happened then, too. Kane's eyesight, along with that of his teammates and Nergal's faithful all around them, reverted back to that strangely dimmed view of the world, painting the pyramid, sky and ground in muted shades of gray and black.

"Sacrifice," Nergal said in his eerily distant voice. "You are the chosen of Nergal."

Kane didn't like the sound of that, and he could sense the mood of the crowd as they fell back under the thrall of their sun-bright god.

"Run!" Kane shouted to his companions, shoving

aside one of the warriors who stood in his path. Surprised, the man fell, tumbling down the black steps of the pyramid. Kane ran, clambering up the pyramid steps, arms pumping as he scrambled away from Nergal's throne.

ON THE GROUND, Grant, Brigid and Mariah were still surrounded on three sides by the massing audience. Their mood had changed as if a switch had been turned back on—going from bewildered surprise at the strange way that their god had reacted, to anger at the dangerous interlopers in their midst.

"Get moving," Grant instructed, sweeping his Sin Eater over the crowd's heads with a burst of expelled bullets. "We'll regroup on the far side, yeah?" He asked this last via Commtact as well, and heard Kane's grunted acknowledgment over the sound of his firing Sin Eater.

Brigid swung the blade before her in a wide arc, forcing three approaching crowd members to step back or be cut. With her free hand she snagged Mariah by the wrist. "With me, on three," she said.

Mariah's mind was awhirl. After its momentary repair, her eyesight had reverted back to the foggy gloom she had suffered ever since seeing the brilliant visage of the Annunaki Nergal. She wasn't like Brigid and the others; she had received only rudimentary training and she was uncomfortable around weapons. She gasped as something hot and liquid splashed against her face, realized it was a man's blood as Brigid hacked the Sword of Heaven across his grasping hand. The man fell back with a howl of pain, and Brigid kicked him hard, driving him in an awkward stumble into his mate.

Then Brigid pulled at Mariah's wrist. "Three already!" Brigid shouted. "Come on, Mariah!"

Mariah realized she had been so horrified by the chaos around her that she had not even heard Brigid do the count. She ran, legs scrambling as Brigid found a path through the confused mob, batting people aside with the flat of her sword.

THE LEVELS OF the pyramid were tall. They were not designed for climbing like this—there were shallower steps for that—but they were guarded. Each level needed Kane to lift his knees high to get over it. Still he scrambled, outpacing the few members of Nergal's entourage who tried to chase him. Kane kept himself in the prime of physical fitness, had done so ever since his days as a Magistrate—he was a survivor; he figured you never knew when you might have to run for your life.

Twelve steps up, twelve of thirty, Kane turned and began to run along the level. He glanced back, already sensing that he had outpaced his would-be killers. The closest of them was four levels below Kane, and he looked weary as he clambered up the next tall step.

Kane bolted, taking fast breaths, sprinting along the level of the square pyramid to the corner, slowing only momentarily to take the corner before he shot around it and picked up his pace once more.

Behind him, the devotees of Nergal seemed to be giving up the chase. After all, what was one sacrifice when there was a whole world of them out there?

DOWN ON THE GROUND, Grant blasted another shot over the heads of the crowd. He was getting dangerously close to running out of ammunition here, and while his captors had failed to find the pistol hidden beside his wrist, they had removed his spare ammo along with his Copperhead, knife and other items from his field kit.

Two of the mob were closing in on Grant and so he made a decision. Grant commanded the Sin Eater back to its hiding place against his wrist, and lashed out with his left elbow, belting one man hard in the face so that his jaw cracked. The man went down, and Grant was already moving, driving his now empty right hand at the second attacker, the hand now clenched in a pile-driver fist.

Grant was a big man, and his strength was like something from a legend. His second blow knocked back his attacker before the man could even get a punch in, then Grant moved on to the next and the next, grabbing two men by the sides of their heads before smashing their skulls together with a resounding thump.

Grant was a whirling dervish then, despite the over-whelming odds. He kicked, he punched, he leaped and rolled, each carefully coordinated movement sliding into the next, each punch or kick delivered with precision, dropping man after man as he created a path out of the angry mob.

Two men came at Grant with weapons, a long knife that was about two inches short of being a full-on sword and a long baton that the user wielded like a nightstick.

Grant bounded at the first man, delivering a sweeping roundhouse kick at his chest, his foot slipping through the gap in the knife man's defenses and striking a mighty blow. The knife man staggered back, stumbled, regained his footing.

Grant was already onto his ally, ducking and weaving as the man swung the baton at his head. With the third swing, Grant lurched back while thrusting his right hand forward, grabbing the baton as it whooshed past his brow. The man on the other end was suitably surprised, and he stumbled in a weird two-step before collecting himself and trying to pull the baton free. Grant pulled harder, snatching the staff with both hands and wrenching the man who had wielded it off his feet. He fell toward Grant as the Cerberus warrior pulled, and Grant kneed him hard in the groin with enough force that the man sank to the ground, relinquishing his grip on the baton.

Grant turned to face the knife man who was only just recovering from the roundhouse kick he had endured. "You want to rethink this?" Grant taunted. "No?"

The man came at him with a battle cry, swishing the knife through the air as he tried to drive it at the hulking Cerberus man. Grant swept the baton in a low arc, clipping the knife man by the legs so that he was suddenly in the air, toppling over himself.

Grant jumped the man as he fell, saw his opening and ran for the cover of the trees. In a moment, he had disappeared.

Behind him, the ghostly voice of Nergal intoned: "Sacrifice! Blood is required!"

THE CERBERUS WARRIORS regrouped on the far side of the pyramid, hiding in the lush foliage there in the shadow of the towering structure. Grant was the last to join them, using a series of recognized bird calls to discover where Kane and company had entrenched themselves.

"Everyone okay?" Grant asked breathlessly as he emerged from the cover of green.

"Our eyesight is still messed up," Kane explained, and Brigid and Mariah agreed. "How about you?"

"I can see," Grant said, "kinda. Same as before, not

much color but the shapes are clear. What happened back there? To Nergal?"

"I threw someone into his throne," Kane said. "It seemed to make him flinch out of existence for a moment. We figure he's a hologram!"

"You've been discussing this, I take it?" Grant asked as he adopted a crouch amid the greenery, hunkering beside Brigid and Mariah.

"The way Nergal was disrupted," Brigid said, "seems to suggest it's a signal of some kind, either a projection or a broadcast."

"Or both," Grant said, remembering something that Kane had said earlier about their current location. The Cerberus warriors had been here before, under very different circumstances, and they had discovered ancient Annunaki technology still in use here then.

"Maybe there's something in the throne," Kane proposed. "A projector maybe." He had his hand pressed against a leaf as large as his skull, pushing it back to watch for enemies approaching. It would not be easy to spot them with his eyesight, but, if nothing else, Kane knew his foes were struggling under the same restrictions.

Brigid shook her head with uncertainty at Kane's proposal. "Could be," she said, "but it wouldn't explain how we also saw Nergal inside the mirror room."

"Mirror room?" Mariah asked, evidently confused by the term.

"We've been here before," Kane said, picking up the story. "About three years ago we got involved with a local mess concerning a mystical item called the Mirror of Prester John. It turned out to be an Annunaki device—"

"No surprise," Grant opined bitterly.

"—predating the Christian reference," Kane concluded.

"So where are we?" Mariah asked. "Prester John would be—what?—India?"

"The Congo," Brigid corrected. "Although you're right. That part of the locals' story never really made sense. Prester John was a Christian patriarch said to be active in India, Asia or perhaps Ethiopia, depending on the telling."

"But you say this is the Congo," Mariah confirmed. "We're a long way from any of those places, even the closest of them, Ethiopia, is still—what?—sixteen hundred miles away."

"Legends get muddled in the retelling," Brigid reminded her. "Probably someone made a mistake and the mistake stuck."

Mariah nodded thoughtfully as they sat among the teeming plant life, the buzz of insects a steady drone in her ears. "This mirror," she asked. "What was it? I mean, I take it that it wasn't *just* a mirror—Annunaki materials are usually something else, right?"

"Right," Grant agreed.

"It was a remote viewer," Kane explained. "Kind of like closed-circuit television for Annunaki. It was used by Anu to spy on his fellow Annunaki.

"He had a little paranoia thing going on," Kane added after a moment.

"Didn't they all," Brigid said. "The Annunaki were viciously competitive and they thrived on their opponents' weaknesses."

Mariah rubbed at her eyes, trying to ignore the way they seemed unable to process color once again. At least she had some sight, albeit restricted. "Where's the mirror?" she asked.

"Overlord Utu tried to gain control of it when the Annunaki reappeared on Earth a few years ago," Kane answered, "but we intervened."

"I blasted it to dust with the cannon of my Manta," Grant elaborated, unable to hide his smile at the memory. "Utu got hit with the debris and it burned out his eye sockets."

"Sounds gross," Mariah said, making a face.

"It wasn't dust," Brigid corrected thoughtfully. "It shattered. They were shards—small shards but still shards."

"So Utu got hit with superheated shards of metal," Kane confirmed. "Doesn't matter now; he's gone."

Had any of the Cerberus team been able to see properly at that moment, they would have seen the sudden expression of realization on Brigid's face. "They're not mining for diamonds," she said. "They're mining for bits of the mirror—the Mirror of Prester John."

"Meaning?" Kane asked.

"Meaning," Brigid said, drawing out the word as she assembled her thoughts, "that a remote viewer would also very likely be a recording device."

"No point spying on your enemies if you can't check back what they said," Grant reasoned.

"Nergal doesn't exist here," Brigid said. "Nor does Ninurta. What we're seeing is old data, transmitted or projected by whatever is left of the mirror."

Kane was shaking his head. "That doesn't make sense," he said. "How could it interact with—"

"Did Nergal really interact?" Brigid asked. "Did Ninurta? Maybe they appeared to respond, maybe Nergal displayed some rudimentary independence, but it was mostly down to interpretation, wasn't it?"

"Nergal spoke," Grant said.

"About worship and sacrifice and slavery," Brigid said. "All pretty normal stuff for the Annunaki. Old data. His people added the context, his followers."

"Followers of an old recording?" Mariah asked, horrified.

"And Ninurta couldn't interact at all," Brigid continued. "He just hung there."

"I couldn't see him," Grant said. "Still can't."

"I think that there's a reason for that, too," Brigid said excitedly. "Frequencies."

"Frequencies?" Kane queried. "You're going to have to explain."

"You understand wavelengths and frequencies, yes?" Brigid asked them all. "Like the way you tune a radio, finding different frequencies. Sight works in essentially the same way. We see within a certain range of wavelengths, tuning in, if you will, to a certain frequency. Color is created in this way—other creatures see in different wavelengths, some, like dogs, barely see any difference in color, others, like honeybees, are especially tuned to the ultraviolet end of the spectrum so that they see plants and flowers in an entirely different manner than the way our eyes perceive them.

"We haven't been blinded," Brigid said, "not really. Each of us can see, but we're seeing in an altered way, the details coming to us in a manner we are not used to. We're tuning into a different frequency than what we've used before."

"Like infrared or night vision," Kane said, nodding in understanding. He was thinking about the polymer-coated lenses the Cerberus members sometimes employed to see in the dark.

Brigid smiled. "Yes, and if that manipulation was subtle, each of us might be tuned to see slightly differently. Hence, the soldiers that we walked in on in Libya being almost unable to perceive us at all. And Grant's inability to see Ninurta when he could see the more powerful signal of Nergal."

"When blindness isn't blindness at all," Kane said incredulously. "It all makes a kind of sense."

"But what's caused it?" Mariah asked. "If Nergal is just old data, as you say…"

"The Mirror of Prester John," Brigid said, "which is to say—whatever's left of it. When Grant shattered it, the pieces were superheated and strewn across the interior of the pyramid, which included an interphase window used for access—a kind of security door."

"Yeah, I remember," Kane said.

"We know that Annunaki technology is organically based, *alive*," Brigid continued, "in a rudimentary manner at least. Shattering the mirror might have destroyed it, but the pieces still retain data—the same way a shattered hologram retains information from the whole image. If you break a hologram, you don't see a part—you see a smaller hologram of the same projection."

"And we're seeing those projections?" Grant questioned.

"I think that what we're seeing is an effect known as Troxler's fading," Brigid said. "Troxler's fading is an optical illusion that affects one's visual perception. In essence, when a person fixates on a particular point, even for just a short period, an unchanging stimulus away from that point will fade away and disappear."

"So we stop seeing the background," Kane said.

"It's how we focus," Brigid said, "and it probably derives from a survival mechanism, ensuring that we spot predators rather than being bewildered by peripheral input. The brain is also inclined to fill in the gaps in our perception, generating data for the mind so that we do not get distracted by our physiological blind spots.

"Simply put—what you see isn't always what you get," Brigid concluded.

"So the mirror fragments are affecting our vision," Kane said, "and the vision of those around us, making everyone susceptible, to a greater or lesser extent, to seeing the old Annunaki recordings of Nergal and Ninurta. How do we test this?"

Grant shrugged. "Shoot Nergal?"

"That's…not going to do it," Brigid said after a moment's thought. "If the shards of the mirror are the transmitters, then we'd need to somehow stop their broadcast."

"And how do you propose we do that, Baptiste?" Kane asked.

To Mariah, with her twentieth-century sensibilities, it sounded as though Kane had just hit on the sixty-four-thousand-dollar question.

Chapter 17

Brewster Philboyd looked up from his monitoring screen as Lakesh came striding past. "CAT Beta are not responding," Philboyd said.

The Cerberus ops room was enjoying a midmorning lull as operatives took coffee breaks away from their screens. There were still staff in situ, with several running monitoring algorithms for the satellite eyes that orbited Earth, tracking anomalies and supplying Cerberus with data.

Like others, Lakesh was enjoying a hot beverage—in his case, a cup of tea, brewed to golden brown with perhaps just a little too much milk. He stopped in his tracks at his colleague's words, the tea in his cup slopping dangerously close to the rim. "Did you say CAT Beta?" Lakesh asked.

"Uh-huh," Philboyd confirmed with a nod of his head. "They jumped to Redoubt Mike fifty-seven minutes ago and they've not reported in since then."

"Since the jump?" Lakesh asked, and Philboyd nodded. "Do we know that they arrived?"

Philboyd tapped an instruction into his keyboard and the image on his monitor screen changed, flickering to a chart showing energy usage for sender-receiver stations in the mat-trans grid. Redoubt Mike's station showed a spike in activity confirming the arrival of someone or something. "The figures match up time-wise," Philboyd stated. "There's no reason to doubt their arrival. Unless, perhaps, they were intercepted and replaced at the moment of dematerialization."

Lakesh nodded thoughtfully as he looked for somewhere to put his cup down. There was established precedence for what Philboyd proposed. Such a thing had happened before to Cerberus when an Australian faction called the Original Tribe had piggybacked on the mat-trans signal, sending their own operatives in place of CAT Alpha during a return trip to the Cerberus redoubt. However, such an occurrence was a one-off, and the protective firewalls and other safety measures that theoretically ring-fenced the system had been strengthened tenfold in light of that attack.

"Let's presume not," Lakesh advised as he placed his cup of tea on the desk adjacent to Philboyd's and rested in the swivel chair there. "An hour's delay between arrival and confirmation is not unprecedented," he said, "but it is certainly cause for concern. I trust that you have tried hailing Beta?"

"Yes, of course," Philboyd said. "No answer."

"Telemetry on the biolinks?" Lakesh queried.

"No response. Which could be a side effect of the redoubt's being underground."

"Almost certainly so," Lakesh agreed. "But an hour is a long time to not receive a report. Who was leading the team?"

"Edwards," Philboyd confirmed. "With Sinclair and Domi." He looked uncomfortable as he said the last name, aware that Lakesh had a romantic arrangement with the petite albino woman and not wanting to make this a personal matter.

"Why were they going to Mike?" Lakesh asked.

"They received a tip-off," Philboyd said, "the nature

of which Edwards chose not to elaborate. The trader Ohio Blue brought them information that led them to check the redoubt."

Lakesh nodded solemnly. "Keep on top of it, Mr. Philboyd," he said. "Keep trying their Commtacts every ten minutes and let me know if you receive any response."

"Yes, sir."

GATHERED CLOSE TO the base of the far side of the pyramid in the sweltering Congo, the four Cerberus rebels were pondering all that Brigid had intuited.

"How did the mirror shards get to Libya?" Mariah asked, breaking the silence that reigned among her colleagues. "That's a journey of over two thousand miles, isn't it?" Thanks to her discipline in her chosen field of geology, Mariah's knowledge of geography was impressive.

"Something like that," Brigid agreed. "And you're right—how did the broken slivers of the mirror make their way so far across land and end up buried in a mine?"

"The mine wasn't there before," Mariah said with certainty. "The earth tremor I detected that started all of this was indicative of its appearance, I think."

"What was that earth tremor?" Brigid asked, questioning herself as much as Mariah. Before her colleague could respond, she proposed an answer. "You called it a sinkhole, back when you spotted it on the data filtering through from the area. A sinkhole is relatively sudden, appearing almost instantaneously, isn't it?"

"There are changes below the surface creating it," Mariah said, "but from the surface it does appear instant."

"But what if this wasn't a sinkhole?" Brigid questioned. "What if this was an instantaneous transfer of the hole, the mine, the whole camp?"

"How?" Mariah asked.

"Matter transmitter," Brigid said. "The Annunaki had access to the interphaser network, used it for their own transportation. Heck, they used it as the doorway into this very pyramid, hiding the entry in an almost inaccessible pass. If an interphase window was used, it could have shunted the mirror's shards two thousand miles north to Libya."

"That's one big interphase window," Grant said.

"Like the pillar we came through to get here," Brigid reminded him.

"But why would anyone want to do that?" Kane asked. "Move the broken bits of the mirror of Prester John thousands of miles away."

"They weren't moving them," Brigid said, "they were *gathering* them. The interphaser, like the mat-trans, uses a focusing beam to dematerialize and rematerialize a subject. If that beam could be widened somehow, like casting a net, then theoretically it might be used to regather the parts of an object like the mirror. Cast the net wide enough and make the rematerialization sequence focused enough and you'd end up gathering things on a molecular level, squishing them all together until you could, theoretically, re-create something that had been destroyed. I think."

"You think?" Kane repeated, a challenge in his voice.

"Why else would the mirror fragments end up where they have?" Brigid asked.

"*If* they have," Kane reminded her. "It's still just a theory, right?"

"If I'm right, then we've been fighting something here, in Nergal, that's trying to re-create the Annunaki pantheon from the scattered memory of a recording device," Brigid said. "Memories whose wavelength spectrum has been compromised to the point that the results can only be seen through particular fields of vision."

"Which leads us to the question," Kane said, "who's trying to put the Annunaki back together?"

Before anyone could respond, Grant made a gesture, warning everyone to hush. Someone was approaching, a figure moving through the lush vegetation whose movements were loud to his trained ear. "Company," he whispered.

Kane stood and so did Grant, their movements barely making a sound. Without a word, they disappeared into the dense foliage, leaving Brigid alone with Mariah. Brigid rested her hand on the grip of the stolen sword, her only weapon at this moment.

KANE AND GRANT moved swiftly through the trees, splitting up and coming around the back of the group that was approaching. There were four men in the group, young, agile and muscular—more than that was hard to tell with their compromised eyesight. Each man held a weapon, knives mostly, though one had what appeared to be a spear. Two of them had the blindfolds over their eyes, though they seemed to be able to see as normally as their colleagues. That whole radiance of new vision, Kane realized bitterly, cursing the Annunaki.

Kane crept behind a broad tree trunk, pressing himself against it and peering out to watch the four men as they made their way through the cover. They were searching left and right, checking under bushes and behind trees. It was obvious that they were looking for the

Cerberus team, and Kane presumed there must be more men out there searching in different spots.

Kane slipped back behind the tree as the group came closer, ducking his head down and creeping away to the next tree in the dense jungle.

Grant's voice reverberated in his ear as Kane reached the next tree. "In position," Grant said.

Kane surveyed the surrounding area, was unsurprised that he could not spot his partner. Grant knew how to hide, even when his own eyesight was drawn in shadows and grays. "Position," Kane confirmed, slipping around the tree like a serpent.

There was no noise. Grant simply emerged from the huge leaves of an overhanging bush, stepped up behind the rearmost of the armed men and dragged him back, his hand clamped over the man's mouth.

Grant delivered a nerve pinch to the man's neck and the man drooped in his grip. He rolled him gently to the ground.

One of the search party turned, not alerted by the noise—for there had been none—but simply alert enough to check where he had been as well as where he was going. His voice rose in alarm as he saw Grant drop his unconscious colleague to the dirt.

Kane leaped at that cry, seizing the opportunity to attack the men's flank as they turned to see why their colleague had shouted the warning. Kane was behind the closest of them, reaching around the man and pulling him up off his feet even as they charged toward Grant. The man flipped in Kane's grip, legs tangling as he went crashing to the ground, face-first.

Grant had adopted a fighter's crouch as the other two came at him, rolled his shoulders and barged into the man on the left—who was wielding the spear—flipping him in an instant. The one on the right lurched to follow Grant, cutting the air with a swish of his knife. Grant dropped, coming in below the man's attack before driving both hands upward to knock the man's knife hand aside. Grant's foe stumbled, dropping the knife as sudden pain fired through his arm.

Grant was upright again in an instant, swinging a haymaker at his opponent's jaw with enough force to knock him off his feet.

At Grant's back, Kane was tackling the other opponent again. The man rose, bringing his knife up to stab at Kane. Kane blocked, diverting the passage of the arm holding the knife, twisting it so that the man was forced to step forward or fall.

Kane stepped back in the same instant, his arm still locked with his opponent's, dragging him another step, two, until he was lurching in an awkward stumble. Kane spun, driving a forceful kick to the man's posterior and sending him crashing into the trunk of a nearby tree. The man hit it headfirst with a strike that sounded like a hammer hitting a coconut, birds alighting from its higher branches. In the aftermath, the man sagged to the ground, losing himself in the dense foliage that grew around the foot of the tree.

The man with the spear was back on his feet, moving more warily this time as he circled toward Grant. Though his eyesight was compromised, Grant fixed his attention on the end of the spear.

The spear jabbed, and Grant stepped back, judging its length and his adversary's reach. His opponent tried again, jabbing out with the spear, forcing Grant back. Kane was coming around the side of the man now—any moment and it would be two against one.

The spearman took his chance, stepping into his lunge as he thrust the spear at Grant a third time.

Grant was ready this time, grabbed it and twisted, turning the spear in the man's grip so that he lost his footing. At the same time, Grant raced forward, leaping up on one leg and delivering a high kick to his opponent's chest. The blow struck like a clap of thunder, sending the man reeling backward, his grip on the spear slipping.

As the spearman came lurching toward him, Kane drew back his fist. "Buckle up, buttercup," he muttered before driving his fist into the man's face with enough force to knock him out cold.

"All done?" Grant asked, standing amid the strewn bodies in the clearing.

"Four for four," Kane confirmed. "But I guess it won't be long before someone else comes looking. We'd better get moving."

KANE AND GRANT returned to their two colleagues, wary of pursuit. "They're sending out search parties," Kane explained dourly. "We aced the first one but they're going to keep coming unless we do something about the Nergal-ogram and his glowing brother."

Brigid nodded, eyeing the shadow pyramid where it waited on the horizon of her altered vision.

"We figure out who's behind this?" Kane asked. "Who's trying to put the Annunaki back together?"

Brigid shook her head. Kane's was a good question but she did not have an answer; she couldn't even guess who would do such a thing, let alone why. There had been some really wacky devotees to Ullikummis, the stone god whose presence on Earth had been accompanied with a growing cult of fanatic followers. Those followers still existed, albeit in small clumps scattered across the US. But this thing—not just here but in the recent incidents in Spain and Italy—pointed to either a larger group or a lone operator with vast reach.

"Baptiste?" Kane prompted after a few moments.

"Sorry, lost in thought," Brigid replied.

"So," Grant asked, "where does this leave us with the whole mirror-broadcast thing?"

"It's obvious that we need to stop the broadcast somehow," Brigid said, "but with so many fragments—"

"Plus my eyesight still ain't so good," Kane reminded her. "Yours?"

"No," Brigid said. "But I think if we can nix the broadcast that will return. You pretty much confirmed that when you threw the wrench in the works back there."

"The wrench being one of Nergal's adoring fans," Kane said, smiling.

"I can't figure out a way to destroy the whole thing in one sweep," Brigid concluded. "We can do parts but we need to get to the source or it will just keep broadcasting."

"Why don't we do what we always do and blast it to hell?" Kane asked.

"You mean the mine?" Grant asked.

"That's possible," Mariah told them, much to her colleagues' surprise. "Well, not blast exactly, but you could bury it. The mine in Libya was created, we think, by shunting the materials that were here through an interphase wormhole. That's disrupted the soil, which is why we had the sinkhole effect."

"Meaning?" Kane encouraged.

"Which means the ground is still moving," Mariah explained. "It wouldn't take much to drop the whole thing under the earth and just bury it for good."

"When you say it wouldn't take much," Kane asked her, "how much?"

"A big enough explosive planted deep enough," Mariah theorized, "would cause the walls to collapse."

"There were people inside there," Brigid reminded them. "Innocents."

Kane glanced up at the pyramid. Its walls were drawn in shadow black to his altered eyes, and the people gathered close by looked like wraiths. But atop the pyramid, two figures glowed furiously, as if they had been ejected by the sun itself.

"We could use the Mantas," Grant said, referring to the TAV aircraft that the Cerberus team used. "Drop a bomb down the mine."

"Okay, but what do we do here?" Kane asked. "We have two sources, right?"

Brigid shook her head slowly. "I think we just have one source, and one very big, very scattered, receiver," she said.

"Then where's the source?" Kane asked.

"The mirror originated here, which means the signal originated here," Brigid theorized. "It was bright silver when we last saw it, before Grant put a ton of ordnance through it."

Grant laughed at the memory. At the same time, Mariah issued a warning that the locals seemed to be amassing once more and turning to Nergal—false Nergal, hologram Nergal—for instruction.

"Of course," Brigid said, snapping her fingers. "Nergal!"

"Nergal?" Kane queried.

"His head, his face—" Brigid said. "It's blinding. It's not his head, it's the mirror. The mirror embedded in the throne."

"Then we need to find a way to counter that signal," Kane realized, "before it's too late."

"Kane," Brigid said slowly, an idea forming in her head, "do you remember what I did when we went back to Saskatchewan and the landing site of Ullikummis's space prison?"

Kane thought for a moment. The incident had occurred just a month before, and had seen himself and Brigid infiltrate the cult of Ullikummis's followers as they investigated persistent rumors of the stone god's resurrection. The whole thing had been a bust, but Ullikummis's acolytes had managed to bring a stone creature to life, utilizing the ferrous content in human blood to drive it. Brigid had managed to turn the acolytes away, falsely assuming the role of her other self, Brigid Haight, who had been created through brainwashing techniques and had worked as Ullikummis's so-called hand in darkness. Haight was revered as some kind of demigoddess by the faithful, and so Brigid—Baptiste, that is, not Haight—had been able to command them as if she were still in the thrall of that Annunaki brainwashing.

"You pretended to be—um—someone you weren't," Kane said ruefully, avoiding mention of the dark personality that Brigid had once adopted.

"Precisely," Brigid said. "And I figure we can do it again. Only question is—who wants to play god?"

Chapter 18

Brigid explained her idea via shared Commtact to the Cerberus ops room. "Brewster, I need you to boost the Commtact signal," she told Brewster Philboyd on the comms desk, "and home in on a frequency you'll be able to find if you triangulate on our location."

"Triangulating," Philboyd responded, running the locator program on the biolink transponders through his system. "I see a weak broadcast signal," he said once the data came up on screen, "very localized, roughly fifty feet to your east."

From her cover amid the foliage, Brigid eyed the black pyramid, estimating the distance. "That'll be the one," she confirmed.

"Signal currently appears to be on a long loop," Philboyd informed her as he analyzed the wave algorithms, "frequently breaking and re-forming.

"What is it I'm looking at here, Brigid?" Philboyd added as he worked his desk in the Cerberus operations room.

"An ancient Annunaki recording," Brigid replied with a nonchalance that suggested it was an everyday occurrence. "So old that the data keeps glitching."

"I'm copying the frequency over now," Philboyd assured her, working his computer desk. "What is it you're after, exactly?"

"Narrow-beam broadcast," Brigid told him, "Commtact to signal."

"From you?"

"No, use Kane."

"Care to give me an idea of what it is you guys are up to out there?" Philboyd asked, a note of surprise in his voice. "I thought we shot you to Libya, two thousand miles north."

"You did," Kane assured him, speaking over the linked Commtacts for the first time. "We got shanghaied into another jump shortly after. We'll tell you all about it when we get home. Which reminds me—you think you can send a squad and an interphaser to our nearest location when we give the signal?"

"I guess we can," Philboyd told him reassuringly. "You need arms, a mop-up squad?"

"Just a quick exit," Kane said.

"Our interphaser was compromised," Brigid elaborated.

"Shot," Kane said. "Compromised by being shot."

"Signals are locked," Philboyd confirmed. "Say the word and I'll cut you into the broadcast."

GRANT HAD SNEAKED back inside the pyramid. His eyesight was functioning the best, which meant he was the logical choice to try to find the weapons and equipment that the locals had stripped from him and his companions. Returning to the pyramid after what they had concluded about their location was strange, like visiting a place you didn't know that you knew.

There was no one inside. Everyone had been outside to witness the arena and sacrifice ritual that Grant and his companions had been caught up in, and they had remained outside to search for the Cerberus teammates when they'd absconded in all directions. What the locals did not know was that the Cerberus people had a hidden way to communicate via Commtacts, which meant it was far easier for them to coordinate their movements and work together than anyone suspected.

Right now, Grant could hear the discussion between Kane, Brigid and Cerberus HQ, and he knew that their time here was running short. Good thing, too, as he was getting sick and tired of seeing everything through a gray filter.

Grant turned a corner in the lowest level of the pyramid, and almost walked into the guard who had first assisted him from his cell. The man jumped in alarm on seeing Grant—a little bloodied from his battle in the arena—come striding around the corner toward him.

"Monsieur, you are—" the guard began.

Without slowing his pace, Grant walked up to the guard and slugged him across the jaw with his fist. "Shut up," Grant said as the man fell to the floor in a dead faint.

Grant checked the room that the man had been posted outside. He had to be guarding something—right?

OUTSIDE, KANE WAITED in the foliage beside the pyramid, with Brigid and Mariah close by his side. They had moved around toward the front of the structure and could once more see the glowing figures that waited at the throne and beside it, unmoved from where they had left them.

"Nergal's definitely connected to the throne somehow," Kane confirmed. "A chunk of that mirror must have gotten embedded in it when we shattered it the last time we were here."

"Needn't be a chunk," Brigid said. "Just the right part for the recording to replay."

Mariah shook her head. "I don't care how sophisticated we pretend to be," she said, "the Annunaki tech still seems magical to me."

Kane gave her shoulder a reassuring pat. "You're a caveman," he said cheerily. "But don't worry—the snake faces have always played on that when they've dealt with humans. You're in good company."

"Are you ready to do this, Kane?" Brigid asked as they watched the figures massing at the base of the pyramid.

"Yeah," Kane said. "Give Brewster the signal and count me in."

"Okay," Brigid said. "And remember, Kane—no hamming it up!"

"My brother Ninurta needs assistance with…matters," Nergal was saying as the crowd watched. His head glowed like a miniature sun, dazzling the senses of all who had felt its brilliance.

No one in the crowd suspected that Nergal's words were a part of a secret recording that had occurred thousands of years before, that the data was repeating in various configurations where it had been brought back to life by a hidden sliver of *Tiamat*, one that had been brought to the local Waziri tribe months before by a dark-skinned woman named Nathalie. The Waziri were a people with little knowledge of the outside world, and they had accepted the gift and the instructions that had come with it without question. Nathalie had told them to take it to their most sacred site and leave it there. The seed had triggered changes, had brought things Annunaki back to life. Life from death, the Annunaki way.

And then Nergal pronounced something new, his words still distant as the stars. "People of Waziri," he said, "your time has come."

If one were to listen closely one might have detected the subtle change in Nergal's accent, but the weakness of the broadcast covered a multitude of sins.

"I need not this chair," Kane said, speaking through Nergal. "It has served its purpose and has no place in the ascent to Heaven."

"Ascent to Heaven," Grant muttered as Kane's words were transferred via the Commtact. "Good one."

He had found the stash of arms that had been stripped from him and his colleagues, not in the first room where the guard had been posted but two rooms along, laid out neatly on a stone plinth as if they had been put out for display.

"Remove my chair," Kane said, his words broadcast through his link to Nergal. "Crush it into powder and bury every piece."

Brigid rolled her eyes. "No hamming," she reminded Kane.

"With its destruction I will ascend," Kane continued, ignoring her. "Do this for your god, do this for me and my brother."

Then he cut the link, and, as per instructions, Brewster Philboyd continued to jam any further broadcast emanating from the memory core that had become wedged into the throne.

At the pyramid, people were hurrying up the steps, bringing axes and club-like branches with which they intended to destroy the chair as they had been told. Brigid felt sorry for them, the way that they had been duped—not once but twice.

"Time we were going, I guess," Kane said, attracting Brigid's attention.

One of Nergal's adherents was taking an ax to the throne, and as it struck the dazzling figures of Nergal and Ninurta flickered and died, the old recordings destroyed forever. With their passing, something else happened— Kane's eyesight, along with Brigid's, Mariah's and that of everyone else who had been under the fractured mirror's spell, seemed to suddenly become brighter, normalizing.

"Man," Kane swore, rubbing a hand over his eyes, "who switched on the lights?"

"The signal's been disrupted," Brigid said. "It's not broadcasting into our perceptions anymore."

"Yeah, but does it have to be so bright?" Kane grumbled as he led the way back inside the pyramid.

"Normality can be dazzling when you're used to darkness," Brigid told him. "I guess that's a lesson for anyone who's been in the thrall of alien dictators."

Kane glanced at her, his eyes watering. "Or human ones," he said.

TRUE TO HIS WORD, Brewster Philboyd had come through, sending Farrell and Beth Delaney to pick up the team, using Cerberus's second interphaser. They arrived via the parallax point in the pyramid, both dressed in Cerberus whites. Farrell had a shaved head and a goatee beard and hoop earring, and Delaney was blond haired with just a little paunch around her midriff.

Grant joined them as Kane, Brigid and Mariah found their way back into the room where they had originally materialized and seen the throne and its illusion of Nergal.

"I found them," Grant said, handing Kane and Brigid back their respective blasters. He also had the backpack with the broken interphaser in it, wearing it over one massive shoulder.

"How's your eyesight?" Brigid asked.

Grant nodded. "Better," he said. "Shaky, but it kind of eased back to normal about two minutes ago."

"That's about the time someone put an ax through Nergal's throne," Kane confirmed.

"Troxler's fading," Brigid observed wryly, "has faded."

A moment later Cerberus Away Team Alpha and their entourage stepped into the quantum window opened by the interphaser and disappeared from the African continent.

Chapter 19

"The she-dog stabbed me," Nathalie said, her voice cracking with pain. She sat on the floor on the *djévo* room, slumped over and clearly in pain, a tourniquet tied to her upper left leg above where Domi's knife had severed the artery. The dark red of spilled life issued from the wound, which continued to bleed out.

The room was imperfectly symmetrical. It had no windows, for it was located deep within the bowels of Redoubt Mike, under the earth of the Louisiana swampland. It always felt too warm to Nathalie, too warm, too dark, and it clung on to the dry smell of burning dust like an obsessive-compulsive hoarder unable to throw anything out. She was light-headed now, from the blood loss, and that only contributed to her impression of heat and rot and claustrophobia.

The space was small, made smaller yet by the drapes that had been hung from the walls and over the doors, covering it in the dark colors of blood and red wine intermingled with the purples and blacks and deepest blues of bruises on human flesh.

Where once there had been fluorescent lighting functioning on automated circuits, now there were candles, three dozen of them scattered across every cluttered surface and dotted across the floor like seeds scattered from a farmer's hand.

The room was cluttered by an odd selection of mismatched objects—feathers and bones, driftwood and skulls, jars of dried spices and plant roots vied for space along the walls, everything lit by the flicker of candle flames. Everything looked tired and worn, and the flickering light cast by the candles could do nothing to disguise that.

Papa Hurbon sat across from her in his wheelchair, before the black mirror that dominated one wall opposite the room's sole door. His gold tooth flickered in the candlelight as he opened his mouth to speak. "Don't call your enemy a she-dog," he advised. "Calling an enemy names only diminishes them in your eyes, not in theirs, and makes you underestimate them when the time comes. Like a child calling everyone they loathe dumb-ass—it only serves to confirm to others that the name caller is dumb, and all the more of an ass."

Nathalie writhed on the floor, her head swaying as she tried to keep upright. "Please, my beacon, my light. I am dying," she said. "The white woman wounded me, wounded me bad. Look."

Hurbon did not move, though his eyes flicked for a moment to the blood-soaked rag that had been wrapped around his assistant's leg. "Where are the Cerberus people now?" he asked.

"Food store," Nathalie said. "Dead or dying. My poison work..." She stopped, losing her mental thread as her mind threatened to slip into the unconsciousness that precedes death.

"Okay," Hurbon soothed. "Hush now, child."

Before the voodoo houngan, Nathalie keeled over, her body slapping against the floor with that awful sound of flesh turned heavy with illness. She lay there, eyes losing focus, facing the wall and the open doorway, her back to Papa Hurbon. "I'm dying," she said, her words just a whisper now.

"Not dying," Hurbon assured her. "Evolving."

With that, Hurbon leaned forward until he could reach the sodden tourniquet tied to his assistant's left leg. He plucked at it, pulling it down until he had exposed the bloody wound, his fingers red with the woman's blood. Then, he reached beneath the blanket that covered his missing legs, and into the old leather bag he kept there. The bag was a pouch, large enough for Hurbon to get both hands in, and it had a strap by which it could be carried, like a woman's purse, its brown surface scuffed, frayed threads showing at its edges. The pouch was full of items that Hurbon found useful—charms and vials and secret powders used in Bizango rituals, the type that even the most adept voodoo practitioners cautioned against handling for fear of displeasing the mystic loa.

A moment later, Hurbon had withdrawn the item he was searching for, nine months after he had placed it there among the bones and the twisted, colorful ribbons and the fith-fath dolls that looked like people in caricature. The object was yellow-white and small, no longer than Hurbon's thumbnail. And it was sharp, sharp enough to prick a man's finger if he grasped it unawares.

Hurbon leaned down, using the stubby fingers of his left hand to pull apart the skin on Nathalie's wounded leg, blood budding across the rent like scarlet condensation.

Nathalie whimpered, aware of the new pain in her leg.

"Be brave, child," Hurbon said, plumping the flesh to make the wound wider. Then he reached forward with his other hand and placed the white shard into the gap in Nathalie's flesh, pressing it there with his thumb the way a man might push a tack into a pin board. Nathalie gasped again, but weakly, her strength and her life having almost departed.

The white shard was a sliver of dragon's tooth, shaved from the remains of *Tiamat*, the dragon city which had been grown—not built—on the banks of the Euphrates by the Annunaki sky god, Enlil. Hurbon had amassed pieces of the dragon's teeth, and through ritual and chemical input he had ignited the genetic code hidden within them, the code that was hidden in all things Annunaki—the code to bring to life the Annunaki once again.

The space gods had first visited Earth in prehistory, had settled here and been worshipped by the planet's mortals as gods. Their technology had been far in advance of anything man could imagine—then or now, in fact—and had been mistaken for the supernatural acts of deities. Millennia after their departure following internal squabbles, the Annunaki had been reborn through a genetic download from *Tiamat*, the wombship. But those Annunaki had been taken down by their own squabbles once again, and *Tiamat*, a sentient spaceship grown through organic technology, had despaired, committing suicide to end the feuding between members of her brood. Each part of *Tiamat* had retained the codes, however, each section geared to regrow the eternal Annunaki, re-creating them like photocopies, over and over and over again. All it took was a little organic material to start the process, planting the download in the soil of human flesh.

Hurbon forced the sharp sliver of dragon's tooth farther into Nathalie's leg, watched impassively as the leg twitched and the woman moaned, her cry so soft, so lost. He kneaded the flaps of skin back together, holding them there with his stubby fingers as he smeared a little binding gum over the flesh. Bloody and jagged though it was, the fix held and the shard of tooth was lost beneath the surface of the woman's flesh.

Nathalie had slipped into unconsciousness by then, her eyes clenched tight, her lips peeled back from gritted teeth.

Hurbon watched in the flickering candlelight as the flesh on Nathalie's leg seemed to ripple around the wound. The skin buckled, the blood sliding down where the skin beneath had folded as it began to re-form and reshape.

And yes! There were scales.

And yes! There was hunger. Ravenous hunger, as from a thing just born.

"Welcome, goddess," Papa Hurbon murmured to the darkness. "Welcome back."

Chapter 20

After they had returned to the Cerberus redoubt, Kane, Grant, Brigid and Mariah were rushed to the medical wing, where physician Reba DeFore checked them over. DeFore was dressed in the standard Cerberus operations uniform of a white jumpsuit with diagonal blue zipper, and she had tied her ash-blond hair back from her face in a French braid.

In the darkened examination room, DeFore ran an otoscope across Brigid's eyes, testing for her reaction. "And you say you were blinded?" she asked.

"Kind of," Brigid said as she followed the light with her pupils. "It's hard to describe. It was like I was blind, but I could see in a sort of muffled way, like only seeing a thing's outline or shadow."

"Sounds strange," DeFore admitted.

"It isn't the first time—" Brigid began, then stopped herself.

"Isn't the first time what?" DeFore encouraged after a moment's silence.

"The more I've worked with Cerberus over the past few years," Brigid said, "the more I've become aware that what we think of as reality is not an absolute. We may not always be seeing the whole picture."

DeFore stopped, switching the light of the otoscope off. "Well, your eyes seem to be back to normal now," she said. "Any special reason you reached the conclusion about reality not being absolute?"

Brigid shrugged dourly. "Ullikummis," she said.

Reaching for the light switch, DeFore stopped, her hand against the switch. Brigid heard the woman's breath catch, and for a moment there was a thick silence in the room that seemed almost to manifest in a physical form. The physician had suffered at Ullikummis's hands, Brigid remembered, and it had taken a psychological toll on her, as it had many members of the Cerberus operation.

"He's not coming back, Reba," Brigid assured her colleague as she waited in the darkness. "We threw him into the sun. He's never coming back."

DeFore worked the light switch and was shaking her head slowly when the light flickered back on in the room. "Didn't you also say that about Enlil and Marduk and Lilitu and all the others?" she said gravely. "But they all came back to cause misery, didn't they?"

Brigid nodded gravely. "They used genetic downloads," she said, "stored on their spaceship. The ship is dead, and so are they. All the Annunaki are dead."

"You say that having just come back from facing— who was it?—Nergal and Ninurta," DeFore said. Then, responding to Brigid's surprised look, she added. "Grant told me when I examined him."

"Then he told you that they were insubstantial," Brigid said firmly. "Ghost things, recordings."

"And Ereshkigal?" DeFore challenged, referring to the Annunaki goddess of the underworld whom Grant had run into in Spain.

"Not fully born," Brigid said. But the denial seemed to trigger something in her own mind, a realization that the Cerberus team had been chasing branches of the same foe, reborn gods, each one failing on some molecular level. Were they all being played, somehow? Was there a mind behind these disparate attacks?

"Brigid?" DeFore probed, bringing Brigid out of her reverie. "Everything okay?"

"Fine," Brigid said. But her expression told a different story.

BAXTER HAD BEEN trying to solve a wooden Chinese puzzle when he heard the old woman call for him. He pushed himself up from the high stool he sat on when he heard the cry, his body all muscle and sinew. Baxter was over six feet tall, with broad shoulders and the hard body of a man who worked out ritualistically, with well-defined muscles down his arms and a six pack visible beneath the clinging material of his white undershirt. He was a guard in Ohio Blue's employ, posted belowdecks where he currently was tasked with monitoring their guest, Dagmar Gellis.

"You okay, ma'am?" Baxter called as he rose from the stool. His guard position was semicasual, he was free to wander the corridors of the boat just so long as he returned to check on their guest every half hour or so. He placed the Chinese puzzle box on the stool as he rose, a trinket from one of Ohio's acquisitions teams that had somehow found its way aboard the fabulous riverboat that now sat rocking gently with the subtle ripples of Bayou Lafourche.

Gellis called again, mumbling something that Baxter could not make out. With a weary sigh he paced up the corridor and knocked at the door of Gellis's cabin. "Did you call?" he asked.

A groan came from within, as if the woman were answering him in her sleep.

Working the door knob, Baxter pushed the door open and put his head inside. "You need something, ma'am? You hungry, or maybe a drink?"

Something struck him the second that Baxter opened the door, hitting him hard across the back of the head. He tumbled forward, shouting in pain as he flailed toward the floor.

Baxter stumbled, righted himself and turned, all in a swift three-step movement. The woman called Dagmar Gellis was standing against the wall by the door, the handle of a glass water jug in her hand, her fake limb in place of her missing leg. The jug had been left for Gellis should she become thirsty. Before Baxter could say a word, the older woman swung again, smashing him across the face with the heavy glass jug. Baxter slumped back against the wall in a shower of water and shattering glass. In a moment, the jagged handle was all that remained in Dagmar's hand; its body and its contents were strewn across the wooden floor of the cabin.

Baxter struggled to stay upright, feeling the telltale warm trickle of blood as it leaked from his nose and burned at several cuts across his cheeks.

The woman was walking toward him, a grim expression on her face, her teeth fixed around a single item she held in her mouth.

"It's okay, ma'am," Baxter said, running a hand through his hair to brush shards of glass from it. "I'm not going to hurt you. You're not a prisoner..."

The woman lunged at the guard with the broken remains of the water jug, swiping the jagged stump of handle at his face. "I need blood," she declared, but the words were delivered through the item she was holding between her teeth so that they came out as *I neeg glood*.

"I'm afraid I don't understand," Baxter began, dodg-

ing out of the way of the jagged handle. He was a guard,
what they used to call a sec man many years before; he
knew how to handle himself in a fight—especially one
against a weak old woman.

"Glood!" the woman barked, throwing herself at
Baxter and swiping the jagged glass at his throat.

Baxter shoved her back—hard—feeling the glass
graze against his Adam's apple. Gellis tumbled backward at the blow, her ugly ginger wig slipping so that
it almost covered her left eye.

Baxter moved swiftly then, grabbing the woman by
her wrist and shoving it against the wall of the cabin
so that it struck with a loud crack. He did this three
times, and on the third the woman let go of the jagged
remains of the jug, still struggling with her free hand
against the man's attack.

Baxter saw the thing clenched in the woman's mouth.
It was as long as a wisdom tooth and similar in shape
and color, a kind of yellowed off-white, and it was attached to a length of thin gold chain.

"What the hell—?" Baxter muttered, seeing the gold
and white flash in the woman's mouth as it caught the
light.

The woman was reaching for his face, hitting him
with her free hand, blows made strong by anger.

Baxter shoved her other hand aside as it grasped for
his face, his undershirt, and pushed her bodily against
the wall so that her feeble frame struck it with a clonk.
"What's gotten into you?" he shouted. "Calm down.
You almost—"

The woman hissed something through her clenched
teeth, ancient words, words of power, spoken in French
Creole. Then she moved her jaws, and the thing she held
between her teeth slipped out of sight, chain and all.

The guard grabbed for the woman's mouth, shoving her jaws together with as much force as he dared. "What is that?" he demanded, pushing her jaw so that she was forced to stand on tiptoe. "What do you have there?"

Gellis squirmed against him, her eyes going back in her head as if suffused with ecstasy.

"Spit it out," Baxter insisted, shoving her against the wall again. "Spit it out, I tell you!" Then he pulled her forward, yanking her savagely by the back of her neck so that she fell forward. The woman staggered several paces as she fell, stumbling over herself as if in a rush to meet the floor of the tidy cabin, tripping on her false leg. Her wig dropped as she fell, spinning across the floor.

Baxter was behind her then, grabbing her in a bear hug and wedging his arms low under her rib cage, amid the layers of cloth she wore. He yanked hard, once, twice, until she was forced to spit out the thing she had tried to swallow. It shot from her mouth with violent force, whipping across the cabin before striking a wall and finally coming to rest.

The muscular guard let go of Gellis, and she sank to the floor defeated as the support he provided disappeared. He paced across the cabin, knelt and picked up the toothlike item where it had dropped, covered in saliva. He saw now that the item was held on a long gold chain, just a fraction of an inch in width, the kind that the woman might have worn around her neck.

"What is this?" Baxter asked, thrusting the toothlike charm at the woman.

Gellis shook her head. "There are powers you don't understand," she told him. "Ancient powers, things older than our civilization."

"What is it?" Baxter repeated angrily. "What does it do?"

"Strengths can be tapped by ingesting parts of the great ones themselves," Dagmar Gellis chanted, her eyes unfocused. "Fear is the only barricade holding man back."

Baxter stood there, disturbed as the woman bit down hard on her own tongue, swallowing it an instant later. Within seconds she was choking, blood streaming down her jaw.

The guard moved then, tried to force the woman to spit out the hazard she had swallowed. He tried for a long time.

EMIT PART.

The sheet of paper stretched before Brigid was written in her own hand. She was sitting at the table in her apartment suite, high in the Cerberus redoubt complex, studying a chart outlining all the Annunaki gods in their complicated structures and substructures. It was a chart she had made herself, trying to figure out the multitude of different names and aspects that each of the Annunaki had been known by in the varied mythologies of Mesopotamia, Sumeria and others.

Enki... Enlil... Ninlil... Ninurta... Nannar... Marduk... Zulum... Gishnumunab... Lilitu... Kinma the Judge...

The list went on and on, a vast family tree of links and crossing lines, like the Mercator map on the walls of the ops room two floors below.

At the bottom level of the chart was Ullikummis, son of Enlil and Ninlil, one of many children sired by Enlil. And at the top, two names: Anu and Ki, the first of the Annunaki, sires to them all; the first Annunaki to appear in Earth's mythology, the first to walk the Earth.

Brigid's eyes scanned the chart, then flicked for a

moment to the notebook at her bedside table. "Emit part." What did that mean? What if they were Annunaki words? Could something in her subconscious, something of the aspect of her that had been Haight, have been trying to send her waking self a message?

Brigid's emerald eyes flicked from the notebook to the chart and back, trying to piece it all together. There was something there, just out of reach, a grand plan she was a part of, but she could not put her finger on where or how or who was pulling the strings.

Had some *part* been *emitted* from the family tree of the Annunaki? Was that part already loose, moving the players across the globe like a chess master moving pieces?

"What if the apocalypse is happening and no one can see it?" Brigid asked herself, tracing the line of the family tree upward with the tip of her finger.

At that moment a wall-mounted comms device hummed to life with a pleasant tone, glowing a soft pinkish red where it was located beside the suite door. Heeding its call, Brigid did not get up, instead activating the Commtact that had been surgically implanted in her skull.

"Brigid," she acknowledged.

"This is Lakesh," Lakesh's voice came over the Commtact, directly into Brigid's ear canal. "Would you be able to meet me in the operations room as soon as possible?"

"Is there a situation?" Brigid asked.

"Everything shall be explained when you get here," Lakesh replied. "I'm calling Grant and Kane also."

"Gotcha."

Abruptly, the communication feed faded. Brigid took one last look at the family tree that lay atop her desk before folding it back up and replacing it in its plastic wallet. She left the pad where she had found it that morning, at a twenty-degree angle to what it had been the night before.

NOT LONG AFTER they had all been examined, the three members of CAT Alpha regrouped in the ops room under the watchful eye of the operations staff. Along with Brigid, Lakesh had requested Kane's and Grant's presence as soon as possible. As the top field agents for the organization that request was hardly unusual, but when they arrived, coming from separate locations within the vast mountain base yet somehow meeting at the doors to the ops room almost in unison, they could not help but sense Lakesh's concern as he welcomed them into the room.

"Something wrong?" Kane asked, perceptive as ever as Brigid and Grant were ushered in to join him.

Lakesh nodded gravely. "Your point-man sense has alerted you once again, my friend," he began, but Kane corrected him.

"Not my point-man sense," Kane insisted. "It's just, well, I know body language and yours is telling just one story, and it's a pretty negative one."

"Quite so," Lakesh agreed, leading the three operatives over to one of the consoles in the twin aisles of computer screens. Brewster Philboyd sat at the screen, monitoring a satellite feed with a separate screen linked into the Cerberus communications input. "Brewster, if you would?"

Philboyd tapped the satellite feed screen with the end of his pen. "Recognize this?"

The screen showed an overhead shot of what appeared to be an overgrown patch of swampland. The canopy of green leaves all but hid a dirt track that wended through the terrain, leading somewhere to the top—or north—of the feed image.

Brigid pulled a pair of square-framed spectacles from the pocket of her jumpsuit—a necessity thanks to her farsightedness—before picking out the details of the image. As she did, Kane looked gruffly at Brewster and Lakesh.

"Instead of playing twenty questions, why don't you just tell us what it is we're looking at," Kane said. "It's been a long day already."

"Redoubt Mike," Philboyd announced with a momentary apology concerning his occasional flair for the dramatic. "CAT Beta journeyed there via mat-trans roughly five hours ago—"

"How 'roughly'?" Grant asked, theorizing that the details of this case were about to become relevant.

"Four hours and forty-seven minutes," Philboyd said, glancing up at Lakesh as if he expected the man to respond. When he did not, Philboyd continued. "Redoubt Mike is located in Louisiana. You guys went there in—"

"Yeah, we remember," Kane said, brushing the details aside. "Go on."

"The redoubt should have been sealed when you left, but we suspect that protocol was never executed," Lakesh chipped in.

"Kane's old friend Ohio Blue contacted us early this morning requesting a meet-up at a location about forty miles north of the redoubt called Bayou Lafourche," Brewster stated. "There was no reason to suspect duplicity..."

Kane emitted a bitter bark of laughter at that. There was always reason to suspect duplicity with Ohio Blue, he knew—she was a trader working outside of ville law, where the motto was "anything goes."

"Ms. Blue gave CAT Beta a lead," Philboyd continued, "which directed them to Redoubt Mike, the scene of Lilitu's incarceration almost two years ago."

Lakesh took up the story. "Following that lead," he explained, "CAT Beta requested a mat-trans jump directly to Redoubt Mike to investigate. Brewster provided said jump. They have not been heard from since."

Kane nodded, realizing how much Lakesh was not saying. He took the welfare of all of his team personally, and would naturally be concerned that CAT Beta had been out of touch for so long. Furthermore, Lakesh had been in a romantic relationship with CAT Beta's Domi for several years now, and it would no doubt be eating him up to think she might have jumped headlong into danger. "What was the lead?" he asked.

"As we understand it, a member of Papa Hurbon's *société* brought evidence to suggest that something was happening in Redoubt Mike," Lakesh stated. "Something relating to the trouble Hurbon had been a part of two years ago."

"Trouble we had to sort out," Grant rumbled dourly.

"And they definitely made the jump?" Brigid confirmed.

"Yes, their biolinks confirmed the movement before they winked out," Lakesh stated.

"It may be nothing," Kane said, trying to sound reassuring. "The Commtacts don't always work underground. We had trouble in Redoubt Mike, couldn't get a signal out."

"Five hours, Kane," Lakesh replied. "That's too long not to have someone reach the surface and report in. I fear we have sent them into the lion's den."

Grant sighed heavily. "And now you want to send us, too, I take it?" he said.

Lakesh nodded grimly. "If you…if you are recovered," he said pathetically. It was clear what he really meant—that he needed them to go, that they were the best hope for recovering the missing away team.

Kane was thoughtful. "Could be they walked right into a trap," he suggested. "Likely, even, from the circumstantial evidence. But a trap has to be sprung."

Brigid looked at Kane, cockeyed. "What are you thinking?"

"We approach from another angle," Kane said. "Use the Mantas—they have firepower and they'll allow us to survey the landscape despite the vegetation. We'll go in low, check out the redoubt and see if someone's hiding, I dunno, an army amid the trees. After that, we can enter, recover Beta and find out what the shit is going on."

"You make it sound easy," Lakesh acknowledged.

Kane placed one hand on Lakesh's arm. "Domi's alive," he said. "Her, Edwards, Sinclair—they're all alive. They're too smart and too tough to die. Trust me, when all of this is over you'll realize this weren't nothing but a taxi mission."

Lakesh nodded, the worrisome expression still evident on his face. "Thank you, my friend," he said. "It's been a long time we've worked this beat, and I've asked you—all three of you—to take some strange diversions along the way. But I do appreciate how much you have invested in Cerberus as a team."

"We're not a team," Kane told him with a smile. "We're a family. And families watch out for each other, especially when one of their number gets lost in the woods."

With that, the three-person team of CAT Alpha exited the ops room and made their way to the hangar bay via the basement armory. It was time to find out what was going on at Redoubt Mike.

Chapter 21

"On-site," Kane said, speaking via Commtact to the Cerberus ops room from inside the cockpit of his Manta craft. His was one of two such craft that now cut through the skies over the Louisiana bayou, close to a settlement called Amox in the late-afternoon sunlight.

The Mantas were slope-winged aircraft constructed from a bronze-hued metal that seemed to shine where it caught the sunlight. Their graceful designs consisted of flattened wedges with swooping wings curving out to either side in mimicry of the seagoing manta, and it was this similarity that had spawned their popularized name of Manta Craft. Each Manta's wingspan was twenty yards and its body length was almost fifteen. The entire surface of each vehicle was decorated with curious geometric designs; elaborate cuneiform markings, swirling glyphs and cup-and-spiral symbols. Aerodynamic, flat in design, each vehicle featured an elongated hump in the center of the body that provided the only indication of a cockpit.

The Mantas were alien in design and had been discovered by the Cerberus warriors during their many investigations into mythological artifacts and sites.

Inside, the transatmospheric vehicles, or TAVs, were as slick as their exteriors. The cockpit featured two seats, one behind the other, and a very basic control board featuring the bare minimum of indicators. In fact, most of the indicators were projected directly onto the pilot's eye in a heads-up display, operated through a bulbous, spherical helmet fixed into the pilot seat and finished in the same bronze as the aircraft's exterior.

Kane piloted the lead vehicle, with Brigid sitting behind him working a laptop running a minute-by-minute analysis of data beamed directly from Cerberus's satellites. Beside Kane's Manta flew an identical craft piloted by his wingman, Grant. The two had flown more missions in these vehicles than they cared to recall, taking them beneath the sea, outside of Earth's atmosphere and even into a cosmic rift where alien technology flourished at a level unsuspected by the people of Earth. Right now they were weaving through the high clouds as they cut sky toward their destination, Redoubt Mike.

"Acknowledged," came Brewster Philboyd's response as Kane sent his brief report.

Kane juked the joystick, bringing his Manta lower in a first reconnaissance of the site.

From above, the redoubt looked like nothing more than a mound of dirt in the center of the swamp. It was buried beneath the earth, only one single overgrown dirt road giving any hint that there was anything out here at all, in fact.

"Looks clear," Grant said as the Mantas made a north-south pass, crossing close to the body of the hidden redoubt.

"Picking up life readings," Kane stated, eyeing his heads-up display. "Baptiste? You getting anything back there? People, vehicles, weapons?"

In the seat behind Kane, Brigid worked a laptop computer, running through a scan program. "Two vehicles," Brigid said. "Land wags, armed. Just bringing up an analysis now."

On the fold-up screen of the laptop, the diagnostics for two vehicles began to flash, scurrying up the page as the details filled in, including wire-frame models that highlighted fuel tanks and weaponry. They were large-wheeled land wags, each as big as a Magistrate Sandcat but with four wheels instead of caterpillar tracks. The vehicles ran on gasoline—an extravagance here in the Outlands—and featured roof-mounted gun turrets armed with double USMG-73s very similar to those mounted on the Magistrate Sandcats. Additionally, each vehicle had a second set of weapons located beneath the high-riding front grille, a Sidewinder missile launcher whose kick would surely make forward movement with the vehicles impossible—indicating to Brigid that they must only use those weapons while stationary.

"What have we got?" Kane asked, working the controls of the Manta to bring his vehicle back around in a long, graceful arc.

"Two land wags, heavily armed," Brigid said, relaying the information over her Commtact to Grant at the same time. "Parked a half mile out from the redoubt entrance on the single road leading to it. I'd guess they're guards."

"Guards," Kane muttered the word. "Yeah, well, we'll bypass them, go straight over their heads."

Over the Commtact frequency, Grant laughed. "Bet they never expected someone to approach by air, huh?"

He had a point. The Mantas were unique vehicles in the modern world, used solely by the Cerberus organization and, by and large, considered a closely guarded secret. There were other air vehicles in use, Deathbird helicopters and a few other aircraft across the globe, but for the most part air travel was an occasional sight in the skies, a means of transportation reserved only for Magistrates and barony officials.

Flying in formation, Kane and Grant drew their Manta craft around and searched for a suitable spot to bring them down amid the wild foliage. The Mantas were VTOL—or vertical take off and landing—equipped, and could turn on a dime. Fast and nimble, they were ideal for reaching tight spots.

Kane searched through the view scan for a landing site, spotted a clearing amid the vegetation roughly five hundred yards from where he pegged the entry to the redoubt itself. "Ten degrees north of entrance," Kane said via the Commtact, "about five hundred yards out."

"I see it," Grant agreed. "Looks ideal."

As Grant finished speaking, his voice was marred with sudden distortion. In their Manta, Kane and Brigid reacted with surprise—the Commtacts were largely infallible, offering crystal-clear broadcasts of such precision that one could easily be mistaken for being in the same room as the individual to whom one spoke.

"Grant, you okay—?" Kane began.

"Greetings, oh sweet prince," a female voice spoke over the Commtact, cutting into the signal. Kane identified it instantly as the female trader called Ohio Blue. No one else ever called him sweet prince. "Is that you up there in the sky?"

"Ohio, get off this frequency," Kane growled, trying to keep the irritation out of his voice. The Commtact signals were encrypted and scrambled as a matter of course; it should not have been possible to tap into them like this, and certainly not to override a linked discussion as Ohio Blue had just done. But Ohio had some remarkably talented people in her organization, and she trod the wrong side of legality as a matter of course.

Laws are only there for the masses, she had once told Kane, they are not for the likes of you or me.

IN THE CERBERUS operations room, sudden pandemonium seemed to break out. Stationed at the comms desk, Brewster Philboyd almost fell out of his seat where he had been monitoring CAT Alpha's transmissions as the trader's voice came abruptly over their encrypted frequency. Two desks over from him, Donald Bry saw something blip on his screen and realized they had a hack in the heart of their system, running directly into the Keyhole commsat.

"How the hell is she doing that?" Philboyd spit, flicking a switch on his console. "Kane, do you hear me? Cut transmission now, you're compromised."

"Thanks for the heads-up, Cerberus," Kane deadpanned in response. "Great job."

Lakesh had leaped from his desk as soon as he had realized that something was wrong, and he stood now behind Bry's desk, where the computer expert was churning through numerous lines of data to try to discover the tap. "Donald, Brewster—what is occurring?"

"We have a tap," Bry said, "going directly into the commsat."

"It's that trader, Ohio Blue," Philboyd explained. "She's on CAT Alpha's frequency, talking to Kane even now."

Lakesh looked at both men, turning his attention rapidly from one to the other. "Let her," he decided. "She has earned some leeway."

"But she's compromised our—" Bry began.

Lakesh hushed him with a gesture. "She has earned some leeway," he repeated, making a two-inch gap between his thumb and crooked index finger. "Although only a very small amount of leeway. I want you both to come up with a workaround for the very second that we may need it. Understood?"

Bry and Philboyd nodded, turning back to their monitors and immediately running diagnostics programs that would locate the source and nature of the communications hack.

KANE, MEANWHILE, WAS still talking to Ohio Blue as he worked the pilot's controls of his Manta.

"Might you reconsider, sweet prince?" Ohio broadcast as Kane prepped for landing. "I believe I have some information that would be of benefit to you, and a meeting would be to our mutual advantage."

Kane gritted his teeth, expelling a breath of irritation between them. Ohio was a wily woman at the best of times, but she had proved a valuable ally when the chips were down, and she'd protected Cerberus personnel when it seemed that the rest of the world had been turned against them. "Okay, you have my attention. Two minutes," Kane said, "start explaining."

"Darling," Ohio replied with a kind of mocking superiority, "you know me better than that, surely? A meeting is a meeting, not a chat over an open channel like this."

Not that open, Kane thought sourly, but instead he said, "Where?"

"We are close. You can see us," Ohio replied.

Brigid whispered in Kane's ear from the seat behind him. "The land wags. Not guards—Ohio's people, maybe?"

Kane nodded, the movement oddly unsettling while in the bulbous spherical helmet. "Gotcha." Then he activated the Commtact link again, trusting Ohio's miraculous hackers to pick up the signal. "Did you bring two wags to the meeting?"

"We did," Ohio replied. "I knew you could see us if you looked."

Even as the woman's mellifluous voice trilled over the Commtact frequency, something flashed in the shadows of the vegetation, once, twice, thrice. On the third flash, Kane spotted the source—the headlights of one of those land wags that Brigid had identified on their first pass.

The Mantas drew down amid the haze of vegetation, the whine of their jets mingling with the sounds of life emanating from that cesspool of moisture and green.

Kane, Grant and Brigid had visited Redoubt Mike before and seen horrors there that should never have been given life. Returning filled them with trepidation and something else—determination. They were warriors; they had to believe in their purpose, even out here amid the muck and grime of hell on earth.

Kane brought his Manta down to the landing spot he had identified, and Grant followed a few seconds later, bringing the golden-winged aircraft down with a gentle bump.

Kane was helping Brigid down from the sloped wing as Grant emerged from his vehicle's cockpit. "Kane?" he asked, his brow furrowed with concern. "You sure about this? Ohio can be a tricky customer."

Kane nodded. "She's a law unto herself," he agreed. "But I've started to realize, after all these years away from the system—the villes, the barons, the Magistrates—that it has always been this way. We never made the laws, Grant. We never even enforced them. All we did was hold chaos back from a tiny speck of earth that someone had built a wall around, deluding ourselves into thinking that somehow that tiny speck meant something.

"And you know what?" Kane asked rhetorically. "All it meant was that we had bought into all that shit the Annunaki had drummed into our ancestors all those thousands of years ago when they treated us as slaves. People like Ohio, they're what we should have been fighting for all along, people who were actually trying to get humanity back on its feet and out of the villes and all the evil they perpetrated."

Brigid looked solemn as she listened to Kane's words. "We didn't create the system, Kane," she said.

"But we've always supported it, supported organization," Kane said, "even when we thought we were breaking away."

"It's a dangerous world," Grant said, checking the breech of his rifle to be certain that it was loaded. He had brought a Swiss-made SSG-550 sniper rifle from his cockpit, a good long-range weapon with a twenty-five-inch barrel that made up over half its length. The rifle also sported a magnification scope that attached to its top and could handle thirty shots without the need for reloading. "If it wasn't, guys like us would be put out to pasture."

"Sometimes pasture doesn't sound so bad after all we've been through," Kane said sourly, checking his Sin Eater before flicking it back to its hidden wrist holster under his sleeve.

As Grant slipped off the safety on the SSG-550 and carried it under one arm, the three warriors took in the entryway to the redoubt where it loomed just a few hundred yards away. The dirt road ran directly into the redoubt, disappearing into a sloped tunnel that was sunk under the earth. When they had last been here, that entry was unobtrusive, a ditch beside a mound of dirt overgrown with lush vegetation. It had not changed much, but now there were things hanging before the entrance and to its sides, animal skulls and bones suspended from stakes and a cross bar that had been placed over the tunnel entrance. Feathers fluttered in the breeze, tied to a line of posts that had been cinched into the ground on the run up to the tunnel, more fluttering amid the propped bones and skulls.

"Looks like somebody's had the decorators in," Grant said sardonically.

"The trinkets are classic voodoo," Brigid stated, her analytical mind always in motion. "There's a lot of that around here."

"Yeah, we both know," Kane said, turning away from the shadowy entrance. "Let's find Blue before we go exploring."

KANE LED THE WAY from the redoubt entrance, along the dirt road to the meeting spot where Ohio and her people were waiting with their land wags.

Grant held back, finding a convenient bit of cover to the side of the road where he could hide without being seen. He pushed the leaves back and dropped down to his belly, resting the sniper rifle before him until its scope peered through the overhanging leaves. The ground was soft here and damp, feeling squidgy underfoot. Grant arranged himself into a comfortable position and lined up the scope until he could see Ohio Blue and her people. It didn't pay to send everyone into a potential ambush.

Through the scope, Grant saw that the two land wags had been parked across the road in such a way that no other vehicle could pass, their front ends facing in opposite directions for all-around visibility. Armed men and women waited in the vehicles and along the road, eight of them in all that Grant could see, though he suspected more were hidden in the dense foliage of the swamp.

Ohio sat on a chair to the side of the road, directly before the passenger-side door to the leftmost of the two wags. The wag would shield her from any kind of sneak attack, and a guard stood at her side three feet away with an AK-47 held in his hands. The man looked emotionlessly up the road as Kane and Brigid approached. His face was hard and square, his shoulders seemed too wide for his head and his sleeveless shirt revealed tattooed arms. He had a second blaster at his hip, a modified Sin Eater like the Magistrates used to use before they began to employ the retractable design that functioned with the wrist holster.

Ohio's chair looked antique, with a velvet backing in the same sapphire blue as the long dress she wore, its high back arched and framed in mahogany. Ohio sat cross-legged, wearing a long blue dress whose slit fell open to reveal almost the full length of her uppermost leg. Her peekaboo hair hid her left eye, as it always did, blond bangs falling until they almost brushed her cheek. She held a glass of clear liquid aloft in salutation as she spotted Kane and Brigid approaching. The chair and the woman looked incongruous amid such earthy surroundings, the sounds and smells of the swamp impossible to ignore.

"Drink?" Ohio asked when the Cerberus warriors got close enough that she would not need to shout.

"We'll have to decline," Kane told her. "Running a tight schedule just now. Care to tell me how you knew we'd be here? How you broke into our comms signal?"

Ohio took a long, slow drink from her glass, her eyes fixed on Kane's, never leaving his gaze. When she drew the glass away, she had left a lipstick stain on its side, and she smiled a tight-lipped smile. "You take such pride in your independence," she observed, "that you do not always know when to accept help, sweet prince. I have something for you, and my people here have gone well beyond normalinquiries to reach you."

Kane's eyes flicked to Ohio's guards as he stood before the blond-haired trader. He figured she was tracking him, somehow—probably with the same transponders that Cerberus used. Under different circumstances he might even be impressed. "What do you have?" he asked.

Ohio raised her free hand, the one without the glass in it, fist clenched, palm down. She opened her fingers and something dropped from her hand, dangling there on a thin loop of gold chain. It looked like a shark's tooth to Kane.

"What is that?" Kane asked, stepping forward.

"Ah, now you are intrigued," Ohio teased him. "You realize that perhaps your anger was misplaced, sweet prince."

"What is it?" Kane asked again, reaching for the yellow-white object on the length of chain.

Ohio dropped it into his hand with a smile. "This was worn among other trinkets by an old woman who came into my presence. Her name was Dagmar—she came from around these parts, worshipped at a local temple."

Brigid's eyes widened at that, recalling their own dealings with a voodoo priest called Hurbon. "Do you know where? With whom?"

"Your colleagues met with me and spoke with her," Ohio replied, brushing the questions deftly aside. Ohio was a trader and information broker, so she was not in the habit of giving away data easily, and almost never freely. Kane and Brigid knew instantly that she was talking about Edwards, Domi and Sela Sinclair, however. "She was wearing this around her neck," Ohio continued.

"Do you know what it is?" Brigid asked, leaning closer to take a look. Beside her, Kane was holding back, watching the guards and the covering of vegetation, wary of an ambush.

"No," Ohio admitted. "It appears to be a piece of bone or tooth. It was brought to our attention when the woman tried to swallow it—one of my assistants caught her in the act and removed it from her mouth, though with some degree of trouble."

"She tried to swallow it?" Kane asked. "Chain and all?"

"I am told that she spoke of ancient powers," Ohio explained. "Of strengths gained by imbibing parts of the great ones themselves. Voodoo hogwash, of course."

"Of course," Kane agreed, peering at Brigid as she stared, almost transfixed by the white shard. She knew what it was, he felt certain. "Baptiste?"

"We've seen this before," was all she said.

Kane knew not to ask anything further at that moment. He would speak to his colleagues out of hearing range of the wily trader and her people. His eyes flicked back to Ohio where she reclined in her eccentric chair. "Where's this Dagmar woman now?" he asked.

"She…struggled," Ohio said, clearly uncomfortable.

Kane nodded, feeling as if a coiled snake was sitting in his gut. He'd had few dealings with voodoo, but all of them had been creepy, and frequently their resolutions had been unclear. "Thank you. Was there anything else?" he finally asked.

Ohio shook her head and smiled. "So much. But it can wait. I see that you are busy."

Kane saluted Ohio with his fingertips, turned and marched back the way he had come, Brigid keeping step beside him with the charm now in her hand.

As Kane and his companion left, Ohio watched the way he walked, the lithe movement of his muscles. She liked Kane, he was her prince, but there was something that always kept them apart. He was reticent, always had been, but perhaps she was partly to blame for that because she had never been truly honest with him. She reached up to her hair, and touched the thing that her peekaboo hairstyle hid, on the left-hand side of her face. One day, perhaps, she would share that little secret with him.

"I HATE ALL this voodoo shit," Kane muttered once he was satisfied that they were well away from the trader and her guards. "Symbols and bloodletting and weird little ugly dolls with ribbons tied to their waists."

"Agreed," Grant said, joining them from his hiding place in the bushes, hefting the scoped rifle in his hands.

"So?" Kane asked, turning an inquisitive eye to Brigid.

Grant looked from Kane to Brigid, feeling the electricity between them. "You guys find out something?" he asked.

"Better than that," Kane said. "Ohio handed us a trinket that was being used by one of the locals."

Brigid was turning the white shard over and over in her hand as they walked toward the Mantas and the entrance to Redoubt Mike.

"That it?" Grant asked, and when Kane told him it was, he peered more closely. "What is it?"

Brigid was still looking at the white shard, her emerald eyes fixed rigidly on its pitted surface.

Kane saw now that she was pale even for her; in fact, she had gone white as a sheet. "Baptiste?" he prompted.

"I think it's a piece from *Tiamat*," she said, "the dragon ship of the Annunaki."

Chapter 22

Kane and Grant looked at Brigid with complete astonishment, a single question on both their lips—though Kane was the first to give it voice.

"How can you be sure that's *Tiamat*?" he asked.

"Because I can remember the shade of the dragon ship's bones," Brigid explained, "exactly."

Brigid had perfect recall, Kane knew, something she called an eidetic memory, which meant she could remember the most intricate detail of the things she had seen with photographic exactitude. But this was not an object that they held, it was a splinter from one. For Brigid to remember a color—no, not even a color but a shade of white, only infinitesimally different from all the other shades of white that were out there—seemed incredible.

"You're sure?" Kane asked, knowing the question was redundant even as it left his lips.

Brigid glanced up from the white rock on the necklace chain and smiled at Kane, that beautiful, genuine smile she reserved only for those moments when she recalled how far behind her Kane mentally was. "You remember in Iraq, on the banks of the Euphrates," she said, "when Enlil regrew *Tiamat* from a seed?"

Kane and Grant did, of course. The seed had grown but it had corrupted, so that instead of forming a new spaceship it had grown only the parts, leaving the bone substructure on show in something that the locals had called the Dragon City. Grant had fought his way into the city twice over, ultimately battling with Enlil and his son Ullikummis in the ship's engine rooms before Kane stepped in via astral projection and managed to trap Ullikummis in an interphase wormhole.

"The ship never fully formed," Brigid said. "It was instead left with its framework—its bones and teeth—on show.

"I think that this is one of those teeth," she said, "or, more accurately, a part of one."

"A dragon's tooth," Kane pronounced with gravity. "And just what would an old lady be doing with a dragon's tooth?"

"It was found on an old lady?" Grant asked, his eyebrows raised in surprise.

Kane nodded. "She tried to swallow it and kill herself. Two separate acts done at the same time."

"No, she didn't," Brigid said as they neared the overgrown entrance to the redoubt. "She tried to shed blood as she swallowed the tooth. Subtle difference. We're talking about sacrifice here, sacrificial blood. It's a standard tool in voodun ceremonies, though usually they would use the blood of an animal such as a chicken."

"No chickens about, I guess," Grant said, catching on.

"But why would you swallow a dragon's tooth?" Kane asked, baffled.

Brigid racked her brains, making new connections at lightning speed. "Dragon's teeth were said to have great power in ancient times. The Spartoí were the children of Ares, the Greek god of war. They were powerful soldiers grown from the teeth of a dragon. But they were walking dead and that made them almost invincible."

"How did they grow these teeth warriors?" Kane asked.

"According to Greek legend, they were sown in the ground," Brigid recalled. "But that only means that they required some kind of nurturing, an organic base in which to flourish."

"So if you put one inside a person—?" Kane began.

Brigid swore then, her frustration suddenly bubbling over. "Of course. Ereshkigal was the same thing! Dammit, why didn't I see that at the time?"

"What are you talking about?" Grant asked. He had met Ereshkigal, the reborn Annunaki goddess of the underworld while vacationing with his girlfriend Shizuka in Zaragoza, Spain. Ereshkigal had manipulated the dead, building an unliving army and bringing about a momentary revolution that had threatened the local populace and almost caused a whole city to die. Kane and Brigid had joined Grant in a showdown with the reborn goddess, whose physical coherence was threatened by some kind of rot that caused her strength to ebb, leading to her defeat.

"Ereshkigal was unfinished," Brigid said. "Reborn, but incomplete. Just like when we faced Ezili Coeur Noir on this very site two years ago."

"You think voodoo was involved in Ereshkigal's re-emergence?" Kane asked, realization slowly dawning.

"Yes, and not just hers," Brigid said. "Charun and Vanth in Italy, everything that just happened to us in the Congo. Gods—dark gods, the kind of bastards who ruled over their own legendary hells—have been appearing all across the globe with no pattern, no reason. But how do you make a god?"

"Spartoí," Kane said solemnly. "The undead born from the dragon's seeds."

"Exactly! Exactly!" Brigid said, holding the pendant before her. "This little sliver of Annunaki debris works like a seed. Like everything else the Annunaki ever made, it's organic technology, DNA twisted in a way that can be grown to make whatever they need. Dragon ships, obedience stones, gods..."

The Cerberus trio had halted before the entrance to the redoubt and saw now that the rollback doors had been pulled back, leaving the access tunnel—concrete walled and wide enough to drive a Sandcat down—open to the elements. Mold grew up the walls, specks of green and darkness intertwined.

"How can one broken tooth do all that?" Grant asked.

"Not one," Brigid said. "Dozens. Maybe even hundreds. The Annunaki were humankind's first gods, their escapades became the templates for myths that traveled far beyond their reach, and touched cultures far and wide. Their stories were rewritten and reworked, turned into new tales with new gods and new heroes, but all the while the same core concepts lurked beneath the surface—Ezili was Lilith was Lilitu, for example. All those histories, all those templates, are contained in the pieces of the wombship *Tiamat*, the place where all the genetic templates resided, waiting for rebirth."

"And now somebody's gotten ahold of them and has been using them to—what?" Kane asked.

"Raise Hell," Grant growled.

"They weren't gods," Brigid said. "They were seeds. Seeds that used genetic matter to revive their data, giving rise to Ereshkigal and Nergal and Charun and so on. Someone spread them across the globe deliberately, guys."

"But why would anyone do that?" Grant asked.

"Control," Kane answered without missing a beat.

"The same reason the barons made the villes, the same reason we became Magistrates. The same sick reason that the system keeps coming back—to control people."

"They used voodoo," Brigid said, eyeing the shadowy entry to Redoubt Mike, voodoo iconography drawn into the once-precise lines of the military base. "They mixed dark magic with the supercomputer nature of these fragments of *Tiamat* to make things come to life."

Kane looked from Brigid to the darkness of the redoubt entrance. "We're at the belly of the beast, then, I guess."

"I guess," Brigid said, trying to pierce the gloom with her eyes.

"You think they have any more of this stuff?" Grant asked. "These dragon's teeth?"

"I think we had best keep our eyes open," Brigid said, "and stay on our guard."

With that, the three Cerberus warriors pulled darklensed glasses from their pockets and put them over their eyes. The electrochemical polymer of the lenses gathered all available light to give them a form of night vision as they entered the darkness of the cavernous tunnel into the complex. As they walked, all three drew their weapons, Kane his Sin Eater from its hidden sheath at his wrist, Grant his Copperhead subgun, leaving the SSG-550 on its sling across his back, and Brigid her TP-9 semiautomatic.

As they went farther along the sloped road, disappearing deeper underground, they saw figures strewn on the road, dead men and women, their bodies rotted away, just piles of bones and rags. All three of them remembered this place, remembered their frantic escape in a rotting truck as undead things came back to life to stop them.

The redoubt was dead now, almost noiseless. And yet, all around them as they went deeper into its subterranean confines, the sense of something organic, something alive, seemed to seep from the mold-covered walls, the soft, moss-covered ground where once there had been tarmac road.

The last of the distant daylight ebbed away like the reflection of the moon on the ripples of a lake, and the Cerberus warriors were walking in darkness, down under the earth, where the dead things had been. They reached a wide rollback door at the end of the tunnel, beside which stood a guard's monitoring station. The rollback door was wedged cockeyed into the wall. The guard post featured burned-out television monitors and a large red panic button whose works had been overcome with rust.

They pressed on, Kane taking the lead as they stepped through the door and into the redoubt itself. They had been here before, their previous excursion hectic and disturbing, a rush of escapes from dead things brought back to life.

A vehicle elevator waited at the end of the road a dozen feet from the rollback door. Overhead, lights flickered and blinked, activated by motion sensors but no longer functioning properly, instead casting the whole chamber in a stutter of illumination, like lightning at midnight.

Within, the redoubt seemed to pulse. It was quiet, but not quite silent—the distant noise of swishing water, things dripping, creaking against their tethers or against one another echoing through the distant corridors. There were scars on the wall, gashes like blood, as if the walls were the flesh of something living that had been attacked and left for dead. Figures lay against the walls, mold growing over their long-rotted bodies,

one a man with a concave rib cage within which mush-
rooms grew.

Kane glanced past the elevator, searching for the
telltale door that would open onto the stairwell that ran
through the redoubt. He pushed at the door, then pulled,
then pushed again until it opened—inward, stiffly, accompanied by a groan of unoiled hinges.

Inside, wall lights flickered and died, flickered and
died, sputtering like candles against a hurricane. Kane
trotted swiftly down the stairs, their hard surfaces
marred by spreading mold, diffusing the sound of his
footfalls and the *tap-tap* of Brigid's heeled boots that
followed.

Without a word, Kane halted at the doorway to the
next level, pressing himself against it as he listened for
any signs of company. Nothing, just silence—creaking,
dripping, silence.

Kane pulled the door, stepping around it with his
blaster nosing before him, using the wall for cover.

He was in a wide area now, the stairwell opening
onto a vehicle garage with the wreckage of stripped-
down jeeps and military trucks that had not been used
in two hundred years. A pool of water dominated the
room, dark with debris, bones and weeds swirling
within its shallow depths.

Kane gestured in the darkness, commanding his
team forward without making a sound.

They joined him, moving through the waterlogged
garage, past the vehicles and crates where two years before they had tangled with living dead things.

It was slow, Kane regretted. Slow progress, checking places like this, searching for his lost colleagues
while avoiding traps an enemy might set. Grant and

Brigid peeled away, checking the nooks and crannies, searching for signs of Domi, Edwards and Sela Sinclair.

The motor pool was devoid of life, just water and the dinosaur carcasses of ancient vehicles. As they checked the vast space, Grant spotted something in the water, its flat line like a streak across the polymer night lenses. He trudged into the water until it was as deep as his midcalf. Reaching down, he plucked the item from the water and stared at it with a chilling sense of familiarity.

Kane and Brigid stopped what they were doing and turned to look at Grant, somehow sensing that the big man had discovered something. He held it aloft for them to see, not saying a word. They all recognized it—Domi's knife, the one she had kept with her like a good-luck charm ever since she had tried to gut Guana Teague with it all those years ago in Cobaltville. Like any good-luck charm, this was one item that Domi would not intentionally leave behind; it was precious to her, a razor-edged hunk of sentimentality with blood in its past.

The discovery did not bode well. CAT Beta had not reported in since mat-trans jumping here. All the knife confirmed was that they had arrived—what had happened to them once they got here was still in the realm of speculation. But if Domi had discarded her knife then things could not have been good.

Kane motioned toward the far doors, recalling the layout of the redoubt and the location of a second stairwell back there. The team followed him, weapons ready, alert to dangers as Kane led the way past a stack of mold-dappled crates and through an open doorway into another passageway.

Kane's nose twitched. There was a smell here, emanating from somewhere down the corridor, a kind of perfume that he could detect even over the smells of mold and stagnant water. He held up a hand, indicating to the others to cover him while he investigated.

Grant dropped back, pressing himself against the wall to give him the optimal view of both the motor pool and the corridor. Brigid, meanwhile, stuck with Kane, her TP-9 held ready as he led the way down the corridor.

They passed several sealed doors for storage rooms. Then, to his right, Kane peered through an open door that led into a long, narrow cafeteria featuring two long tables arranged with their short edges together so that they ran the length of the room. There was water on the floor here, three inches deep and dark with detritus.

Behind Kane, Brigid took a moment to check the doorway on the other side of the corridor. An aging sign declared that it led to the facility's restrooms, and there was a little mold growing along the bottom sill of the door.

Kane sniffed the air again, sensing that scent wafting from somewhere within. Cooking? No, it couldn't be that…could it?

Kane moved into the darkened cafeteria, everything brought into stark, unforgiving clarity by his night lenses. There were more bodies in here, slumped at the tables in an almost comical manner. Kane checked them swiftly, recalling the nightmarish things he had faced here once before.

The smell was coming from deeper in the room, from behind the serving hatch with its shuttered window.

Kane turned back, motioning Brigid to join him in the room. He had a sense of unease here now, the old point-man sense ringing like an alarm in his mind. His heartbeat sounded loud in his ears, his breath seemed shallow. Was it the smell, the air or just the memory of what had happened here all those months before, when he had used a blessed sword to fight the legions of the undead, that made him so tense?

An open doorway was located beside the wide serving window, leading into the food preparation area for the redoubt. Kane stepped through, feet shushing in the water that flowed in ripples from room to room.

Like the rest of the redoubt, the food preparation area was in darkness—but this only drew attention to the single green light that was located on a far wall. The light seemed bright in Kane's night-vision glasses, burning like a miniature sun at the back of the room.

He paced forward, walking toward the light, Brigid Baptiste hanging back inside the doorway to the room. The light was knuckle small and square and it was affixed to the wall on a metal plate, molded into it as part of the design. Kane had seen one like it before, recalled it from the Cerberus redoubt, but it still took Kane a moment to recognize what it was; an activation light for a refrigeration unit.

The fridge was still in use. Kane was amazed. It didn't seem normal, not when everything else was broken and shut down the way it was.

But the smell was coming from the fridge, a sickly smell up close, like rotting fruit—or meat.

Reaching for the chrome-plated handle to the refrigeration unit, Kane pulled at the door, feeling that familiar heavy weight as the seal broke to allow freezing air to escape.

It was cold in there, ice-cold, and a brilliant light came on as the door was pulled back.

Inside, three human bodies hung upside down like cured meats. Three familiar human bodies: Edwards, Sinclair and Domi.

Chapter 23

Kane drew a sharp intake of breath as the bodies gradually rotated in the breeze he had created when he pulled the door open.

"Edwards? Domi?" Kane whispered. "Sinclair?"

His breath hung in a cloud in the wake of his whispered words, dissipating slowly like mist on the wind.

The bodies had been hung from hooks by chains that had been cuffed to their ankles. The result left them swinging with their arms hanging down so that their fingertips remained just above the floor.

Domi's face turned to face him first, and Kane saw that her eyes were closed. There was blood on both of her legs and across her belly, a cut on her arm. The others had suffered similarly, Kane saw, his gaze flicking from one figure to the next to the next, trying to process everything with the emotionless clarity of the Magistrate.

Kane took a step into the room, seeing other things hanging behind these three, some people, some animals, mutated things he did not even have a name for. It was a walk-in refrigerator, designed to store food enough for all the personnel who might be stationed at a redoubt of this size. Some of the figures were incomplete, people with arms and legs missing, chunks of their torso removed...eaten? There were shelves along the walls, more shelving units to the rear of the room, with white tiled floors and ceiling and walls.

"What happened to you?" Kane whispered, reaching gently for Domi where she hung like the Hanged Man on the Tarot Card. The smell he had detected earlier was coming from her, or at least from the room, the sickly sweet smell of meat decomposing. He was standing in a meat locker, a vast meat locker where people were stored before...

Before what?

Kane could imagine some things—strange rituals, cannibalism. He had witnessed some truly disturbing behavior during his lifetime as a Magistrate and a Cerberus operative. His eyes flicked for a moment to the other bodies in the room, human and animal, the ones with pieces missing, neatly sawn off while the rest of the meat was left to hang and to twist.

Sickened, he stepped from the refrigerator and made his way through the kitchen area and out into the canteen, leaving the refrigerator's door open behind him. "Baptiste," he called, keeping his voice low. "You need to see this."

Brigid was leaning against a table at the far end of the room, close to the entrance, her TP-9 held ready in a steady grip. "What is it?" she asked without turning her head.

"I've found CAT Beta," Kane said.

WAITING AT THE FAR end of the corridor, Grant had heard the sudden noise of a motor at about the same time that Brigid had disappeared through the canteen doorway after Kane. He turned, searching for the source of the noise, the Copperhead ready in one hand while the other still clutched Domi's knife.

It was the elevator, he realized after a moment. The damn thing was working, or it sounded as if it was—the whirring was coming from the shaft.

Grant quietly paced across to the elevator, its doors sealed, glancing just once behind him to make sure nothing was coming from the motor pool.

Then he pressed his ear to the doors, listening to the sound. It was definitely coming from the shaft, a faint humming that echoed up its enclosed length as the elevator ascended. He might not have even noticed it had the redoubt not been so deathly quiet up until now.

BRIGID JOINED KANE in the kitchen area, staring into the walk-in refrigeration unit.

Brigid crossed the tiled room and pressed her hand to Domi's face, feeling the icy chill. "They're frozen," she stated.

"Yeah," Kane agreed. "We need to get them down from there and get everyone out of here."

Brigid pushed a stray lock of red-gold hair from her face, frowning with concern. "What are they doing here?" she asked. "How did they get here?"

"Something got them," Kane explained. "See the wounds—" he pointed "—here and here. Something in this redoubt attacked them."

"But why hold them here?" Brigid asked.

"Prison," Kane said, "or food store. Look around you. I suspect the latter."

Brigid's eyes flicked to the corners of the room, took in the state of the carcasses hanging from the ceiling hooks. "Damn," she muttered. "This is sick, Kane. Sick."

Kane grasped the chain from which Domi was suspended, pulling it closer and causing her body to sway where it hung. "Let's just get them down."

As he spoke, Grant's voice hissed from somewhere just beyond the threshold of the kitchen, calling to Kane and Brigid in a low tone.

"Guys, we've got company. Nasty company."

Less than a minute earlier, Grant had stepped away from the elevator and considered calling for Kane and Brigid to join him before realizing there would not be time. Swiftly, he trotted backward down the corridor, keeping his gun pointed at the elevator doors as he skipped to the open doorway where he had seen Brigid and Kane disappear.

He had almost reached it when the sound came to an abrupt halt, accompanied by a thump like a drumbeat in an echoing hall. A moment later, the twin doors to the elevator began to part, flooding light into the water-logged corridor. The light flooded across the darkness, casting a widening rectangle of luminescence across the floor where it spilled. And framed in that widening rectangle were two silhouettes.

One was a low, boxy shape with a head—someone in a wheelchair, Grant realized.

The other was a tall and broad-shouldered humanoid figure with the added protrusion of a thick, serpentine tail. *Annunaki*.

Grant ducked into the open doorway to the cafeteria just as the figure emerged from the elevator, glancing behind him to see who was in the room.

It was empty, but there was a light—showing as a firework glare on his night lenses—emanating from another open doorway in the farthest corner of the room. The doorway was located beside a serving hatch, two long, twenty-four-seater tables between it and Grant.

"Guys, we've got company," Grant hissed, hurrying back toward the illuminated doorway. "Nasty company."

KI HAD AWOKEN feeling ravenous.

She emerged from the elevator with Papa Hurbon at her side, ducking the frame as she strode into the waterlogged corridor. Hurbon followed, wheeling forward with his hands on the rims of his chair's wheels, pushing with a little effort against the water that slowed his progress.

It was dark here, dark as pitch beyond the little rectangle of light cast by the open doors to the elevator. Hurbon stopped just beyond the lip of the elevator doors, reached into his bag for a candle.

Despite the darkness, Ki saw everything in vibrant tones through her reptilian eyes, well beyond the reach of the rectangle of illumination spilling from the elevator cage.

Behind her, Hurbon lit his candle, casting a tiny circle of flickering light around himself. He watched in awe as Ki walked forward. She was magnificent, graceful and sleek, a sight to behold.

Ki was older than most Annunaki, mother to Enlil and his fractious siblings. She was considered the first female of the Annunaki, who had walked the Earth with her brother and consort, Anu, long before the family had arrived. Anu had loved her so much that he had named the planet after her, dedicating it to her as a lover's gift.

She stood reborn, eight feet in height, naked, her scaled skin like armor plate rippling across the muscles of her newly reborn body. Her scales were luminous blue, the color of the ocean in sunlight, almost translucent in its purity. A great spiny crest protruded from

her skull, seven sharp spikes poking in a radiant circle
that began roughly two inches above her brow. Beneath
those pointed spines, her heavy brow protruded down
to her eyes, which were the brilliant, deep orange of
sunset in the tropics, and beneath that her face was almost flat, her mouth a cruel slash across the scaled skin.

Her body was muscular, and each step she took gave
the impression of a giant moving with a heaviness and
determined balance to every stride. Behind her, a prehensile tail swished and curled, wrapping itself momentarily around her left leg before unlooping and
swinging free once again, assisting her balance as she
strode down the corridor in search of the apekin meal
located close by.

Ki was reborn, walking on Earth for the first time in
millennia. Ki was reborn and she was hungry.

And if she had any inkling that she had once been
Nathalie, had once worked with and admired Papa Hurbon, houngan of the Louisiana *société*, then that thought
had been lost once the transformation had taken hold.
That transformation had burned through the organic
building blocks that the woman's shell had provided,
using them like fuel to create this majestic and graceful creature.

"This way," Hurbon urged, casting the light of the
candle ahead of him as he wheeled through the water,
leaving twin trails of water in his wake. Ki remained a
few paces ahead, hungry for food and for experience,
new experience after all those millennia locked away
as a sliver of DNA coding.

"TWO OF THEM, I think," Grant explained from the doorway to the kitchens as he slipped Domi's knife into his

belt. "Only saw their shadows. One's in a wheelchair, the other looks Annunaki."

"The wheelchair will be Papa Hurbon," Brigid said.

Kane shot her a sideways glance. "You're jumping to conclusions," he said, warningly.

"Fits the facts," Brigid insisted. "Location and the voodoo ephemera. If I'm wrong, I owe you a meal."

Grant hurried back to the cafeteria doorway, hefting the Copperhead in both hands. He had put the rifle down—its weight would only slow him here and its long-range advantages became hindrances in close quarters. He could see flickering light emanating from the open doorway, getting slowly brighter as it moved closer. He could hear the splash of water, too, as whoever it was drew near.

Kane and Brigid followed, moving swiftly out of the food-preparation area and into the cafeteria. As Kane emerged from the kitchens, the first figure came through the open doorway at the far end, beyond the two long tables laid out with their sad, skeletal occupants.

The Annunaki stood in the doorway, her skin an almost luminous blue in the flicker of the candlelight that followed. Grant raised his Copperhead, aiming through the laser sight. The Annunaki turned its head, glaring at him with a piercing stare. It had seen him.

"Apekin," the Annunaki spat in a mellifluous duotonal voice that sounded as if it were being spoken through a spirit flute. "I've been waiting for a hot meal longer than your feeble mind can comprehend."

"Hot meal?" Grant growled in response. "Try hot lead!" He raised the barrel of his Copperhead a half inch, squeezed the trigger and sent a bullet just over the Annunaki's head.

At that moment, Papa Hurbon wheeled himself to

the doorway, just as Grant's bullet streaked past in a whistle of parting air. "What th—?" he began, dodging back so swiftly that he almost tipped.

"Hurbon!" Kane called, recognizing the wheelchair-bound houngan where he was framed in his night-lensed vision. "What's going on here? What did you do?"

Hurbon wheeled himself away from the doorway in retreat, rapidly disappearing from view.

As Hurbon wheeled back, the blue-scaled Annunaki leaped at Grant, clambering over the furniture in the room with bared teeth.

It was *so* on!

Chapter 24

Grant squeezed the Copperhead's trigger, sending a swift burst of fire toward the approaching Annunaki as she rushed toward him. A line of 4.85 mm steel-jacketed slugs spit from the subgun's muzzle, striking against the Annunaki's hard skin with momentary flares of metal on armored flesh. The Annunaki ignored them, kept coming for Grant with her arms reaching forward.

Grant ducked as the first grasping hand reached for him, fired again sending a second burst of bullets at the reptilian creature. Once again the bullets struck uselessly against her shell, dancing away in lethal ricochets.

Behind Grant, Kane and Brigid were providing covering fire, splitting up as they directed a cross fire of bullets at the reborn Annunaki.

"Who is that?" Kane shouted over the loud reports of gunfire.

Brigid, whose eidetic memory made her the expert on such matters, cursed. "I don't know," she admitted. "No one I've ever seen before."

Kane held down the trigger of his Sin Eater, launching a cluster of 9 mm bullets across the room at the blue-scaled Annunaki as she reached again for Grant's neck. "Fair enough," he growled. "Appreciate there aren't many photos of the Annunaki, what with them first being here however many millenniums ago it was!"

"Millennia," Brigid corrected automatically, her own

blaster sending bullet after bullet at the Annunaki figure as she scrambled across the room. "Kane—someone needs to go after Papa Hurbon! He's tied into this somehow, and if he has one pet Annunaki, then chances are he could have another!"

The Annunaki female roared as she heard this, and for a moment the Cerberus warriors wondered if their bullets had actually wounded her through her impenetrable scale hide. "Pet? Be careful whom you call a pet, apekin girl. Ki is no one's pet."

"Key?" Grant muttered, trying to place the name.

Brigid recognized it, racked her brains for just a nanosecond to realize who Ki was and what threat she represented. As the name flashed through her mind, she recalled with dread who Ki had been in ancient Sumerian myth. "Kane, Grant—Ki is the mother of all Annunaki!" she shouted to her colleagues.

"I thought that was *Tiamat*," Kane said as he rattled off another shot from his Sin Eater, scrambling over a table to get a better bead on his target.

"*Tiamat* held the genetic codes," Brigid summarized, "but Ki was like the firstborn, the most ancient of the Annunaki along with her consort, Anu."

Ki had been reaching between chairs for Grant where he had rolled beneath a table, his Copperhead still booming at her. But as Brigid spoke, her words carrying over the hubbub of gun reports, Ki halted and looked up, her luminous eyes meeting with Brigid's. "What do you know of my brother, apekin?" she growled, her forked tongue darting between sharklike teeth.

"Brother?" Kane muttered. "I thought you said—"

Brigid shot Kane a look. "The legends contradict themselves. Sometimes she's consort, sometimes sister and sometimes just a place—Earth."

Striding across the table's top, Ki stalked toward Brigid, ducking her head to avoid hitting it against the ceiling. "Anu named the planet after me," she stated in her strange duotonal voice. "It was mine—it's always been mine. You apekin are just tenants whose lease is about to expire."

As Ki moved away from him, Grant slipped out from under the table, drawing himself up from the watery floor and taking that moment to reload his Copperhead with a fresh clip. Kane caught his eye and made a gesture, running the index finger of his free hand along his nose for just a second in the old 1 percent salute. The salute was something the two men shared, a little superstition dating back to their Magistrate days, and it referred to the 1 percent margin for the unexpected to ruin an op, no matter how controlled it seemed. On this occasion, Kane hoped that Grant realized that the 1 percent in question was not their chance of success, but that of the reborn Annunaki. Because Kane had a plan.

Grant watched as Kane gave a signal they both recognized and, following his partner's lead, he reached into his coat pocket for two tiny earplugs he kept there for just such an occasion.

Brigid had rattled off several bursts of fire from her TP-9, watched in increasing frustration as the bullets skimmed the surface of the Annunaki's body and were lost in the darkness of the room. She backed farther away as Ki strode toward her, and suddenly her back was pressed against the wall where the shuttered serving hatch was located. Ki loomed before her, climbing down from the table and sniffing the air.

"All these years and apekin still smell the same," she said, licking her lips with her writhing, forked tongue. "I wonder, do you taste the same, too?"

But as Ki reached for Brigid, there came an almighty explosion, so bright that it lit the room. The brilliance was accompanied by a burst of noise like clashing cymbals, the whole thing seemingly feet away from where Ki stood. The Annunaki fell back, clutching at her eyes where the explosion had momentarily blinded her, hissing with pained irritation.

The explosion had been caused by a weapon that the Cerberus warriors habitually carried in their arsenal. Called a flashbang, the device was similar in size and shape to a palm-sized ball bearing, and was designed as a nonlethal part of the standard Cerberus field-mission equipment. As its name suggested, the flashbang brought an almighty flash of light and noise when it was triggered, similar to a genuine explosive being set off, only the flashbang did no damage. As such, it was used by the Cerberus personnel to confuse and disorient opponents—be they human or a reborn space goddess.

In the explosion's wake, Brigid rocked in place, dazzled by the sudden burst of sound and light. But Kane had thrown the device and he and Grant had been prepared, using earplugs and turning away from the brilliance as the flashbang went off.

"Come on, Baptiste," Kane said, grabbing his partner's arm. "The bitch here wants to eat, so we'll go find her something to eat."

Kane guided Brigid through the doorway and into the kitchen area while Ki continued to writhe where she stood, swiping at the patterns that danced across her eyes. Ki had incredible night vision, which meant that hunting her prey in the darkness had been easy, but it also left her especially vulnerable to the dazzling effects of the flashbang.

Grant, meanwhile, made his way back through the

room, skipping in a backward run through the water that pooled on the floor, his Copperhead trained on Ki's staggering form. He worked the Copperhead's trigger, firing round after round into the great Annunaki form, using the laser target to ensure he struck the same exact spot again and again.

Ki wailed at the force of those impacts, swaying in place as she blinked back the afterimage of the explosion. Inevitably, she stepped away from the source of the attack, stumbling against the wall where the shuttered counter was located. Her eyes opened wider and her expression fixed in a grimace of anger as her vision returned. Ki eyed Grant with pure hatred burning behind her eyes.

"Check your privilege, apekin," she shrieked as she took a pace toward Grant where he stood on the far side of one of the long dining tables.

Grant seized the opportunity, triggering his own flashbang and throwing it toward the reborn Annunaki. The silver sphere arced through the air, its short timer counting down to explosion as Grant turned his head away.

Then—

Boom!

The flashbang ignited in a burst of noise and light, rocking the cutlery that had waited in drawers for two hundred years.

Ki stumbled back again, shrieking in pain as the blinding force of the explosion seared her eyes. The shutters clanged as her muscular body struck against them, rattling in their treads.

Grant glanced back, located his target and threw another flashbang right at her head, firing his Copperhead to cover the toss. "One for luck," he muttered as the flashbang sailed through the air toward its target.

There was another explosion, this one just two feet from Ki's blue-scaled face and accompanied just a fraction of a second later by the pained shriek of the Annunaki goddess.

Ki clawed back, away from the brilliance, trying to get away from the pain it brought. Powerful muscles worked, ripping at the thin metal shutter into the kitchen, tearing it apart like tissue paper.

Grant fired again, sending another burst of 4.85 mm bullets at the retreating Annunaki as she clambered blindly through the revealed serving area, dropping awkwardly over the sill.

She's all yours, Grant thought as the lizard creature disappeared from view. He would have stayed, provided back up, but Brigid had made it clear that someone needed to keep track of Papa Hurbon before the demented voodun priest unleashed something else. Grant figured he was that someone.

Without pause, Grant ran for the exit to the cafeteria, booted feet splashing in the layer of dark, swirling water that carpeted the floor.

THROUGH THE AUGMENTED sight provided by their night lenses, Kane and Brigid saw Ki come stumbling through the hatch in the wall. She moved without grace now, flopping and falling over the sill and worktop behind, limbs tangling in the steam-tray units that had been designed to hold hot food while it was being served to the soldiers who had once operated this base.

Grant had bought them a precious few seconds in which Kane and Brigid had been able to pull down their colleagues from the meat locker, dragging them out into the open area of the kitchen itself. Kane had just been hefting Sela Sinclair's body from the open refrigerator when Brigid had alerted him with a hiss.

"Incoming," she had said before ducking down out of sight.

Now Kane placed Sinclair's frozen body gently down behind a freestanding, island-style worktop, his eyes watching the reptilian figure come barreling through the ruined shutter. As Kane let go of Sinclair, leaving her beside the other two members of CAT Beta, he commanded his Sin Eater back into his hand with a familiar flinch of his wrist tendons. The gun appeared in his palm in a fraction of a second, and Kane was already rising from behind the counter with the weapon poised before him, index finger locking on the trigger.

"Hey, snake face." Kane shouted as the Sin Eater bucked in his hand, sending a stream of 9 mm slugs at Ki's rising form. "How's it feel to meet a meal that fights back?"

Ki rose from the floor, slipping a little in the slick blanket of water there as she tried to regain her balance before finally standing, her head hunched forward. "Apekin," she said, "I'm going to eat you alive—*slowly*."

"Talk is cheap," Kane said. "Why don't you come get me, Your Highness?"

Ki took a step forward, and as she did Kane took a step back, causing Ki to laugh. "You're scared," she said, between guffaws.

"Not me," Kane said, but as Ki took another step, he took one, too, away from her.

"Your body betrays you," Ki told him. "Weakling apekin. See the way you back away from what you know to be your destiny?"

Ki bared her teeth then, snapping them together as she took two more steps toward Kane. "I'll eat you bit by bit, leave you just enough so you stay alive for a very long time indeed, just enough life so you feel every bite."

Kane took another step back, his blaster held out before him. "I hope you choke," he said, sounding a little less sure of himself now.

Ki strode forward, butting against the worktop island with her hip, angrily knocking the things on its surface to the floor as she pushed herself aside.

Good, thought Kane, her vision's still impaired. That made things easier.

She was almost upon him now, and Kane was right at the threshold to the walk-in refrigerator, his heels against the sill of the illuminated open doorway. "Come on," he taunted. "Come get me."

Ki pounced, leaping the last five feet to where Kane waited, her feet rising off the ground. Kane scrambled back in that same instant, turning around and shooting behind him, sending a continuous stream of bullets at the blue-scaled Annunaki as she charged toward him. The bullets struck her hide armor, clanging against the scales with momentary flashes like fireworks, before being cast away in all directions.

Ki was beyond the threshold now, into the illuminated space, her feet striking the floor of the refrigerator as she continued to scramble after Kane. Kane leaped, reaching high with his left hand, grabbed the hook-and-chain that Edwards had been hanging from barely a minute earlier. As Ki grabbed for Kane, he swung on the chain, throwing himself out of her reach by the narrowest of margins. Behind him, he heard the material of his jacket tear as Ki caught it with the hook-like talons of her claws.

Still hanging in the air, Kane twisted, shifting his

weight so that he rotated, locking the Sin Eater's trigger down and sending a vicious storm of bullets at his opponent.

Ki laughed the bullets off, taking just a moment to flick some aside as they struck against her torso. Ricochets hurtled across the locker, striking the tiled walls with clangs and thuds. Several bullets had embedded themselves in her superhard skin, but it was the work of just a moment to pluck them out with a claw before letting them drop to the ground.

As Ki continued to stride toward him in the confines of the large refrigeration unit, Kane felt something hit him—hard! He let go of the hook and chain and went flying toward the side of the room. He landed awkwardly, rolling into a freestanding shelving unit before he brought himself back to his feet.

Ki was on Kane then, shoving him back against the floor so that he struck there hard on his back. Then she was looming over him, reaching out with lethally sharp claws, grasping for his face.

Kane fired again, the familiar wail of the Sin Eater echoing in the hard-walled confines of the room. Bullets lashed Ki across the face and shoulders, striking and flying away as they were repelled by her impenetrable scales.

And then Kane's Sin Eater clicked on empty.

Chapter 25

Papa Hurbon was waiting at the end of the corridor beside the elevator, listening to the sounds of gunfire as the battle played out within the cafeteria, watching as the brilliant white explosions rocked the room. It was taking too long, he realized. His goddess should have dispatched these interlopers by now—even hungry from rebirth, her strength should have been more than enough to repel their bullets and to finish them. Plus, she had the instincts, somewhere deep down, of Nathalie, didn't she? And Nathalie had been deadly.

It was hard to see in the darkness, as the lightning stutter of the flashbangs provided the only illumination other than the candle Hurbon bore aloft in one hand. Every time one of those explosions went off, the brilliance seemed to draw his attention to the watery floor below him, its color a black sheen like oil. It was eerie, unnerving, seeing it in flashes like that, as if it were alive.

He heard another explosion, immediately followed by the rending of metal. But there was something else, another noise, getting louder—splashing, running footsteps. Someone was coming!

Hurbon reached to the call button beside him, found it by touch and jabbed it with his stubby index finger as he watched the entryway at the end of the corridor. The elevator's doors drew back beside the wheelchair-bound figure, as he waited to see if it was Ki who was approaching or someone else.

He saw the silhouette then, like a moving shadow, as a figure emerged from the cafeteria. Human. All too human.

"Hold it!" the man shouted in a voice like rumbling thunder.

Blast, thought Papa Hurbon, reaching for his wheel rims, those Cerberus people are tough.

He pivoted his wheelchair, turning himself into the elevator car and jabbing the floor button. The damn thing didn't go to the surface; in fact, this was as high as it went. Still, he had items down below, where he had set up his *djévo* and stored his many items of witchery... and a more traditional arsenal of weapons.

Hurbon watched the darkened corridor as the doors rocked closed, shuttering him alone in the elevator's cage. He had seen the Cerberus man come running down the corridor with a gun in his hand, heard the shot as he sent a bullet toward Hurbon and the elevator. The doors had closed on the bullet, blocking it with their heavy sheets of metal, accompanied by a noise like someone hitting his skull with a hammer. He was safe...for now.

Damn those Cerberus people. They weren't just tough, they were lucky as all get-out, too.

The elevator shuddered as it began its descent.

GRANT HAD COME hurtling out of the cafeteria like a freight train, leaping through the open doorway and out into the corridor beyond with his Copperhead sub-gun raised and ready. There were two ways of executing that exit—you could either go all sneaky-sneaky, checking for an ambush and trying to stay out of the line of fire; or you could come out like a lion from a cage and trust that the speed and surprise of the action would be enough to throw off a would-be attacker's aim. Grant chose the latter only because he knew time was at stake, that if he didn't get after Hurbon soon, the current situation could escalate from already bad to preposterously worse.

He recognized Papa Hurbon as soon as his night-vision lenses lit on him. Brigid was right anyway—she'd said it would be Hurbon in the wheelchair.

"Hold it!" Grant shouted, drawing a bead on Hurbon as a rectangle of light grew larger beside the man.

Hurbon was running, Grant guessed, making a break while he still could. That was like him. Grant had met the guy twice before and on both occasions he had shown himself to be a cowardly rat when the chips were down. He had lost his legs to his goddess, Ezili Coeur Noir, and then he had lost his consciousness to her, becoming shut-tered within a technologically enhanced hallucination created from his own desires. Grant had been forced to wake Hurbon from that dream, and the Cerberus crew had enlisted his help in stopping Ezili Coeur Noir and her sisters, each one in actuality a template fragment of the Annunaki goddess called Lilitu. Hurbon had helped, but he had remained away from the final battle, using mystical means to influence the fight itself.

And now here he was, large as life and operating from the same darned redoubt where CAT Alpha had trapped his wicked goddess. It was as if he had been playing them all along, as though he had wanted to be left with the trapped energies of the dead Annun-aki so that he could follow an agenda of his own. On the way here, Brigid had speculated that someone was using *Tiamat*'s teeth to distribute the genetic traits of the Annunaki, Grant recalled. Could it be that Hurbon was that someone, the person behind the widespread reemergence of the death gods of multiple religions? Yeah, Grant wouldn't put it past Hurbon for a second—in fact, it was right up his alley.

Grant thought all of this in the flash of a heartbeat, even as the doors to the elevator opened and the corpulent figure of Papa Hurbon wheeled himself inside. He was escaping, Grant saw, and there just wasn't time to worry about being delicate any longer, not with that Annunaki monster called Ki still on the loose.

Grant raised the Copperhead and fired, sending a single 4.85 mm bullet in Hurbon's direction just as the elevator doors slid closed. The doors closed on the bullet, snapping shut against it in a ringing clang of metal on metal.

"Dammit," Grant muttered, jogging along the corridor toward the sealed elevator. He looked at the display to the side of the call button, wiping away the mold that had clung there over the recent months since the redoubt had been opened up to the elements. The elevator was descending.

Grant glanced back at the cafeteria, detecting the familiar roar of Kane's Sin Eater amid the cacophony of crashes and booms. He could stay, help Kane and Brigid, or he could go after Hurbon and finish this.

With a determined jut of his jaw, Grant turned and strode to the heavy fire door that opened onto the stairwell, pushing it aside and hurrying within. A moment later he was scampering down the stairs, his footsteps echoing down the chasm of the stairwell shaft.

DEEP INSIDE THE REFRIGERATOR, Kane's Sin Eater had clicked on empty. Ki was on top of him, clawed hand reaching for his face, larger than any Annunaki that Kane had ever seen. He had fought bare-knuckle with Lilitu and with Enlil, but Ki was larger, more powerfully built. What was it Brigid had said? Ki was the first, the archetype, the mother of the whole line.

Ki's smile broadened as she saw fear cross Kane's expression, even though his eyes were still hidden behind the darkened lenses of the night-vision specs. Her breath smelt of rot, of the dryness of sleeping too long, of birth or rebirth.

"Your weapon is empty," Ki said, the duotonal words coming with a wash of rancid breath on Kane's face. "Poor, helpless apekin, too proud to bow to your master."

"Maybe I'm just too stupid," Kane replied. "Did you think of that?" As he spoke, Kane squirmed beneath her, pushing Ki away with the clenched fist of his free hand. Ki just laughed at the feeble attempt.

"I'll start with one of your eyes, apekin," she promised in her weird, duotonal voice, "but you'll still see and feel everything that follows. I'll leave you the other right up until you finally die." A droplet of saliva dripped from her salivating tongue onto the left lens of Kane's shades.

"I'm sure I'll appreciate that," Kane said sarcastically, pushing at Ki's forehead with his left fist to try to hold her back. Behind the dark lenses, he had closed his eyes, screwing them tightly shut. Then Kane activated the thing he had clenched in his left fist, opening his fingers to release it as it went off in his hand. It was a flashbang.

Suddenly, the refrigerator was filled with a brightness like the sun and its accompanying boom as the flashbang went off, right in front of Ki's face. She shrieked, the duotonal scream of a creature whose existence crossed the boundaries of dimensions, a scream heard in places far beyond the confines of the underground redoubt.

Ki reared back, blinded by the cruel proximity of the explosive charge. Her ears were ringing, too, the reverberation of the explosion like a tolling bell inside her head.

As Ki's weight shifted momentarily from him, Kane pulled himself aside, rolling over and scrambling free on hands and knees. Like a sprinter at the starting blocks, he got to his feet from that swiftly moving crawl, kept pushing himself forward as Ki flailed just a few feet behind him.

"Now, Baptiste!" Kane shouted. "Now!"

AT THE DOOR to the refrigerator, Brigid watched as Kane came sprinting toward her, the temporarily blinded form of Ki regathering herself to give chase. Brigid shoved the door, its cold metal heavy against her straining muscles, for it had never been designed to be shut quickly like this.

Legs pumping, Kane came running toward the gap in the door even as Brigid swung the heavy door, driving it with all her strength, both hands pressed against it, handle and front.

Kane leaped through the closing gap, still running as the door slammed shut and Brigid drew the handle up to lock it.

The kitchen area was plunged into sudden darkness once more, only the green activation light on the refrigerator glowed eerily in the gloom. Kane was still running, Sin Eater clutched in his right hand, dodging to avoid the central island worktop as he shed the burst of speed that had driven his body to freedom. Behind him, he heard something heavy slam against the far side of the refrigerator door, crashing against the metal.

Standing at the door, Brigid took a step back, alarmed by the sound as Ki came slamming against the door. It held, the chromium not showing so much as a dent, as the muscular Annunaki crashed powerfully against it from the inside. The refrigerator was designed to seal as tight as an airlock, trapping all of the cold inside.

There came another crash against the far side of the door, and another, but the door remained unmoved, holding in place without so much as a scuff showing on exterior surface.

Kane came over to join Brigid a moment later, his breathing racing from the adrenaline that had driven a shock through his system in the ultimate fight-or-flight response against one of humanity's very first monsters.

"You okay, *anam-chara*?" Brigid asked.

Kane smiled at the nickname, one he could not recall Brigid ever using out loud for him. It was a much-needed reminder of their relationship, of how they were soul friends throughout all of time, locked together in a clinch that existed somewhere much deeper than the physical plane. "Yeah," he said between hurried breaths.

Then Kane reached forward for the control panel beside the green indicator light, seeing it clearly through the electrochemical polymer lenses of his night-vision spectacles. He worked the controls for a moment, adjusting the temperature in the refrigerator with a twist of a dial and a double tap of a button. *Deep freeze.*

"There," Kane said. "That ought to do it."

The refrigerator would freeze Ki in place, holding the lizard in the room until such time as Cerberus could return and deal with her more fully. Lizards were cold-blooded, they did not function well in freezing temperatures.

When Kane turned back, he saw that Brigid was staring at his chest. "What?" Kane asked, looking down to see what she was looking at.

His shadow suit had a two-inch rip across his left pectoral, the material puckered against his chest. The tiny window it left exposed Kane's bare chest beneath. There was something dark and metallic there, pressed against the flesh, round like a coin. Kane reached for it, but Brigid stopped him, grabbing him by the hand.

"Kane, you've been shot," she said.

Chapter 26

"What?" Kane repeated, trying to process what Brigid meant even as the hammering against the refrigerator's metal door continued just a foot away.

"It's a bullet," Brigid said. "Your shadow suit must have reduced its velocity, but not enough to stop it going in."

Brigid could see better than he could, Kane acknowledged with emotional detachment, had a better angle on what had happened. He thought back, remembering something striking against his chest, forcing him to let go of the hook-and-chain where he had originally intended to use one of the same to hook Ki.

"I've been hit," Kane said, echoing Brigid's words from just a few moments before. He stared at the bullet, his chin pressed against his chest.

"How do you feel?" Brigid asked, the concern obvious in her voice.

"Bruised, kind of," Kane said after a moment's thought. "The adrenaline's wearing off now, I think that and the shadow suit helped blunt the pain."

"We need to get it out, get you proper medical assistance," Brigid told him.

But Kane was shaking his head. "Grant will need our help," he said. "This whole thing isn't over till it's over."

"It looks like it's missed your heart, but we don't

know what the bullet's pressing against," Brigid said doubtfully.

"It'll wait," Kane assured her.

"What if it can't?" Brigid told him. "I'm not a doctor, Kane—"

"It'll wait because it has to, Baptiste," Kane told her, his voice firm. "Now, let's go find Hurbon and see what other monsters he's been hiding down here."

Without waiting, Kane strode toward the entryway that led into the cafeteria. He halted in the doorway, turning his head back to Brigid. "Baptiste? You coming?"

She nodded and began to trot after him. "You know, Kane, we always fought the Annunaki because we believe they restricted humanity's free will, forcing us into a submissive position."

"Yeah," Kane acknowledged, leading the way through the bullet-marked cafeteria, reloading his Sin Eater as he walked.

"Well, I just realized that they don't have anything on you," Brigid teased, "you hard-assed bastard."

Kane turned to her and smiled, offering a snort of laughter as his reply.

Brigid frowned at him. "Doesn't mean you should go catching any more bullets, though," she admonished as they furtively made their way toward the entrance of the cafeteria to try to locate Grant.

GRANT SCURRIED DOWN the stairwell, listening to the muffled groan of the elevator mechanism as it lowered the car carrying Hurbon through the redoubt.

He knew the redoubt—kind of. He had been here roughly two years before, when an incursion had occurred that had been flagged by the Cerberus mainframe. That time, he and his colleagues, Kane and Brigid, had checked every floor, searching for the source of the incursion before locating it in a laboratory that branched off from the motor pool.

He thought back, trying to picture what they had found on each level. Storage, living quarters, sleeping quarters, some computer rooms that had fallen into disrepair, some ancient food stores. Not much worth hanging around for.

The lowest level had been the only point of interest. Here they had emerged from the facility's mattrans chamber, and had discovered it was powered by an experimental cold-fusion generator located on the same level. If anyone was setting up anything here, Grant guessed it would be in that lowest subbasement level.

He took the stairs two at a time, still listening for the whine of the elevator as it finally came to a halt. Even if he had not been listening out for it, Grant could not have missed the halt—it was accompanied by the loud *ch-chunk* noise of the brakes activating and bringing the car to a stop in the shaft next to the stairwell.

Grant was one floor above the lowest level by then, and he vaulted the banister and leaped down to the next flight of stairs, moving swiftly toward the door there. A sign had been painted on the wall identifying the floor and area. It read "BO55 Level."

There was a small window in the door made from reinforced glass with a familiar crisscross pattern of wire running through it. Grant checked the window, wary of attack.

Outside, the corridor was cast in a soft, red glow. Papa Hurbon was just exiting the elevator to Grant's left, the back of his wheelchair retreating from Grant as he wheeled down the corridor, away from the yellow rectangle of illumination spilling from the open elevator doors.

There were other things illuminating the corridor, candles in jars and on stands, one flickering inside the blackened face of a human skull like some ghastly jack-o'-lantern. And the whole thing was cast in a soft redness that emanated from somewhere beyond the window's frame.

Grant cursed as Hurbon disappeared from sight, moving beyond the reach of the window. The Cerberus warrior waited a moment, listening. Then, quietly, he pulled open the door and stepped out into the red corridor.

Hurbon had already disappeared, but there were two figures standing at the far end of the corridor, lit by the flickering candles and a square of redness that seemed almost organic in nature, as if they were all inside a body. The men were dark skinned and bare chested, and they stood perfectly still. They momentarily reminded Grant of the men who had functioned as Ereshkigal's Terror Priests in Spain.

Grant raised his Copperhead, training it on them so that they could see it. "Hands where I can see them, and no sudden moves," he instructed.

The two figures ignored him, standing perfectly still like statues. To their side, Grant saw the redness seemed to be emanating from a doorway, though from this distance and this angle it was hard to make out quite what was causing it. It cast the scene in a red wash like blood on teeth.

Grant jogged the blaster a little, raising it to draw attention to it. "I ain't kidding, guys," he said. "Hands up high, right now."

"They won't obey you," Hurbon's voice called, emanating from somewhere nearby.

"Papa Hurbon," Grant called in response, "whatever is going on down here it needs to stop."

"Is that so, Mr. Grant of Cerberus?" Hurbon replied from wherever he had hidden. The voice was emanating from somewhere close to the two figures who stood sentry in the bloodred corridor.

With his blaster still trained on the two men, Grant paced forward. "We've been following the trail of chaos you left right across the globe," he said, raising his voice. "Spain, Italy, the Congo. That was you, wasn't it?"

"Experiments," came the response. "I'm a medicine man, Grant, you know that. Medicines need to be tested, refined. That was all it was. Surely you don't resent me for that."

"People died," Grant said, pacing slowly along the corridor, still watching the two bare-chested figures who stood statue still. "A lot of people. Hundreds.

"And worse," Grant added, "some were killed just so they would walk again, dead soldiers brought back to life."

"The difference between life and death is far less than most people outside of the path acknowledge," Hurbon said, a throaty chuckle to his words.

Grant was close to the motionless men, still watching them cautiously.

"But then, you never walked the path, did you, Mr. Grant?" Hurbon added.

The two static figures suddenly moved, lunging for Grant and grabbing the end of his weapon in a flash. Grant pulled the trigger as the blaster was yanked from his grasp and, for a moment, propellant lit the red corridor as Grant went dancing backward. In that momentary flash, Grant saw the men's eyes clearly for the first time—they were pure white, like the eyes of a marble statue.

Chapter 27

Zombies! Grant realized as the two men piled on top of him in the tight confines of the candlelit corridor.

Not the shambling undead, risen-from-the-grave types, but the other kind, living men whose wills had been drained through the use of drugs and herbs. It was an old voodoo trick, sapping the will of the living, leaving them in an impressionable haze where they would follow a houngan's orders like the hypnotized volunteers at a magician's show.

One of the figures shoved Grant hard—harder in fact than he would have expected even given the impressive muscular on show across the man's naked torso—as if he had no sense of self-preservation, just the desire to knock his enemy back.

Grant staggered backward, only remaining upright by striking against the wall at his rear. He watched as the other man, the one who had grabbed his blaster, threw the Copperhead dismissively aside. The weapon clattered to the floor, kicking up water from a puddle that had accumulated there.

Grant was a highly trained combatant; even a momentary advantage for an enemy was short-lived unless they knew how to press that advantage. Grant rolled his shoulders as his enemy came for him again, swung a punch at White Eyes's jaw that crossed the space between them like a rocket. The man's head whipped back under the impact as Grant's fist connected, a crunch of crushed gristle or bone accompanying the strike. But the man did not so much as grunt, just flopped back with a stagger, falling against the wall.

Grant moved forward, closing in on his second attacker. They had caught Grant unawares, as he had let his guard down for just that fraction of a second as he spoke with Hurbon. But he was a trained hard-contact Magistrate and they were just civilians. Putting them out of commission, even if they had no sense of pain or self-preservation, would be a matter of a few seconds, not minutes.

The second man strode toward Grant, arms outstretched, teeth catching the flickering candlelight as a wicked grin appeared on his face. He swung a punch, but Grant blocked it, overturned it and threw the man off balance so that he staggered wildly in a three-step spin.

Grant kicked out with his right leg, delivering a hard blow to the tottering figure's belly as he circled past. The man crumpled at the impact, doubling over himself like balsa wood struck by a sledgehammer.

Grant turned as his foe dropped to the deck, ready for the first man whom he sensed was rising. He was right—the man was just pulling himself up off the floor where he had gone slamming against the wall.

Grant leaped, delivering a double kick to the man's jaw, knocking his head so hard it spun. Grant landed with a splash of displaced water as his foe went down, the other man dropping to the floor, all the fight gone out of him.

Grant turned back to the end of the corridor, eyeing the doorway that loomed there. He saw now that the doorway had no door; instead the entrance was masked by a scarlet blanket draped across it, and through this

Grant could see the flicker of a candle, turning the material into a bloodred rectangle and casting the whole corridor in its scarlet hue. Hurbon had to be behind it, Grant knew. His hand twitched as he felt for the Sin Eater strapped against his wrist, drawing it into his palm. It was time to finish this.

THREE FLOORS ABOVE, Brigid and Kane had left the waterlogged cafeteria and were carefully making their way along the corridor beyond.

"Grant?" Kane growled. "You out here?"

"The elevator's gone," Brigid pointed out. "You notice?"

Kane glanced at her and nodded. "Yeah. Someone's used it."

"Probably Papa Hurbon," Brigid proposed.

"Then either Grant went with him or he followed," Kane reasoned.

The two Cerberus warriors halted before the closed elevator doors. The muck had been brushed from the indicator panel, leaving a dirty smear. It showed the elevator was now at the lowest level of the redoubt.

"It only goes down," Kane said.

"Yes, I remember," Brigid said, nodding. She had used this elevator once before, as an exit from the laboratory that was located close by. Brigid never forgot anything.

Kane marched away from the elevator, down the wide corridor and into the motor pool, urging Brigid to stay back. At the doorway to the motor pool he stopped, surveying the waterlogged expanse for any sign of Grant or anyone else. There was no one, just the still-life image of sinking jeeps and rusted trucks, the bones of dead things drifting slowly in the water.

Kane turned back, joining Brigid at the elevator doors.

"Anything?" she asked.

Kane shook his head. "Let's go explore," he said, reaching for the heavy fire door that led to the stairwell. "I have a feeling Grant's going to need our help before all this is done with."

Together, the two warriors stepped into the stairwell and began trotting down its water-slick steps, heading for level BO55.

STANDING TO ONE SIDE of the doorway, Grant reached for the scarlet curtain with his left hand, his right thrusting the Sin Eater pistol out before him. Gently, he moved the drape a fraction of an inch, alert to an ambush or the sound of movement.

Nothing happened, and Grant let the curtain slip back to where it had been before.

Then, using the barrel of the Sin Eater, Grant pushed the bloodred drape again, shoving it swiftly aside.

The movement was met with the loud boom of a shotgun coupled with a wad of shot which cut through the swishing curtain before peppering the wall behind Grant in a radial smudge. Grant withdrew his Sin Eater even as the other weapon discharged.

Immediately after, the world seemed to drop into an incredible silence. Grant pressed his back hard against the wall.

"You try that again and I'll shoot you," Grant shouted. "Now put the weapon down."

"You think I'm afraid of you, Mr. Grant?" Hurbon shouted in reply from his hiding place behind the red drape.

"Don't matter to me either way, friend," Grant told

him. "Just put that hog leg down before things get any messier than they already are." He was a Magistrate now in his heart—a Mag dealing with a psychotic who needed to be disarmed. Funny how all that training came back to Grant when he really needed it, when the situation demanded it. Mags knew how to survive; his life was testament to that.

Grant waited, hoping that Hurbon would see reason. He gave him a few seconds to consider the proposition, then shouted again. "Look at it this way. You can keep running, keep hiding. Maybe you'll get a lucky shot in, maybe not. But your soldiers are dead, your pet monster's being dealt with, and there are three of us against the one of you. An' that's without factoring in our reinforcements."

"You think I'll run away?" Hurbon asked, a note of incredulity in his tone. "A man without legs don't run."

At the end of the corridor, unnoticed by Grant, the door to the stairwell opened again. Kane stealthily edged out from behind the frame, keeping his movements silent, scanning the corridor for signs of attack. As he did so, Grant made his move.

Grant swept the red curtain aside with his left hand, bringing his Sin Eater around with his right, entering the room sideways to make a smaller target.

He was met with the blast of a shotgun, loud in the confines of the small room of eccentricities, trinkets and charms, bones and swords and herbs in jars, all arranged in such a way as to create a kind of symmetry. Hurbon sat in the middle of the room, still in his wheelchair, resting the double-barreled shotgun across his lap where the blanket disguised his missing legs.

The first blast struck Grant in his side, clipping his left flank with such force that his own shot, fired at the moment he parted the curtain, was thrown off target.

Grant had made the decision out of necessity, to enter the *djévo* room and try to stop Hurbon. Hurbon would hide and fight until he was put down, the same as he had before. Who knew what the man had hidden in here, what he planned to use in his deranged quest to control the world or to destroy it?

Hurbon had played them the last time they had been here, worked his own agenda even as he gave the appearance of cooperating with them. While the Cerberus warriors had toiled to protect the world, Hurbon had been making his own plans, ones fueled by greed and selfishness.

Grant's first shot careened into a glass jar located on a freestanding shelf on the back wall. The jar shattered, spewing its contents—goose feathers—in all directions.

Hurbon retargeted in that instant, firing again, and this time catching Grant full in the torso. The shadow suit took some of the edge off, not much but some, and still Grant was flipped off his feet with the impact, head and shoulders lurching forward even as his legs went out from under him.

Grant slammed against the floor, jaw striking with a loud crunch that seemed to ring in his ears long after the blow itself.

As Grant drifted in and out of consciousness, Hurbon casually reloaded his shotgun.

IN THE CORRIDOR OUTSIDE, Kane and Brigid could hear the sounds of gunfire. They glanced at one another just once, a shared understanding flicking between them;

then they sprinted down the corridor toward the commotion. Better to face it than to hide from it.

Two strangers lay there in the water-slick corridor, bare chested and clearly unconscious, their bodies strewn at uncomfortable angles where they had fallen. Three feet beyond them was the doorway with the red drape, the wall opposite peppered with shot. As Kane and Brigid approached, they heard a second shotgun blast, and the wall was suddenly riddled with another burst of shot.

"Stay back," Kane warned, holding his arm out before Brigid.

"Grant has to be in there," Brigid told him. "What do we do?"

Kane's gaze switched from the torn drape and ruined wall to the Sin Eater in his hand. "We try not to get shot," he said, pushing forward.

Kane shoved the red curtain aside, bringing his Sin Eater to bear as he took in the *djévo* room where Hurbon was poised above Grant's fallen body, shotgun in hand.

Kane fired, and so did Hurbon, the voodoo houngan shifting his aim in an instant from Grant's head to the newcomer framed in the doorway.

The first blast sailed past Kane, spreading out as it reached for the swinging curtain before ruining the wall beyond.

Kane squeezed the Sin Eater's trigger at the same moment, targeting Hurbon's belly with a 9 mm bullet. The bullet struck Hurbon's left forearm where he balanced the shotgun, and Hurbon cried out in pain. Almost immediately, a spray of blood spurt from the wound.

Hurbon fired again, his second shot just as wild as his first, covering the doorway as Kane came rushing toward him. The wad of shot missed his body, but Kane felt something spike against his left shoulder and suddenly he found himself twisting in midstride, thrown off course by the force of the impact. At the same moment, Hurbon bit down hard on something he had hidden in his mouth, breaking it and swallowing.

Kane fired again, midstumble, and his bullet went wild, racing past Hurbon's bullet-shaped head and drilling into a mirror whose surface had been painted black. The mirror shattered in a cascade of breaking glass, shards crashing away from the frame like a waterfall.

The room was small and windowless, lit by candles. Kane could have reached Hurbon in three strides if the shotgun blast hadn't clipped him and thrown him sideways. Now Kane seemed to be falling instead, tripping over his own feet as he ran, crashing toward a wall draped with fabric the colors of bruised flesh. He fired again, launching another bullet out into the ether, trying to kill Hurbon as his vision reeled. The bullet went wide.

Then Kane was on Hurbon, smashing into the man in the wheelchair with the force of a jackhammer, knocking over the man, chair and all.

Hurbon blasted again, reflexively. The shot sprayed out into wall and ceiling, accompanied a moment later by the wispy flutters of shredded material and feathers where the drapes that had lined the wall were rent apart, a glass jar of trinkets exploding.

Kane had his hand on Hurbon's arm now, pressing it down to the floor so that the man could not use the shotgun again. Kane was on top of him, part of the awkward tangle of chair and man.

"Don't do it," Kane warned, bringing his Sin Eater around so that it pressed against Hurbon's skull.

Hurbon let go of his shotgun, allowing it to roll from

his lap. "You're too late, Kane," he said, his mouth frothing. "It's all over now."

As Hurbon spoke, Kane saw something change in his face, a kind of blistering across the skin like acid damage.

"What th—?" Kane spat.

The blistering moved like a wave, covering Papa Hurbon's skin in an unmistakable patina. Kane recognized it through his night-vision lenses, seen as a play of shadows in the flickering light of the candlelit room. Hurbon's skin was changing, turning into scales before his very eyes. Annunaki scales.

"What have you done?" Kane asked, lifting himself up and backing a little away, holding the Sin Eater against Hurbon's skull at arm's length now.

"Kane, what's happening?" Brigid asked from the doorway. She stood before the red curtain, holding it aside with one hand, her TP-9 semiautomatic clutched at the ready in the other.

"It's Hurbon," Kane said bewildered. "He did something. I don't know."

"He's changing," Brigid realized. "Becoming one of them—the Annunaki."

"No, he's not," Kane said, depressing the guardless trigger on his Sin Eater.

Boom!

Chapter 28

And, just like that, it was over. The 9 mm parabellum-jacketed bullet from Kane's blaster drilled through Papa Hurbon's skull as it began to change, ending the whole sorry saga with a bang.

In the immediate aftermath, Kane stood like an angel of death over Papa Hurbon as the voodoo priest's corpulent body sagged to the floor, the ephemeral thing we call life ejected from it in the space of a heartbeat. A hole had appeared on his skull, the left temple missing in a blood-ringed circular wound that went right through into his brain. There—gray matter and blood. Hurbon's brown eyes were wide in shock and something else…still clinging to that contempt he had felt for others even as he died. Hate was strong, but even it had to die eventually.

Kane kept his Sin Eater trained on the body as it keeled lifelessly to the deck.

A second later, Brigid hurried into the room and scooted to the floor beside Grant, checking him for life signs. She had seen Kane shoot people before, had shot people herself, when they had deserved it, when her life had been at stake. But there was something in what she had just seen, the nature of it, like an execution, that felt final and morally ambiguous all at once.

Grant was breathing, at least. He opened his eyes when Brigid touched his face, the trace of a smile appearing on his lips as if he had simply been woken from slumber. "Did…?" he began, but he was unable to put the question into words.

"It's over," Brigid assured him. "Papa Hurbon's dead."

"I think…" Grant began slowly, "I took…a bullet."

"I think you did," Brigid agreed, checking over Grant's flank and locating the buckshot that had embedded itself in his side, puckering the shadow suit in its wake. It felt rough where the ruined shadow suit had mingled with the torn skin, the whole thing lubricated with Grant's blood.

Kane was still watching the fallen form of Hurbon where he was crumpled on the floor. What had he seen in those last moments? Kane wondered.

"Baptiste?" Kane asked, his eyes still fixed on Hurbon's corpse. "You said he was changing, becoming an Annunaki. How is that even possible?"

Brigid looked up from where she was tending to Grant. "I don't know," Brigid said heavily. "We should go. Grant needs medical attention. So do you. So do Domi and Edwards and Sela."

Hurbon's face seemed to be more scaly now, becoming more reptilian as Kane watched. Or was that Kane's imagination? A trick of the flickering candlelight? Kane was spooked, and he was also coming down from the adrenaline high that had ended in killing a man. But things didn't seem right—blame it on his point-man sense, but things weren't how they should be.

"Kane!" Brigid called, snapping him back to the present. "I said we need to move Grant—"

"I c'n move," Grant insisted weakly.

"Yeah, and the others," Kane said. "I heard.

"What was Hurbon doing here?" he pressed without taking breath. "How did he start to change like that?"

Brigid looked up at Kane, exhaustion on her face.

"Organic technology," she said. "The trademark of the Annunaki. They don't create, they build on top of, like someone cladding a house. Hurbon must have used something that the Annunaki left."

"But what?" Kane asked, turning to Brigid.

"Kane," Brigid began, her tone warning.

"This is important, Baptiste," Kane insisted. "How did he—?"

At that moment, the once-dead form of Papa Hurbon moved, reaching for Kane's ankle and yanking the Cerberus warrior off his feet in a sudden movement.

Kane shouted with surprise as he found himself flopping across the floor. Then the hand still grasping his ankle threw him against the back wall, beside the shattered mirror, before it let him go. Kane flew the four feet through the air, smashed there in an untidy splay of arms and legs like a rag doll.

Brigid Baptiste had her TP-9 blaster in her hand in an instant, drawing a bead on Papa Hurbon where he still lay tangled in his toppled wheelchair, trapped beneath it. She squeezed the trigger, sending a 9 mm bullet in Hurbon's direction without so much as a warning.

The bullet hit Hurbon in his face—his cruelly scaled face—and stuck there. No pain showed on his grinning expression; no blood came; he just took it, smiling, as if a gnat had flown past and he had barely noticed its buzz.

Brigid watched wide-eyed as Hurbon's face seemed to alter. The scales were more pronounced now, their sheen no longer the color of human skin, but taking on a golden hue like honey. The edges of the scales were darker, a greenish color as if they had been dipped in duckweed.

And there was more, too: Hurbon's body was growing. Where he had been a double amputee before, now legs were growing, extending, fully formed and double jointed, accompanied by something else—a thick prehensile tail that grew from the base of his spine, tearing his clothes.

Brigid fired again, sending another bullet at Hurbon's face, and another and another at his torso, his heart. The bullets pinged against his new skin, hurtling away in all directions.

"You...were dead," Brigid spat, confused.

"I worship Ezili Coeur Noir," the dead thing that had been Papa Hurbon said in a duotonal voice, "loa of all things dead. Her proximity assures my success and your failure, apekin woman."

Ezili Coeur Noir. A voodoo spirit that had been reincarnated through Annunaki technology, forming from corrupted pieces of an Annunaki female called Lilitu. She had had the power to revive the dead and make them her slaves, and everything living that she touched was killed. Brigid, along with Kane and Grant, had helped incarcerate the woman right here, in this redoubt, forcing her component parts into the cold-fusion reactor that had provided power to the underground military complex. And when they had left, Brigid recalled, the lights had still been working—where now they were not.

Brigid's mind raced, trying to put the whole messed-up mystery together. If Papa Hurbon had somehow channeled the cold-fusion generator to hold Ezili Coeur Noir in one place, despite her dispersal, he could, conceivably, have held enough of her together to keep a level of consciousness operating. Even if it meant diverting power away from nonessential things, like lighting and ventilation. The elevator would have had to remain, of course—a man in a wheelchair needed that more than he needed light. And the refrigerator—cold storage food for the newborn gods.

The cold-fusion generator was nearby, Brigid remembered, on this floor. Close enough, maybe, to affect the status of things living and dead here.

Brigid fired again, scrambling back out of the room, through the scarlet curtain, its material pocked with holes where the shotgun had been discharged against it. Behind her, Papa Hurbon—or the thing he was rapidly becoming—shoved himself out of the tangle of the wheelchair, looming up on two muscular legs to a height of nine feet, head to toe. He bellowed an angry howl as Brigid's bullet struck, flicking at his torso where the bullet failed to leave a mark.

He was not Papa Hurbon now. Hurbon had been snorting the powdered bones of *Tiamat* the dragon ship for nine months, ever since Nathalie had come to him with her find. But that gestation period had needed something more, the fleck of tooth he had hidden in a gap in his own teeth, its substance carefully lanced over and over with a nail and hammer until it had been porous enough to break when he had bitten down on it. Now, the genetic download was running its course, and where Papa Hurbon had been, his body bent and crippled, now stood the first monster, the one who had come to Earth all those millennia ago—Anu.

Anu had arrived in a starship the last time, when he had discovered Earth and treated it as his own personal laboratory, its inhabitants nothing more than fodder for his experiments. This time he arrived via memory download, the genetic imprint of mind and body coded into every circuit, every cell of the dragon ship *Tiamat*. If Papa Hurbon had thought he could control this thing, this deific metamorphosis, then he had been an arrogant fool. Anu was Anu; nothing else could inhabit the space where he existed.

BRIGID RAN.

Through the corridor with its fallen guards and its candles and its pock-marked wall where Hurbon's shotgun had ruined it.

Past the elevator and the staircase, from where she and Kane and Grant had emerged to try to stop this madness.

Along another corridor, the walls painted with a red stripe to show the way in a color scheme that had been forgotten for two hundred years.

She ran and she ran and she ran, her mind racing faster and faster, trying to figure out what was going on and how she could possibly stop it.

There has to be a way, she told herself. There's always a way to stop it—isn't there?

IN THE *DJÉVO* ROOM, KANE dragged himself out of the tantalizing promise of unconsciousness. His side hurt, his right arm hurt, his head…he had hit the wall and lay there now, on the floor amid a scattering of fallen drapes and totems and jars, trying to make sense of where he was.

Behind Kane, something was stirring. Something large and reeking of amniotic fluid and newness. Something alien.

Kane turned, a stabbing pain rushing through his neck as strained muscles tried to function, his breath coming through his clenched teeth. An Annunaki stood behind him, large and saurian, larger than any that Kane had ever seen before. He had fought with Enlil and

Marduk and others, gone toe-to-toe with Ullikummis, whose surgical enhancements made him a towering pillar among his own kind. But this, an Annunaki of gold and green, was something else—something huge and muscular, as though its power was barely restrained.

Kane gathered his thoughts, commanding the Sin Eater back into his hand from its hidden sheath. He squeezed the trigger as Anu turned, the light of recognition appearing in the monster's bloodred eyes.

Blam! Blam! Blam! Blam! Blam! Blam!

And in that moment, Kane knew just who he was looking at!

Chapter 29

Anu.

The name was carved in stone tablets that dated back to the earliest days of humankind.

Anu, who had walked Earth's green hills and lush valleys back when the world was young, when humans had still cowered in the trees from saber-toothed tigers.

Anu, the Earth's first monster, the first of the Annunaki to descend upon her and abuse her children, her bounty.

Anu, who made Earthfall millennia ago, had seen a place where the crippling ennui of his race might be staved off and had adopted the planet as his own private playground.

Anu, who in those earliest days—alone, unimpeded by the others of his race—had taken a single man under his wing, observing and testing him, making him run mazes and jump hoops like the lab rat he was. And in all that time, Anu had never felt affection for the man, the apekin. He had felt something else, though, a surprised admiration that the apekin man could survive such hardships, endure such depravities as Anu heaped upon him, and still walk tall, still push himself to do better. The man had been a survivor, head and shoulders above his fellow apekin. And Anu had named him—

"CAIN!" THE WORD barked from Anu's mouth even as Kane's bullets drilled against his scaly skin, bouncing from its armor with all the effectiveness of raindrops on stone.

"Anu!" Kane snarled, knowing the monster's name without prompting. It was buried there, deep in his psyche, a name that his inner self had clung to for years without number, going back far beyond this life, or the one before that or the one before that. It went all the way back, through to the dawn of time and that first revelation when the golden god had arrived astride his dragon on the plains where Kane had been scrabbling for food. He had not been Kane then, of course—he had been simply "self," an unnamed collection of drives and needs; a survivor.

Kane and Brigid had been described as *anam-charas*, soul friends whose bond stretched beyond the boundaries of time. So, too, had it been with Kane and Anu, as their bond had stretched outside of the confines of time and body, much like the Annunaki themselves. Kane and Anu were *anam-naimhde*, enemies of the soul, whose paths were destined to cross but twice in all of eternity, once at the beginning—their first meeting— and once at their end, when they were destined to cross paths again.

Anu stalked forward, swiping away bullets as Kane pumped the trigger of his Sin Eater. The room was small, confined with ceilings too low for a creature of Anu's majesty. He was forced to hunch as he approached Kane, flying bullets scraping against his scaly hide with clangs like metal on metal.

The Annunaki remembered everything. Their memories were shared, transversing history and time, creating a racial memory that could be dipped into like a well and drawn from at any time. No matter how many births one of their number went through, he or she would always be able to remember the events leading to that moment, remember it from the point of view not only of himself but of the others of his race. Anu's memory of Cain was fire bright, as if he had only trained and tested the apekin yesterday; as if yesterday could have meaning to a creature of the multidimensions. The memory was bright, searing, because Cain had been his and his alone. Anu had owned him, tested and mistreated him, observed and punished him… dismissed him.

When Anu told the other Annunaki about Earth, the planet he had named Ki after his sister-consort, he had neglected to mention Cain. He had spoken of the apekin and how they broke so easily and how they had a streak of compassion that made them love beyond themselves, love the things that could be cruel to them, like Anu. But Cain had been his: his perfect subject, his *first*. He had taught Cain about survival, not through kindness but in lessons shot through with pain and challenge. Cain had to learn new things or he would die. Cain had been a survivor from the first, but it had taken Anu to show him murder, and how it was the ultimate path to survival.

Cain the first murderer, Anu the hand that held his puppet's strings.

Now, after all those millennia, Cain was here and he had turned on his master, his better, his *anam-namhaid*.

"HOW DO YOU defeat a foe who's conquered death?" Brigid asked herself as she hurried away from the *djévo* room with its imperfectly mirrored design. Was she panicking? Was that why she was running?

She could still hear the sounds of battle, eighty feet and two corridors away from where the combatants clashed. The echo of gunshots resounded through the redoubt's many warrens, the familiar note of Kane's Sin Eater. Which meant Kane was alive.

"Did I run?" Brigid asked herself, clinging to the bland gray wall. "Did I leave my friends?"

Why had she done that? It was something inside her, something primal. She had recognized the Annunaki thing that had assumed Papa Hurbon's place on the floor of the underground room, the gold scales with green edging like verdigris. She didn't know its name, not from sight alone, but somehow, deep down inside her, Brigid knew this monster.

It was as though she had fought it before. As though she had been fighting it all of her adult life. The thing from her nightmares, the ones she never remembered even with her eidetic memory—the ones her bedside notepad had waited in vain to record—which only served to make them scarier still. This dead thing had visited Earth before.

"I have to stop it," Brigid whispered, a plan forming in her mind. If Hurbon had conquered death to become this thing, then Brigid would have to find death's weakness. Which first meant finding the dead thing that lurked elsewhere in the forgotten redoubt, the thing with the heart of black.

"Coeur Noir," Brigid said in French as she turned back down the corridor toward a junction she had sprinted past moments before. *Black heart.*

ANU REACHED FOR CAIN/KANE, bullets butting against his impenetrable flesh as Kane held down the trigger of the Sin Eater where he stood by the wall. Anu's golden clawed hand swung out, slapping the Sin Eater's barrel and shoving Kane's hand against the wall in its wake.

Then Anu grasped Kane by the neck with his right hand, its taloned fingers enwrapping Kane's neck with ease. "You have always been a survivor, Cain," Anu said in a voice that echoed with the weight of centuries. "I admired that quality in you."

Kane struggled in the monster's grip as he was lifted from the floor. His feet hung above the deck now, and it was all he could do to kick against the wall behind him as he scrambled for purchase. "See…" Kane muttered through his strained windpipe, "that's…where… we…differ. I ain't…never…found an…Annunaki…I… did anything…but hate."

Anu thrust Kane against the wall, pushing him with such force that Kane's head was shoved hard into the paneling behind the drapes, striking with a hollow thump. Kane's vision blurred with the blow, and he could suddenly taste blood in his mouth.

"Admiration can still be present when there is hate, Cain," Anu informed his foe. "You apekin have such simple minds, perhaps you are unable to appreciate that."

Anu pushed again, stiffening his muscles and driving Kane against the wall with such force that it seemed as though Kane would go right through it. Kane felt himself being crushed, the bones of his spine grinding together as he was pushed harder and harder against that unrelenting barricade.

"Argh!" Kane screamed as the pain became interminable.

And then, incredibly, Anu screamed, too, screamed and let Kane drop as he lurched backward, his grip faltering on the man's throat. Kane dropped to the floor, landing hard on his backside as all the force that had been used to hold him up suddenly relented.

Anu had almost fallen, lurching sideways like a man caught on slippery ice. Recovering, Anu turned his head, bent over as he was in that claustrophobic little room. Something had bitten him, something sharp and vicious, tearing straight into the tendon of his right ankle with such cruel force that it had snapped right through. The dark-skinned apekin—Grant—was lying there, blood smeared down the torn clothing along his flank, a hard grin on his lips. In his hand, Anu saw, a weapon glinted—a knife with a six-inch serrated blade and the dark stain of blood marring its silvery sheen. *His* blood, Anu's, drawn from his leg when the apekin had cut his tendon.

"Domi says hello," Grant said as he plunged the knife a second time into Anu's flesh, its sharp point driving into the hard skin and biting deep into his left ankle.

Anu kicked out, whipping his leg up and out of the reach of the fallen Cerberus warrior, flipping Domi's combat knife away in a lightning streak of silver in the candlelight.

Grant rolled with the movement, dragged a little as the knife left his grip. Then Anu's foot was coming down again, stomping him in the face, once, twice, a third time. Grant was already down; he had barely mustered the energy to use the knife he had secreted when they had arrived at the redoubt. He could not hope to fight back against a larger and more powerful foe in the prime of physical fitness. So instead he sunk into the dream, the one where the pain was just a memory, where the story was already over.

KANE SAW HIS chance in that moment. He was wounded, light-headed, on the verge of collapse from exhaustion and the wounds he had taken. But he was a survivor, just as Anu had said, just as he had always been, and here and now this *anam-namhaid*—this soul enemy whose reappearance here spelled the arrival of an apocalypse unseen—was the only thing standing between himself and survival.

Kane leaped, forcing energy into his limbs, energy he didn't know he had, drawing on reserves of adrenaline that had waited an eternity for this moment. He was on Anu's back in an instant, clambering up the lumpy plates of the monster's spine, reaching for its skull. Kane's shadow suit had been ripped across his left pectoral, two inches of torn material flapping away from his body, threads puckered against the bloody wound in his chest. As he leaped he tore at that dangling strip, ripped it across his body in one almighty yank, unwrapping as much of the fantastically durable material as he possibly could, following the weave. Already weakened, it tore, turned from a two-inch rent to a long cord, an inch across and sixteen long, still connected to Kane's chest at its end like a second skin.

Kane whipped the cord-like strip of the shadow suit over Anu's head, dragging it down across the golden creature's throat. Then, with the two of them connected by the superstrong weave of the material, Kane dragged back with all of his might, using all the strength in his muscles, applying all of his weight, in one last-ditch attempt to strangle this monster and be done with him.

"Die, you abomination," Kane growled, his mouth close to Anu's bat-wing-like ear. "Die!"

Anu lurched back, the pressure of the superstrong material palpable on his throat, as if his flesh were being cut with another blade. He stomped out again, foot crashing down on Grant's shoulder as the Cerberus warrior lay helplessly before him.

Then Anu reached for the cord around his neck, trying to pull it free. His clawed fingers fidgeted and scrambled, trying to find a gap as Kane swung behind him from the cord. For his efforts, Kane just hung there, using his weight to keep the cord tight across the Annunaki's throat, kicking out with legs and feet to try to swing away from the monster.

Anu was dragged backward—a step; another—his head pulled up and back so that the spiny protrusions across his crown scraped against the low ceiling of the room. His hands tore at the nanofiber of the shadow suit strip, thick claws unable to find their way between its snug curve. The pressure was pulling at him, making it hard to draw breath in the pokey, candlelit room.

"Die!" Kane barked again, pulling on the cord so hard that Anu was almost bent backward with the weight.

Anu lurched, giving up on trying to remove the cord from his neck. Instead he reached behind him with golden claws, jabbing blindly at his enemy. He felt a hardness press against the claw of his thumb, then the hardness became softness as it was pierced by that sharp talon. Anu thrust the razor-sharp claw deeper, swiping it to the side as he penetrated his foe's flesh. Warm blood cascaded over his claw, running down his thumb, past the joint and onto his hand in a slick tongue of red.

"Not today," Anu muttered cruelly as he felt his foe sag, the life going out of Kane's body with the loss of blood.

Kane dropped then, crashing to the floor, the torn strip of his shadow suit still attached to Kane like an umbilical cord, fluttering from Anu's throat. There was blood across Kane's throat, blood down his chest and leaking across the floor of the mirrored room. Anu looked down at the apekin, watched the shallow rise and fall of his chest as it grew more shallow still.

They were *anam-naimhde*, these two—soul enemies through eternity. Two meetings was all they would ever have. Two meetings, one at the start and one that would be their last.

Anu stood over his fallen opponent, watching as Kane lay leaking blood and life over the floor of the *djévo* room. Beside him, Grant was curled up on himself, dark bruises coloring his already dark skin like shadows, blood trickling from his ear.

Anu turned, surveying the room and finding the door. He was alive, and there was a planet to conquer.

Chapter 30

Brigid Baptiste was hurrying down a bland-walled corridor of Redoubt Mike, on her way to where she remembered the cold-fusion generator was located, trying to figure out what she could possibly do. For a moment, she stopped, as she felt something pressing deep down inside her, like a pressure against her heart. Something had happened; something bad. She and Kane were tied together, *anam-charas*, soul friends through eternity. She had left him. The pain in her chest—was that sorrow? Or was it something else? It didn't matter now; nothing mattered but finding a way to stop Hurbon before this got any more out of hand.

Papa Hurbon had somehow found a cheat, Brigid realized, a way to bypass death and keep going, the same way that the Annunaki had time and again. But he was human, not Annunaki—his body should not be able to accept such forces. Only a hybrid could do that, which was why the barons had been bred for so many millennia to ensure there were suitable vessels ready when *Tiamat* unleashed the genetic download that saw nine members of the Annunaki pantheon reborn on Earth.

But Hurbon's new form was something different, as was the other one that they had trapped in the freezer—Ki. Hurbon appeared to have tapped something more monstrous than any Annunaki that Brigid had ever seen before.

He had been behind it all, Brigid realized as she stepped into the room where the cold-fusion generator was located. The unit hummed to itself, a neon blue brightness emanating from its single, porthole window, its reinforced glass marred with a cobweb of lines where something had tried to get out. Tried—and failed.

Hurbon had spread the Annunaki genetics somehow, using them in the same way that his mistress had done two years before, after the Annunaki wombship had been destroyed. Then, Lilitu had been reborn thanks to another genetic download, creating a new body to house her mind. But something had gone wrong in the transfer, something had corrupted, and instead of one body she had been born in several, her psyche fractured across each in a sequence of broken fragments. It had been enough to drive Lilitu insane, and it had taken the intervention of Cerberus with Papa Hurbon's assistance to force the multiple Lilitus together, trapping them in the cold-fusion generator where they would be entwined for eternity.

But there had been something else then, when Lilitu had been reborn—she had become a dead thing that moved and touched other dead things with her madness, who could bring the dead to life. Now Hurbon was tapping that same power, Brigid realized, his proximity to the cold-fusion generator here in the subbasement of the old redoubt ensured he was close enough to sidestep the finality of death itself—or perhaps go beyond it.

He must have used that bond, coupled with his own knowledge of mysticism—which was just science in another form—to bring the old data from *Tiamat* back to life, spreading it across the globe through the dragon's teeth. Except it hadn't worked. Ereshkigal, Charun, Vanth, Nergal, Ninurta—all of them had been made wrong, cast from faulty molds, brought only imperfectly to life, halfway houses between life and death. If they had movement, it had only been an illusion, the grave's worms moving beneath the flesh. They had strayed too far from the life giver, the death cheater, the one who had been named Ezili Coeur Noir, who had once been Lilitu. Without her influence, they had all failed, all corrupted and imploded and died…as much as a thing that had never been alive can die.

Brigid peered into the generator's portal, saw the ghost moving within, the hint of a pained face brushing past the cobwebbed glass. There was a way to stop this, a way to bring down Hurbon and his perfect cheat that allowed him to survive the impossible.

"Kill the dead," Brigid realized.

Anu strode from the *djévo* room, his scaled skin glistening in the flickering candlelight of the corridor beyond. His breath was hot, a hint of acid at the back of his throat—the taste of anticipation.

The torn drape swished back behind him as his tail curled into the gray-walled corridor behind his body, providing balance for legs regrown for the first time in uncounted millennia. Two figures lay out there in the corridor, two men with bare chests and dark skin, warrior types who had been roundly defeated as they had tried to protect the other him, the one called Hurbon. Hurbon was not even a memory now—Anu had no awareness of him, nor any interest in learning about him. Papa Hurbon had foolishly believed he could control the Annunaki inside, that he would be the master of the monster he unleashed by imbibing the genetic download from *Tiamat*'s crushed tooth. He had run the tests across the globe to work out the best way to do this, constantly refining the ingredients he added to the mix; for that was the way of the Bizango, the outlawed priests of the blackest voodoo arts—to mix components of their magic like a chef mixing a cake. But Hurbon had been a fool—he had spent nine months preparing for this moment, twice that time getting the pieces in place, obtaining the ingredients. But he had not reckoned for what the Annunaki really were, multidimensional things whose existence crossed space and time. To try to cage that in human form, to restrain that with a human mind, was grand folly.

Hurbon had imagined he would be trading up, swapping his tired, deformed body for one of immense power, an Annunaki god's that he could control. Instead, the body had obliterated him, deleting his consciousness like an unwanted computer file.

Anu's nostrils flared as he took in the scent of the corridor. It smelled of damp, spilled blood, mold.

There had been another, a female, he remembered. Red hair and eyes of green. Hadn't there been another like her, all those millennia ago, when he had tested Cain? Perhaps. All apekin seemed largely the same to the Annunaki, treating them as individuals was like trying to apply specific personality traits to ants.

Anu's stomach rumbled, reminding him of the trauma of rebirth, of how much energy it had taken to grow this form from the DNA shunt. He needed to eat.

The female apekin would provide a warm meal, he realized, nostrils twitching once again. He turned his head, tracing her scent in the abandoned corridor of death. She was close, he sensed.

Anu turned, his great lizard body a rippling flex of shimmering gold on muscle. He would follow his nose to the female apekin, and then he would dine.

IN THE ROOM housing the cold-fusion generator, Brigid reached for the lock on the generator hatch. The hatch was designed to give access to an engineer, and required a code along with a timer delay before it would open. Brigid remembered the code from the last time she had been here, when she had studied the designs for the redoubt that were held in the comprehensive database at Cerberus. Then, this had all been done remotely, but this time she would have to do it on-site.

Hidden magnetic locks clunked as Brigid's code was accepted, and a siren alarm bellowed a single note that sounded something like a duck being strangled. Accompanying the siren, a spinning red light came to life at the doorway to the room, casting the whole chamber in a swirling scarlet light. The countdown from code to final unlock appeared on the face of the lock in bright white digital figures: 02:00.

Brigid's hand rested on her holstered blaster. Two minutes. Now all she could do was wait.

She heard the shuffling noise just a few seconds later, and automatically stepped away from the porthole in the generator. It was coming from outside—something was moving down the corridor. Moving closer.

Brigid paced across the small chamber silently, pressed herself to the wall by the open doorway and peered out. There was no light in the corridor outside, just the flickering illumination of a candle held in the jaws of a tobacco-brown skull. The noise was coming from the far end of the corridor, where the flickering flame failed to illuminate.

Brigid watched, holding her breath, narrowing her eyes to try to penetrate the darkness at the distant end of the corridor. She could make out the edges of door frames, the glistening ripples of the water that seemed to smother every floor of this old redoubt.

And then she saw the movement in the darkness as that shuffling susurrus grew louder. He was closer than she expected, only twenty feet away, skin shimmering, a liquid gold like honey. She saw the leg first, clawed foot striking the watery floor with a splash. Her heart sank in that moment, for secretly she had hoped it was Kane, her *anam-chara*, all right and come to crack some damn-awful joke about dispatching Papa Hurbon's Annunaki form once and for all. He's nothing but voodoo doo-doo now—that was the kind of thing Kane would have said. Brigid smiled grimly as the words ran through her head, Kane's voice locked there with all the other perfect memories that she always retained.

The beast was closer now, muscular legs crushing the floor beneath it with every stomp, right leg dragging from some wound Brigid had not seen inflicted, body seen only in fragments where its golden sheen caught the flickering luminance of the lone candle flame.

It was the thing that Hurbon had become, naked and so tall that the spines atop his head almost brushed the ceiling, even here in the corridor where those ceilings were higher.

Brigid rolled back around the wall, pushing herself out of sight, away from the open door.

"I can see you," the duotonal voice taunted as Brigid disappeared from view, "apekin."

Brigid's hand was still on her blaster, pulling it from the holster at her hip. Her eyes flicked up to take in the timer display on the generator's door: 01:06

Over a minute still. Too long to hide. Nowhere to hide in here anyway, not really.

Anu's voice called again from outside the door, closer now, the splashing of his footsteps loud. "I can smell you," he said. "You smell good enough to eat."

Brigid glanced around the chamber, searching for the angles, the places where her smaller and weaker frame could be accommodated, where the Annunaki monster could not reach. There was nothing, nowhere, only inside the generator itself maybe and even that would not open for another 59 seconds...

00:58...

00:57...

Brigid twisted, reaching for the door frame and pulling herself up, scrambling up the wall like a bug.

00:54...

00:53...

ANU ENTERED THE ROOM containing the generator, favoring his leg where his ankle tendons had been cut. He entered fearlessly—an Annunaki does not know fear—he rules.

There was a countdown glowing on the door to the generator.

00:42

A porthole window glowed an eerie blue, the color of snow seen in the twilight.

But there was no sign of the woman, the apekin with the red hair.

Anu took another step forward, moving farther into the room. He could smell her, almost taste her. He had just been born. He was ravenous.

00:37

Anu took another step, his serpentine tail slithering into the room behind him, the glow of the countdown lighting his black-red eyes.

Brigid leaped, dropping down from her hiding place over the door frame, where she had wedged herself using her arms to press against the ceiling above her while her booted heels jammed down against the top of the frame. She dropped down, landing on Anu's golden back and drilling the muzzle of her TP-9 blaster into his side.

Anu spun, growling, as Brigid clicked down the trigger and fired point-blank into his flesh. She ran the barrel of her blaster up and down the Annunaki's side, trying to find—or make—a weak spot between his ribs.

"Off me!" Anu growled, staggering lopsidedly backward and crashing against the wall beside the open doorway.

Brigid struck the wall, her breath knocked out of her as she tried to hang on to the Annunaki progenitor. The TP-9 shook in her right hand, rattling against Anu's flank as it delivered bullet after bullet into his armor-plated skin. Some pierced, finding their way into the folds of flesh, only to be stopped by the incredible hardness of the muscles beneath.

00:24

Anu lashed out with his tail, flicking at Brigid as she continued to cling to his back. Brigid clung tightly, hanging there as the Annunaki beast thrashed and wailed, the TP-9 still drumming against his side.

Then Brigid shifted her aim, clinging to Anu's throat as she drew the semiautomatic pistol around and targeted the monster's head. The trigger squeezed again, sending a stream of 9 mm bullets into the reptile's face. Bullets flew in all directions as they struck the armored hide and raced away, some rattling against the fractured glass and metal sides of the cold-fusion generator. The generator continued its countdown, the pallid glow of blue light from the porthole dimming.

00:16

"Primitive bitch," Anu growled in irritation. "Learn your place." He flipped his tail, his whole body shuddering as he jumped in place.

Brigid's grip faltered, she slipped and suddenly she was spinning and falling, the world around her a swirl of shadows and candle flame. She landed with a thump against the floor or wall, she could not tell which. Her head was spinning, still caught in the whirl that had gripped her as she was tossed away by Anu.

When Brigid looked up, Anu was looming over her, baring his teeth in the dimming glow of the generator. Her blaster—where was her blaster? It had slipped from her hand as she fell; she could hear the skittering noise it made as it landed, realizing only now what had happened.

00:08

00:07

Brigid had to move. The generator was about to open, and damned if she knew what that would do—if it would kill Hurbon's Annunaki form or strengthen him. She thought...she hoped...that without fusion the death goddess's body would discorporate. It was something she did not want to be here to see. So she moved, against the pain in her body, the fire that seemed to burn in every muscle, every cord.

Anu lunged at her, a clawed hand swiping for her chest as she rose to her feet and ran. The claws snagged Brigid's chest, tearing the shadow suit and plunging deep within, cutting through skin and flesh.

Brigid was still moving, though, still hurtling away, all momentum and desperation, fired through with that thing that Kane had taught her, that survival instinct that drove humanity's progress. She was through the door in a moment, out into the corridor as the timer flicked through the final seconds of the lock release. Another siren alarm like a strangled duck blurted from overhead speakers.

00:03

00:02

00:01

Chapter 31

The door to the cold-fusion generator opened. Above, the whirling red light was throwing its illumination across the four walls of the room in quick succession, Jackson Pollocking the arrival of death.

Anu turned, hearing the click of the final magnetic lock, the hiss of air as the generator shut down and the door pulled back. The familiar thrum of the generator had ceased, its constancy now become an absence, a void.

The figure in the generator lurched forward. It had the body of an Annunaki, a female in form and depleted, savaged, ruined by the way *Tiamat*'s rebirth program had botched her. She was tall, emaciated, with arms like sticks and fingers like twigs. Her skin sloughed from her bony frame, its rippled pattern like that of a lizard, charcoal black and edged with fire as it burned away on contact with the air.

"Lily?" Anu gasped, his eyes meeting the lizard-slit eyes of the woman who was death, vertical red-black stripes in a pus-yellow bed. "Lilitu, is that you?"

The thing that had once been Lilitu, that had been known as Ezili Coeur Noir in her final life, reached for Anu, her ancestor, her grandfather, with arms devoid of flesh, with hands whose component parts were flaking away like seeds on the breeze.

The dead thing touched Anu a moment later, arms

wrapping around him, body flopping into a hug when all her strength had departed. Wisps of her emaciated flesh were burning away, looking like fireflies in the night as they fizzled in shooting embers toward the ceiling of the room, fizzled and went out.

Anu felt the thing's weight lighten even as she fell against him, felt her become lighter still as the body discorporated and she became bones and dust. "Granddaughter?" he asked, his duotonal voice choked as he breathed in the dusty essence of her rapidly disintegrating form. "What did they do to you?"

Reborn Lilitu burned away, her substance becoming nothingness in a matter of moments.

Anu stood alone in the aftermath, feeling the faint press of Lilitu's body—the daughter of Enki, his son, and Ereshkigal, his own granddaughter—still whispering against his skin.

Whisper and burn.

There was burning there, not without but within. Anu felt it racing through his body, igniting his cold blood, eating through the flesh.

When she had been reborn, Lilitu—Ezili Coeur Noir—had been so badly messed up that her touch had brought death to all organic matter. Her touch was the touch of death. Even for an Annunaki.

Anu was eternal, but so was Lilitu. Her touch was as devastating as any plague, any disease. Even the Annunaki could fall. They had suffered the scarabae sickness, a cancer caused by the sunlight on Earth. They had been killed at the end of the Godkiller, a blade carved from Ullikummis's own body. They had been killed through the Boolean algebra of Ereshkigal, who had mapped the secret mathematics behind life itself. And they could be killed by an Annunaki so corrupted that she was now more a dead thing than living, whose very touch came from the inky darkness at the far side of the grave.

Anu fell, his chest searing within, his body quaking and trembling. He struck the deck with a crash like overhead thunder, his muscular body wasting away even as he settled there on the floor.

Above, the red light spun around and around, warning all of the danger.

OUTSIDE THE GENERATOR ROOM, Brigid Baptiste lay propped against the wall, blood oozing from the wound in her chest. She had heard the fusion generator door open, had heard the scuffle as the dead thing had met with the gold-scaled Annunaki. He had called her granddaughter, which meant he had to be Anu, according to the Annunaki family tree that she had drawn back in the Cerberus redoubt, when she had begun to piece the structure of their enemy together years before.

Brigid listened, waiting, not really knowing what was happening, not really wanting to move. She hurt where she had been stabbed by Anu's claw. She hurt in other places, too, aches and scrapes and burns. And there was tiredness, her muscles suffused with it, her mind swimming in exhaustion.

She heard Anu collapse, his gigantic body striking the floor like thunder just a few feet from where Brigid sat...a few feet and a wall away.

She lay there a long time, propped against the wall, listening to the nothingness as Anu's body deteriorated and died, ravaged by the faulty program that *Tiamat* had passed onto the reborn form of Lilitu years ago.

When it was over, Brigid did not know. She was too tired to place when it had happened; her mind was slipping in and out of consciousness and she could not really know how much time had passed.

EVENTUALLY, BRIGID OPENED her eyes and realized she had been asleep. The blood was warm and sticky on her chest, the pain nagging like a stray dog barking after midnight in the next street.

She pushed herself up, hissing between clenched teeth as new levels of pain shot through her. She could hear nothing from the room behind her, no noise, no battle. Nothing had come to kill her while she slept, so she figured that was a good sign.

She moved, shuffling slowly back to the room with the generator, baby steps that were accompanied by straining breaths. At the door, Brigid peered into the generator room. The guttering candle had all but burned itself out. The generator door was open and dark, the subconscious hum of the generator silenced. There were dark spots on the floor and walls—blood, shell casings. And there was nothing, an eerie patch where nothing had bled or fallen or scraped, a space that seemed almost as if it had been swept clean by some almighty hand. Anu was gone and so was the thing from the generator, the unborn thing that should never have been. It was over.

SLOWLY, WEARILY, BRIGID took her first tentative steps along the corridor and back to the *djévo* room where she had left Kane and Grant. Domi and the other members of CAT Beta were on an upper level of the redoubt where Brigid hoped they were safe, and her own away team had to be her top priority just now.

With each step, the wound in her chest seemed to burn a little stronger, ache a little more. That monster had tried to rip out her heart.

Each breath was strained, and Brigid halted, leaning against a wall. She opened her eyes and realized she had drifted asleep for a moment as she leaned there against the wall. She could not tell if she had slipped out of consciousness for a few seconds or for minutes. The darkness of the redoubt, the warmth and her own exhaustion were all conspiring against her now, beckoning her to lie down, to give up.

"If I lie down, I'll never get up again," she told herself in a hoarse whisper. She barely sounded like herself.

With tussled hair and a loping form, the bruised woman made her way to the *djévo*, where the two guards lay outside, dead or something like it. The curtain had become twisted, holes in the material hooking onto themselves in a knotted tangle. Brigid pushed the curtain aside with her left hand, holding her TP-9 pistol with her right, hunched over with the pain and blood loss.

Inside were Kane and Grant. And blood, lots of blood.

"Kane?" Brigid whispered from the doorway. "Grant?"

Brigid fell to her knees and wept, knowing without looking. She knelt there for a long time, with tears flowing down her cheeks, pain in her chest each time she drew breath.

Chapter 32

But it was not over. Brigid cried a long time as the blood drained from her body and the candle at her side finally guttered out.

Selfishly, Brigid remembered the trick she had used once before, when Ninlil had emerged from her chrysalis state and threatened to destabilize humanity forever. An Annunaki trick.

BRIGID THOUGHT BACK to when she was in the ante-nursery of the wombship *Tiamat*. Brigid pressed her hand firmly against the newly born reptilian body of Ninlil, applying all the incredible pressure of her corrupted understanding of the universe. Ninlil's body shook in the stone egg from which it was emerging, juddering in place.

Standing behind Brigid, the dark-haired warrior called Rosalia watched as the astonishing scene took place. Rosalia's brain struggled to comprehend what was happening; it seemed that Ninlil was becoming focused even as the world around her blurred.

Brigid recalled the equation she had used to find the hidden door to Agartha, driving into her mind that different way of seeing, of comprehending. The Annunaki were multidimensional, the static rules of physics did not apply. Backed inside the egg, Ninlil's body wrapped upon itself, becoming smaller to fit the enclosed space.

Time took a half step back; evolution itself was reversed.

Then the stone chrysalis sealed with Ninlil crouched inside it, and Brigid slumped forward, exhausted.

TIME COULD NOT be turned back, but evolution could. The thing that had evolved out of Papa Hurbon, the thing that had killed…

If the Annunaki could be reborn, then why not…?

There was not much time. "I can reverse it," Brigid said in a whisper, reaching inside her pants pocket for the boney shard she had placed there just a couple of hours earlier. "I can make everything how it was."

She drew the dragon's tooth from her pocket, still connected to its gold necklace chain. Dagmar Gellis had tried to swallow it, certain that it would give her ancient powers—powers derived from the Annunaki. Hurbon had done something similar with his own shard of *Tiamat*, tooth or bone, and it had burned through his body and grown a monster in the compost that remained. But Brigid was different. She had been of the Annunaki once, briefly, in a time she had hoped to always forget.

The Annunaki's was an organic technology, utilizing genetic material to create and to build. It needed something of her so that she could access it, she knew.

It was selfish, so selfish. But the alternative was beyond comprehension.

Gritting her teeth, Brigid reached into the wound in her chest, closing her eyes against the indescribable pain, and pressed the dragon's tooth there, pushing it into her body until the hot folds of flesh and muscle wrapped around it.

Hurbon had imbibed the dragon's tooth and it had

overwhelmed him. The others—Ereshkigal, Nungal, Ki—had also begun as human and thus been overwhelmed, their human foundations corrupting and spoiling the transfer. But Brigid had something that they did not—she had been trained in the ways of the Annunaki, forced to see as they see by the god prince Ullikummis, the only human ever to do so. It had changed her so much that she had become a different person then, Brigid Haight, whose worldview was Annunaki. The change had been so traumatic that she had buried the memory of it, had pretended it had never been.

Brigid recalled those lessons now, reached for them, hidden as they were in the dark corners of her memory; her wonderful, flawless, eidetic memory. She had once told her colleagues that it was better to forget some things, that Haight had died. But the lessons she had learned at Ullikummis's indulgence, the philosophies of the alien Annunaki, were all still there. She only chose to shy away from them because she had been so afraid of what she might become if she tapped them ever again.

She tapped them now. As the shard of *Tiamat*, its potency like a genetic bullet fired into its victim, embedded itself in Brigid's body, she tapped those lessons, recalling the Annunaki ways.

There was another way of looking at time. The Australian Aborigines knew this, had utilized it for thousands of years. It held that time was not linear, one event following another, but rather that it was all at once. And being all at once meant that you could travel along it freely, moving from time to time the way you move through the rooms of a house. All it took was disconnecting yourself from time's flow.

Brigid entered a meditative state of *nirvikalpa*, not

accepting time as it stood, letting the change flow through her, through time.

The Annunaki were multidimensional creatures, whose aspects on Earth were but a fraction of their all. A *part* that they might *emit* from the infinite levels of reality.

Brigid reached deep inside her, reached for the power of the dragon's tooth, and drew herself back, Annunaki-style, through the folds of time.

The long walk through the underground passages of the redoubt, the strain each step took, reversed now, heading back to the generator room. Ezili Coeur Noir had discorporated on exiting the generator but now she reformed and returned, hiding herself there, closing the door of her protective home. Before that, Anu stabbed Brigid with his clawed hand, but the mortal wound healed in reverse, his bloody claws drawing free and cleaned, magically, as they drew from the hole in her body that was no longer there.

Things moved faster, images flashing across Brigid's brain too fast to process. Here Kane was alive, the blood returning greedily to his body. Grant wrenched Domi's blade from Anu's leg as the Annunaki lifted one golden foot from his head, and then he too began to absorb the blood he had spilled, his eyes closing as if he needed to sleep through this part of the process.

Hurbon was lying on the floor of the mirrored *djévo* room, his head a bloody wound. Kane stood over him, pointing his Sin Eater at the man's skull, the bullet returning to the barrel, running back to its nest in the ammunition clip.

And then Ki was emerging from the freezer as Kane opened its door; and then Brigid and Kane and Grant were searching the redoubt, entering it, meeting Ohio Blue, leaving in the Mantas, rushing through the skies.

Another chance. It would be another chance to make things right. A chance to live. She just had to avoid all the mistakes they had made before, she just had to *remember*.

Chapter 33

Brigid looked around, her mind reeling. She was in her apartment, on the upper levels of the Cerberus redoubt, standing in the center of the darkened room beside the bed. Lights out. She had done it, then, moved through time, through space, reversed everything that Papa Hurbon had done that had concluded with his bringing Anu and Ki back to life. Had Ki lived through it, trapped in the freezer? This time she could change that.

But already that memory was beginning to fade, like a dream slipping away on awakening. Can you remember a thing that is yet to be? No—she could not forget, not this. Brigid had to write it down, before it was too late, before she forgot what she had done, changing time so that it flowed another way, opening up another path to follow. If she didn't remember, then she ran the risk of repeating the exact same mistake, over and over again, caught in a loop from which the Cerberus warriors could never be free.

She was losing consciousness already, the effort of moving through time. That other her, that past her, was taking control, taking her place in the cosmic scheme. She had to warn herself before the memory faded away like the dream.

Brigid reached for the notepad she kept on her night table, grabbed the pen and scribbled two words, writing them in a circle—widdershins, the way of all magic.

Even as she wrote the final letter—*p*—her time-adrift mind dissipated and she dropped the pad and pen back on the nightstand. It was off by twenty degrees, but there was no time to correct it, she was already fading away, falling asleep. Falling…

BRIGID AWOKE WITH a start.

The sounds of the Cerberus redoubt filtered through the walls and door of her private apartment, faint but offering a reassuring background, reminding her that life goes on.

It was usually quiet here, whatever the time was. The staff at Cerberus worked on shifts, and people respected that someone was always sleeping no matter what hour of the day it was. But the sounds of talking, of laughter, seemed to echo through her door today.

Brigid shifted, turning onto her side and reaching for the lamp. She squinted as she brushed the lamp's side, switching it on with her touch. Beside the lamp, the notebook she kept at her bedside had been moved.

Brigid reached for the notepad, saw in that instant that there were words written upon it. She turned the pad slowly, looking at the words. There were two words— *emit part*—written in her hand, albeit shakily. The words were written not on a line but in a circle, like so:

$$e$$
$$t \qquad m$$
$$r \qquad\qquad i$$
$$a \qquad t$$
$$p$$

Automatic writing, Brigid realized as she looked at the strange words, presumably written without conscious thought while she was asleep. Well, that was new.

But what did it mean? Obviously, something had disturbed her in the night, something had caused her to write those words on her notebook, an item that often seemed like a redundant indulgence when her memory was such a keen tool and yet could sometimes elicit the answer to a nagging problem from the day before. After all, what would a woman with a photographic memory ever need to write down?

She lay in bed, the covers pulled up high to keep her warm, holding the pad and gazing at the topmost sheet.

Emit part.

It meant nothing to her. What was the *part*? What did it *emit*? It was dream writing, the kind that adheres to the logic of the subconscious, whose meaning is lost when the waking mind takes over.

Brigid held the pad before her, staring at the letters until her eyes lost focus and stared beyond, into the whiteness of the page, turning the letters into a blur. From outside her suite, Brigid heard familiar voices raised in a friendly discussion peppered with joyful laughter, the sound barely registering on Brigid's consciousness.

Eventually, she set down the pad, pushed back the covers and got out of the bed. She dressed rapidly, washing quickly so that she could go to the cafeteria for breakfast before grabbing a shower after.

THE CERBERUS CAFETERIA was a large room and it featured several long dining tables covered in wipe-down Formica, their seats affixed to the tables, along with some smaller, cozier tables that sat groups of four.

As Brigid entered, she heard the same laughter she had heard not fifteen minutes ago when someone had passed her suite. It was Domi, talking at her most excited volume, regaling Kane and Grant with some story or other.

Brigid strode past a table where Edwards sat with Sela Sinclair, comparing details from some gun catalog the two had found among the redoubt's ancient artifacts, and headed for the serving area and much-desired pot of steaming coffee. As she passed Domi, Kane and Grant, Kane was offering a friendly denial to the albino woman.

"We've been all the way around the world, Domi," he insisted. "All those myths got busted. They're all just alien meddling, science that got muddled up as supernatural hoodoo in the retelling."

"And the ignorance," Grant added, talking around a warmed bagel at the seat beside his field partner.

"Don't you guys hear yourselves?" Domi challenged animatedly. "You call it science, but it's still magic. Alien science is magic because we still can't really explain it, we just nod our heads and say 'oh, yes, faster than light CCTV in the Stone Age.' You talk about the dumb primitives who were too ignorant to know better, but, you ask me, you're just as dumb as they were, only you're too busy being sophisticated to realize it."

Brigid smiled, moving on toward the serving area. It was an argument that Domi had had with them before, in varying forms—how calling an explanation scientific didn't make it so. And maybe she was right; maybe everything the Cerberus warriors had discovered was still as magical as it ever had been, understood in a different way that was just as ignorant as any other.

Brigid reached for the percolating coffee, pouring herself a cup of java. The new day awaited, whatever it might bring.

Epilogue

Let's say Brigid did fix it all. Let's say everyone lived and the Annunaki were defeated. If the world had been remade, how would you know? If everything was put back in the way you remembered, or thought that you remembered—and maybe even that was a part of the fix, that you only thought you remembered it at all.

And how would you ever know that you were fighting on the right side when the battle is eternal and the sides can change and reverse in the blink of an eye?

How can anyone?

* * * * *

COMING SOON FROM

GOLD EAGLE®

Available December 1, 2015

GOLD EAGLE EXECUTIONER®
FINAL ASSAULT – *Don Pendleton*

When the world's first self-sustaining ship is hijacked and put up for auction, terror groups from around the world are scrambling to make an offer. Mack Bolan must rescue the hostages and destroy the high-tech floating fortress before it's too late.

GOLD EAGLE SUPERBOLAN™
WAR EVERLASTING – *Don Pendleton*

On a desolate ring of islands, Mack Bolan discovers that a reactive volcano isn't the only force about to blow. A Russian mercenary and his group of fanatics are working to destroy America's network of military bases and kill unsuspecting soldiers.

GOLD EAGLE STONY MAN®
EXIT STRATEGY – *Don Pendleton*

One reporter is killed by a black ops group and a second is held captive in Mexico's most dangerous prison. But when Phoenix Force goes in to rescue the journalist, Able Team learns that corruption has infiltrated US law enforcement, threatening both sides of the border.

UPCOMING TITLES FROM

DON PENDLETON'S
THE EXECUTIONER

KILL SQUAD
Available March 2016
Nine million dollars goes missing from a Vegas casino, and an accountant threatens to spill to the Feds. But with the mob on his back, the moneyman skips town. Bolan must race across the country to secure the fugitive before the guy's bosses shut him up—forever.

DEATH GAME
Available June 2016
Two American scientists are kidnapped just as North Korea makes a play for Cold War–era ballistic missiles. Determined to save the scientists and prevent a world war, Bolan learns he's not the only one with his sights set on retrieving the missiles…

TERRORIST DISPATCH
Available September 2016
Atrocities continue in the Ukraine and the adjoining Crimean Peninsula, annexed by Russia in March 2014. With no end in sight, a plan is hatched to force American involvement by sending Ukrainian militants to strike Washington, DC, killing civilians and seizing the Lincoln Memorial as protest against their homeland's threat from Russia. Can Bolan bring the war home to the plotters' doorstep?

COMBAT MACHINES
Available December 2016
What began in a Romanian orphanage twenty years earlier, when a man walked away with ten children and disappeared, leads Mack Bolan and a team of Interpol agents to fend off a group of "invisible" assassins carving their way across Europe…toward the USA.

"We need a new plan," he said, looking toward the building where the majority of the fire was coming from.

"The plan is fine," Spence snapped. "It was fine until you had to start making changes. I shouldn't even be here! I'm not a goddamn field agent!"

Bolan didn't waste his breath arguing. Instead, he looked up. The sun was starting to rise. Once they lost the dark, they'd also lose the only real protection they had. The militants would realize they were facing only two men, and they'd swarm them. Bolan and Spence had to take the fight to the enemy.

Bolan popped a smoke canister free from his harness and pulled the pin. He lobbed the grenade over the wall and immediately grabbed for another. "Get ready to move," he said as he sent the second spinning along the narrow street. Colored smoke started spitting into the night air.

"Move where?" Spence demanded.

"Where do you think?" Bolan asked, pointing toward the building. "You said we needed to bring a gift, right? Well, how about we give them the best gift of all—dead enemies."

"Enemy of my enemy is my friend, huh, Cooper?" Spence said in a tone that might have been admiration. He grinned. "I can dig it."

"Then on your feet," Bolan said, freeing a third smoke grenade from his combat harness. He hurled it toward the building as he vaulted over the wall. Smoke flooded the street, caught in the grip of the sea breeze. He and Spence moved forward quickly, firing as they went. They took up positions on either side of the doorway. The smoke was blowing toward them and into the open building. The gunfire had slackened, and Bolan could hear coughing and cursing within.

He caught Spence's attention with a sharp wave. Spence nodded, and Bolan swung back from the door and drove his boot into it. Old hinges, ill-treated by time and the environment, popped loose of the wooden frame with a squeal, and the door toppled inward. Bolan was moving forward even as it fell, his weapon spitting fire. He raked the room beyond, pivoting smoothly, his UMP held at waist height. The gunmen screamed and died.

Bolan stalked forward like Death personified, his gun roaring.

Don't miss
FINAL ASSAULT by Don Pendleton,
available December 2015 wherever
Gold Eagle® books and ebooks are sold.

STONY MAN®

"As the President's extralegal arm, Stony Man employs high-tech ordnance and weaponry to annihilate threats to the USA and to defenseless populations everywhere."

This larger format series, with a more high-tech focus than the other two Bolan series, features the ultracovert Stony Man Farm facility situated in the Blue Ridge Mountains of Virginia. It serves as the operations center for a team of dedicated cybernetic experts who provide mission control guidance and backup for the Able Team and Phoenix Force commandos, including ace pilot Jack Grimaldi, in the field.

Available wherever Gold Eagle® books and ebooks are sold.

GOLD EAGLE®